ENVY

THE SHADOW-KEEPERS SERIES — BOOK FIVE

JAS T. WARD

BOOK FIVE OF THE SHADOW-KEEPERS SERIES:
ENVY

ISBN-13: XXXX

For Information, address:
JTW Publishing LLC
www.AuthorJasTWard.com
hello@JTWPublishingllc.com

Cover Design: Q-Design & Premades
Amy Queau

Editing: Two Red Pens Editing
Rogena Mitchell-Jones, Literary Editor
Colleen Snibson, Co-Editor

To my Crazy Ladies and the Fan-Fiction Group. Thank you for keeping our world of the Grid alive.

And to Murphy... You are missed from the Ward Herd.

WORKS BY JAS T. WARD

Shorts & Poetry

Bits and Pieces: Tales and Sonnets

Contemporary Romance

Love's Bitter Harvest

A Little Pill Called Love

The Shadow-Keepers Series

CANDYMAN: Before the Madness

MADNESS

BOUNCE

LUST

COWBOY

MURDER

ENVY

www.AuthorJasTWard.com

PROLOGUE

The old woman's voice droned on for more than an hour, but Epsilon needed her words, not her money. He hid his irritation well. Six months had gone by since his father, Lucifer—the dark ruler of Hell—had cut off any assistance, including funds to supplement Epsilon's army. In that time, he had used his trained mercenaries and soldiers to take on specific unsavory tasks.

"I was told you were discreet."

The woman wound down her personal history, and Epsilon smiled as he ran his fingers down the pressed crease of his trousers. Slowly flexing his hand before clasping it in the other in his lap, he gave her a slow smile. "I am. And I am sure you would expect that to continue with this task. However, Ms. Shen, you must also presume that my services do not come cheap. You were told that as well?"

The Asian woman's steely stare must have intimidated everyone she had ever placed in her sights, but not Epsilon. One could not be the son of Lucifer and wither in front of any human, much less an elderly one, almost seventy years old.

Ms. Shen stood, the expensive linen of her gray suit swishing with the smoothness of her moves. "Mr. White, my marriage was one of arrangement between two of the wealthiest families in our region. I accepted that and did not complain. I assisted my husband when our families' companies combined, and he took charge of the operations."

She angled to look back at him, her gaze scathing as if he stood there with shit on his shoe, marring the expensive rug on the floor under it.

"Without me, Shen Enterprises would not exist. Our fathers died, and my husband inherited everything. And I accepted that, as well. When I gave birth to my son, the only male to carry on the family business, that too, I accepted. It was the way of our culture. However, when my son and his wife died in the plane crash..." As her gaze moved away, Epsilon tilted his head, attempting to detect some grief in her tone. But, no, she sounded as cold about the death of her son as she had about the rest of her history—even though the plane crash occurred less than a year ago.

Completely without emotion.

A living, aging statue.

"I should have finally gained control of what I built—built not by grooming the men in my life but by manipulating and controlling them. By whispering in their ears the best decisions and knowing they would follow as if they had hatched the plans. But no..." Epsilon had been incorrect about the lack of emotion. Hate and vengeful venom tainted her words now. "My son gave control of the entire Shen empire to a seventeen-year-old child." Her palm slammed down on the table in front of her, the impact so hard that the lovely tiny carvings chinked together like individual wind chimes made of china.

"Ah." Epsilon stood to approach her and smiled. "A trust fund that converts when your granddaughter, Jade, turns eighteen." He tilted his head. "I did my research. Your son and his wife died in a private airplane crash over the mountains of Montana. And he left your funds, the companies, the properties, everything except your living allowance and this home, to his daughter. That must have hurt. To finally have a chance to hold the reins of a mighty steed, and they are given to a little girl."

"She is a child! A shy, withdrawn, witless child. She has no confidence and loses herself inside of books! Not even intelligent reads but ridiculous volumes of fantasy and fiction. Her father let her go to public school with children of low class—not a school that would groom her for the role of a woman in power! Nor a wife worthy of a powerful man! Just a girl. He allowed her just to be..." she spat out the word as if it tasted like the imagined shit on his shoe, "just herself. No pressure, and no training. She is not *suitable* nor worthy of what I built, Mr. White!" She brought her palm up to her chest, which was rising and falling with deep indignation like she had run to get herself worked up. "And he leaves it all to *her*!" Epsilon reached out to take her hand and stroked his thumb over her wrinkled knuckles, lifting his eyes to hers. "And if she dies, you finally have it all."

Her eyes met his, and Epsilon found her gaze—like that of a viper contained in its basket for too long and wanted to sink its fangs into its charmer's throat. "Yes. I was told you would do this, that the fact it was a child would be no issue. And if you researched, you know I can pay whatever fee you wish. As long as you do this deed."

With a deadly smile, Epsilon brought her hand up to kiss her knuckles and then met her gaze. "I can. And the fee will be one of your son's companies."

"Which one?" Her face went emotionless once more, and the coldness had returned to her tone.

Epsilon pulled out a piece of paper and pressed it into her hand as he released it. "The one in Colombia that makes weapons."

"Ms. Shen, we're here."

Jade pulled her earbuds out when the driver announced they had arrived at her grandmother's home. She hated the rambling mansion above the city with its empty rooms, servants, and ghosts of the past. She hated her room, which she wasn't allowed to change from its museum-type interior—like the rest of the house. The only rooms Jade found any solace in were her grandfather's library and the solarium it opened into. She never knew the man, though, as he had died when her father was a teenager. Sighing as she tucked away her well-worn paperback copy of *The Hunger Games* into her messenger bag, followed by her phone and earbuds, she mumbled a thank-you and exited the sedan. Watching the private driver turn the corner to park the car, she let her head fall forward, her eyes sliding over in puzzlement at the car parked on the curb with a large, intimidating man standing next to it.

Was someone visiting her grandmother? Strange. The woman ran over the schedule every morning over breakfast and had said nothing about any appointments.

Walking up the steps to the front door, she entered and dropped her bag by the front door. "Soba? I'm home. Do we have company?"

"Hello, Jade."

A person moved in front of her, and she creased her brow in confusion as her eyes trailed up expensive suit jacket buttons, over a deep blue tie, and then continued upward to meet startling blue eyes. They were the hue of an iceberg—harmless on the surface but danger far below. "Hello?"

The man smiled, and something about it had Jade stepping back only to hit the large man from outside as he entered the home. "Soba?" Her breath hitched, and fear made the hair on the back of her neck stand like someone or something was whispering in silence against her skin. A warning she could not hear.

The man in the suit stepped close to her, and Jade tried to avoid his hand as it came up as fingers clasped her chin brutally.

"You are a pretty one. What a shame such a pretty doll is about to die."

1

THREE MONTHS AGO

"What do you mean"—Reno glanced over at Witch, who appeared just as confused as he was—"retire?" He let out a bark of laughter and waved his hand at the cowboy. "We all know you're joking. Dude, you love killing and slaughtering and doing all of it in that stupid Stetson." But Jess's face did not show a joking expression. In fact, it looked the opposite—dire. "Oh, wait! You're not joking." Reno stood and gawked before sputtering in disbelief. "But Grid is like... You are like... I..." He gave up trying as his big brother clapped a hand on Reno's shoulder.

"I ain't completely leaving. I'm just retiring from being a fighter." Putting an arm around Beth, Jess kissed the top of her head and met her eyes. His lady cop wore a smile, making it clear to Reno the couple had discussed and were in agreeance with whatever this was. "We are starting on finding a surrogate for a baby, which you all know. And your kids are gettin' more grown by the day. And you're having more"—Jess pointed at Witch's tummy, where the newest Sundowns, in the form of twins, had started to grow even if Emma didn't show yet—"since you two like to pretend you're rabbits in springtime. Even more reason, I want to start a school, one with day care and has grades from kindergarten to high school. I want to run it, well, the administration side."

"And I'm going to help," Lily Devenmore spoke up as she joined them.

Reno looked down at Witch to find her as confused as he.

Lily walked up to Emma to take her sister's hands. "I have a degree in education and library arts. Jess came to me last month to propose it to Bounce. It will be a school that embraces all their supernatural gifts while they get a top-notch education. And be safe doing it."

"A school?" Reno smiled at Jess with a chuckle. "You running a school? Lily makes sense, but you, Jess? Seriously? No guns. No fighting. No badass? Just sitting in an office, making sure kids learn their ABCs and 123s?"

Jess smirked as he sat on the back of the sofa. Beth rested her head on his shoulder, trying not to laugh. She too must have found it silly when Jess told her. She appeared to be all on board now. "Reno, I know it's hard to reconcile but think back to when the two of us were in that orphanage. How I always tried to help those young 'uns. When we had new kids come into the brothel, who was it that taught them to read after Miss Prissy taught me?" He put a finger against his chest. "And once we find a surrogate to deliver us a beautiful baby, I need to make sure I ain't risking my fool ass out in the field." He turned his head to smile at Beth. "Especially since our baby's mama is dead set on staying a cop. I can't have both of us running a chance of not coming home."

Reno knew that it had been difficult for his brother and Beth to come to terms with the fact that Beth was unable to get pregnant. Even though they kept it private, Jess had reached out to Reno and Emma after Beth had a second miscarriage. He decided he would not put his wife and himself in that position a third time, and Beth had agreed. Now, they wanted a baby without that painful possibility, and a surrogate was currently being searched for via Grid services.

Jess's focus returned to Reno. "I know you might not get it, but I want to do this. For our daughter, Sophia. For Eli. For all the Grid kids, including our own. I'm really excited about it. I think it can make a difference. Bounce has already approved it, and so has the High Council, but I need you and Emma to understand. I need the parents of the Grid to support this. Or there ain't no reason to do it."

Witch curled her arm around Reno's. "I think it's perfect. I really do."

She looked up at Reno, and his jaw dropped. Had *everyone* forgotten Jess Bailey once lived as a deadly Old West outlaw? Okay, fine, that was more than two hundred years ago, but still. He sighed when he took in Witch's expression, asking for him to understand, then faced his brother and nodded. "Okay, then. Retirement it is." He nodded but had to add, "But, uh, lose the hat. It needs to retire, too."

"YOU DO KNOW how to swing a hammer with your own damn arm, right?" Jess had officially been retired from active Grid duty for a month. The permits for the school had been approved and filed. He had purchased a large property, which housed a sprawling mansion and a cottage in the front part of the land to be used as an office. The three-acre estate was surrounded by an aging brick wall completed with a high iron gate at both the front and rear driveways. The mansion was four stories, had dozens of rooms, and even had an enclosed pool that would be renovated, so it was pocketed under the floor of the new gym.

The place was built in the early 1900s and had been abandoned when the housing market crashed back in the early 2000s. Sitting empty had not done the place any favors, but with some hard work and more funds than Jess wanted to confess to, the conversion to a private school was underway. Reno, as well as others from the Grid, had thrown in their help. The thought of his brother building anything was a scary thought to Jess.

Reno stood over a cut pile of boards meant to be one of the custom built-in shelves. Jess loved working with wood and using the carpentry skills he had perfected over the years—Reno, not so much. The Keeper snorted and waved the hammer at the shelf parts. "I'm pretty sure I know that this is the business end, and this is not." He pointed to the hammer's head and handle. He even confidently tossed the tool up. And of course, it came crashing down, missing Reno's hand and landing on the man's boot.

Jess's chin went to his chest to suppress laughter as he waited for Reno to stop hopping up and down in pain. Sure as the sun was shining, Jess could guess that Reno's dark half made the man miss catching the hammer for fun's sake. Some things never changed with those two. "Guess Sundown decided to let you feel that one. Take that as a lesson. But let's find you some other less damagin' work to do."

Reno kicked the hammer with a hiss, and it bounced off the boards and, of course, hit the man in the shin. Jess might not be able to *hear* Sundown anymore, but he could bet that the dark side of Reno was laughing his non-corporeal ass off. Further confirmed when Reno started angrily mumbling to himself. To anyone not in the know, they'd think the man was crazy. Which, honestly, he was. But Jess knew Reno was lecturing, to no avail, his dark half.

"Who is that?" Reno's mental chastising abruptly ended as he pointed toward the driveway.

Jess twisted at his hips to see the cause. A sleek, expensive sedan pulled up, complete with a driver exiting to stand by the door. Jess frowned as he fully turned toward the vehicle. "I have no idea. Maybe that fancy car didn't come with a GPS?" He wiped the sweat from his brow with his T-shirt as he approached the car and smiled at the driver. "Howdy. Can I help you all?"

Reno followed and stopped to stand behind Jess. Both most likely appeared casual, but Jess knew that his brother had a gun placed at the small of his back just like Jess had one tucked into his boot. Old habits die hard. While the school was not a battle-based facility and for all appearances and documentation nothing more than an academic facility, it was still linked to the Grid. And confidence was low that Epsilon could not find out those details.

The driver said nothing, his face stoic and closed off.

Alrighty then.

Jess glanced back at Reno, who simply lifted his hands and shoulder in a shrug. The rear window lowered, and an older woman sat in the coolness of the car. She was of Asian descent, and judging by the jewelry, car, and driver, she was rich. Her eyes went to Jess, slid to Reno, then returned to Jess. And if Jess thought the diamonds were icy, her voice was even more so.

"I need to speak to the administrator of your school. Could you please ask them to come to speak with me? Or"—her gaze ran down Jess's frame, which was covered in drywall and wood dust. She did not bother to hide her distaste in evaluating his low standing in the hierarchy of command—"have them contact me."

She held out a calling card or, by modern terms, one for business. However, perhaps the old term Jess knew suited the item. It was on thick, high-quality paper with a name written in black foil lettering—Sigu Shen—and a San Francisco telephone number. No company, website, nothing. Just the name and number.

He gave her a grin. "Fancy, thank you."

Jess tapped the business card on his palm as he leaned down, noticing the woman was not alone in the back seat of the car. A young woman sat there. Her posture was hunched over as if she hoped to go unnoticed. Or maybe be absorbed into the fine leather seat upholstery. Her downcast eyes were on a thick paperback book, but she chewed on her bottom lip nervously. Jess could tell the girl paid attention to the conversation of the adults.

Jess braced the hand holding the card on the roof of the car, and he bent at the waist to give both a smile through the open window. "A'right, Ms. Shen. Your request is real easy. I'm William Bailey. Administrator and chief executive of this here school." He glanced behind him, and it was impossible not to feel pride in what had been accomplished thus far. "Edge Academy. And can I guess you're looking for a new school for"—his voice softened—"your daughter?"

The girl looked up with a look of shock that he had registered her existence at all. That made him feel sad. So much so, he gave her his full attention.

She looked at him before glancing at the older woman. Given a slight, curt nod, the girl said in a shy whisper, "Grandmother," followed by a smile. "She's my grandmother. I'm Jade. Hello, Mr. Bailey."

Before Jess could reply, Ms. Shen touched her granddaughter's knee lightly, and the girl seemed to shut down. Head once again downcast to appear to read the book. Saddest damn thing Jess had ever seen.

Her grandmother cleared her throat and addressed him once more. "This is your Academy. I must say you seem to have a very hands-on approach."

It may have been a joke, but judging by the raised, elegant brow and the thin hard line of the woman's mouth, Jess doubted the woman had a sense of humor. Hell, she might not even have a heart if the way she treated her granddaughter was an indicator.

"Oh, he is. Big time. It's his dream."

Reno had stepped up with his hand held out to the woman in greeting.

She regarded his hand with as much disdain as she had Jess's appearance, if not more. She shrank back a small measure to avoid the touch.

The gesture was not subtle; even Reno picked up on it and said in a low voice, "Okay then..."

"Your dream is to operate a private school, Mr. Bailey? Intriguing."

Jess smiled an easy smile—the topic one he was more than happy to discuss. But he could read Ms. Shen, or any person for that matter, pretty quickly. She wouldn't give one pig squirt how he felt about it. Pushing up to stand, he crossed his arms as his professional gear wound up instead. "Yep. But we've also recruited some of the most talented and awarded educators across the world to teach here. Our curriculum is top-rated and college prep. We are offering classes from kindergarten to high school. And we're even going to have a day care with a Montessorian framework. Add to that, liberal arts such as dance, music, art, and creative writing. We hope to give kids not only a place to thrive but also a place where they can become well-taught and rounded adults. In a protected and balanced environment."

Jess hoped his smile portrayed the sarcasm he felt like throwing at the old bat. "So, if you want to call all that intriguing, then a'right. But to me, it sounds like a damn school. Now, Ms. Shen, care to tell me how I can help you and why you pulled up in our driveway?"

Ms. Shen reached up to touch her necklace. "I had heard through the city chambers office that there would be a school near my neighborhood. You see, Mr. Bailey, my granddaughter, Jade, lost her parents a year ago. She has had a difficult time"—she paused, composed her face, and then smiled the coldest smile Jess had ever seen—"adjusting. I thought perhaps a new place of learning would help give her a new start. Tell me, Mr. Bailey"—she lifted a fancy handbag and pulled out her wallet—"how much is your tuition. I will pay for her first year in full. She will then graduate. I am already researching a suitable college." She brought her eyes to his with that creepy smile still in place. "Abroad." It reminded Jess of a snake, kept hungry far too often, seeing a rat being lowered into its cage.

Jess stole a look over to Jade as he opened the older woman's door. "How about I show you around, ma'am. I have to tell you that we have zero openings for our student body. We've been booked to full capacity for over a month now." That was another fact that Jess held pride in. The moment the Grid notification went out that a school had been approved for all the children who lived and worked with the secret army, they became inundated with applications. Many of the children had supernatural gifts and talents. They would be groomed, trained, and taught to grow in the open within the secured walls of Edge Academy. But Jess could not tell Ms. Shen any of that. He knew there was no way in hell the High Council—the governing body over humans, Heaven, and Hell—would allow non-Grid humans or others to attend.

"But we may have some openings before your granddaughter graduates. Why don't you let me give you a tour? Bring your driver along. Some of the site is rough, and I would hate to have you fall and all, ma'am." His confidence was high, so she would allow that. After all, there was no way a woman such as she would want sweaty construction hands on her fancy suit. He had been correct as the driver held out a white-gloved hand to assist the woman in standing.

"Stay in the car, Jade."

Jess motioned the way for Ms. Shen to follow along with her driver, and he caught Reno's gaze as they passed to receive a discreet, knowing nod.

2

"Hi."

Jade jerked to sit upright in surprise when she heard a man's voice so close and strangely friendly. Lifting her gaze from her book, she looked past the man who had been with Mr. Bailey and saw her grandmother enter the school.

Jade moved her gaze back to the friendly one and nodded before saying softly, "Hello."

He had squatted down and sat on his haunches within the opening of the ajar passenger car door. He was handsome in a boy next door kind of way, and his eyes were a startling, brilliant blue. His hair was soft brown and wavy, a little overgrown yet not. Jade wondered if it was actually cut to look that way. But what Jade registered the most was his open and casual demeanor.

"I'm Reno. You said your name was Jade, right?"

She had ducked her head down to avoid any further conversation until he said his name. She frowned, lifted her chin, and met his eyes. "Reno? Like the city?"

The man smiled even wider, and she let out an alarmed squeak as he climbed into the car to sit on the seat next to her without requesting permission or waiting for an invite. "Yeah, it's a stupid name. But it's mine. Last name is Sundown."

When he chuckled, Jade realized he must have seen her reaction of shocked amusement at his surname being just as ridiculous as the first name.

"Your name is"—she could not stop the smile that twitched at the corner of her lips—"Reno Sundown? Really?" She closed her book, the knowledge she was reading replaced with curiosity for the man who had interrupted its digestion. Jade angled in her seat to give him her full attention. "I thought my name was silly. Jade. But I know it was my mother's favorite stone. It's a mineral. And she had green eyes just like me."

Mr. Sundown's smile faded, and his brow creased in thought. "Was? Had? And that's your grandmother? Oh, yeah. She said you lost them." His lips formed an *O* and then pressed together in a firm line. His gaze slid right and then left before resting on Jade's. "So gone as in dead?"

Jade should have known that question would naturally follow. She internally chastised herself for sharing what little she had. "They both died in a plane crash. A year ago. My grandmother is all the family I have left." She picked up her book and opened it. She had no idea what page she had been on, but she just desperately needed the escape its pages provided from the topic that had arisen. Reaching behind her head as she lowered it, Jade released her hair from its ponytail to toy with it and fidget.

"I don't have any, either. Parents. Jess—I, ah, mean Will was my only family growing up. And me him."

Jade simply nodded as she let her long dark hair fall forward to act as a curtain between them, hoping the man took the hint that she no longer felt sociable. Her anxiety started to kick up, and her foot bounced on the floorboard as she brought the opposite knee against her chest.

"What are you reading?"

He was still there. Why had he not taken the hint? Not that Jade needed him to say anything to know he was there. She felt him in her space. A space that felt like it was closing in by the second. Closing her eyes tight, she mentally listed her favorite reads, one after the other, to conjure up calm and keep a freak-out in check.

Hunger Games

Velveteen Rabbit

Harry Potter

Beauty and the Beast

Percy Jackson

The well-used tactic had begun to work until the man reached out to take the book from her hands.

"Hey!" she yelled and jerked sideways, her dark hair flying back as she gave him an astonished glare. "That's mine."

He nodded, and with one finger placed as a bookmark within the pages, he looked at the cover. "*The Chemical Properties of Natural Formed Toxins*?" His brow went up, and he let out a laugh. "Wow, that's really heavy reading. Bet that it has all kinds of big words." He let out another laugh. "And you're reading this for *fun?*"

He looked out toward the school, and Jade felt renewed hope he would leave the car and join the others. She had been wrong.

"Why did you get kicked out of your school, Jade?" He turned to face her, and she could have sworn there was something else in the blue depths of his eyes—scrutiny, analysis… No, it was something Jade did not recognize. Only one description seemed right to Jade—predator. Whatever it was, it caused her anxiety to spike higher.

She jerked the book from his hands. "I didn't get kicked out. I wasn't getting along with some of the people there."

It was, however, true in reverse—Jade did nothing to merit the friction. No one appeared or tried to get *along* with her, which both baffled and frustrated her. She stayed out of the way and apart from them all. She was the quiet bookworm girl who only wanted to be left alone. She was not the only child from a wealthy family—it was a costly private school. Many of her fellow students had parents in the movie industry, politics, or professional sports. Sure, she had perfect grades and hit the Dean's list each semester, but she was not the only one to achieve that honor, either. Never mind that some of the grades were bought and purchased. Essays purchased from others to pass. Not Jade, but it was a well-known practice that the school did nothing to stop. Why would they do that when the parents "donated" thousands and sometimes millions to have halls, buildings, and stadiums to carry their names. A generational, educational legacy bought and paid for.

But ever since her parents died, the animosity and bullying escalated to a level that caused the school to call in her grandmother to discuss concerns. Jade had complained to the counselor how girls were cruel to her in the bathroom. Taunts in the hallway and nasty notes left on her desk or snuck into the pages of her notebook—from boys and girls, ones Jade had never even spoken to nor known their names. She had hoped the school would help, but instead of assisting her, they accused *her* of being the cause with explanations of spite, jealousy... And of course, her grandmother blamed Jade. The final straw had been when a classmate had locked Jade in a bathroom stall and dumped a bottle of blue toilet cleaner all over her and her book bag. Her phone had also taken damage. Jade had no choice but to go to the office, covered in the chemical, her skin along with her clothes stained a deep blue.

They had called her grandmother to the office with a spare uniform, but it had not been required—she was suspended from school as a "trouble maker." When they arrived home, her grandmother had ordered her to shower and scrub until the tinge of color was removed from her skin. The first shower did little to remove it, so Jade's grandmother told her to shower twice more. Still not satisfied, although Jade could find zero traces of blue, the woman ordered her to strip. She scrubbed her down with a loofa herself until Jade's skin became raw and painful. Jade had pleaded for her to stop, telling her grandmother it hurt. That was halted with a hard backslap to stop complaining. She had brought it on herself. Only after that final traumatic shower did Jade's grandmother declare her decent and clean.

Mr. Sundown's brow popped up as he continued that strange and intense scrutiny. "Okay, so you had a problem getting along with people. I get that. I have had a lot of trouble making friends. Or uh"—he raised his hands to use fingers in an air quote manner —"getting along."

"What is going on here? Sir, remove yourself from my granddaughter this minute!"

Jade heard her grandmother's voice, and she straightened up stiffly in her seat. She looked beyond Mr. Sundown to find her elder standing with Mr. Bailey and the driver. "Ah, oh, he was asking about my book. What I was reading."

Her grandmother's face was mottled in red, livid with indignation as she stepped back to allow Mr. Sundown to remove himself from the back seat. Grandmother took a moment to compose herself, but Jade knew she would bear the brunt for the break in decorum. She always did.

Jade gave Mr. Sundown an apologetic look as she shrank into the corner of the back seat to press herself against the door. She let her hair fall back down and discreetly listened to her grandmother tell Mr. Bailey to contact her if any openings at his Academy presented. Jade chanced a look over at the men and found Mr. Sundown's eyes watching her intensely. A little too much so. It caused goose bumps to rise on Jade's arms and prickle the back of her neck.

As the car pulled away, her grandmother's hand snapped out to grab Jade's knee cruelly in her bony fingers. The pain caused Jade to yelp. The punishment was neither unexpected nor uncommon. But always painful. It would leave a bruise as it usually did. But her grandmother always made sure those marks did not show for anyone to see. She was calculated even in her disciplinary abuse.

"We will discuss this indiscretion when we arrive home, Jade."

Jade turned her head to look at her grandmother. "I did nothing.

He did not ask, nor did I permit him to get in the car. Why am I in trouble?"

The fast movement of the hand from Jade's knee coming up to slap was no more surprising than the rest. In the time it took for the sting of it to make itself known, Jade's grandmother had restored her composure. "A Shen woman is always in control of her situation. Regardless of whom initiates the interaction." Jade's grandmother gave her a sideward reprimanding glare. "You know this. Never let it not guide you." Her hand now came up to cup Jade's chin so their eyes met. Jade knew better than to flinch or look away. It was evident which Shen woman was the dominating one in this situation, and it was *not* Jade. It never was. "That will always state your worth."

The woman's hand fell away, and Jade wanted to exhale heavily in relief but had been trained to control all signs of emotions—including the shudder accompanying the more careful release of air. "Why does it alone state my worth, grandmother?"

Grandmother checked her carefully applied lipstick in a platinum compact. "Because it is all the worth you have, child. You lose the impression you are worthy of respect?" The compact was folded and placed back in the woman's Gucci handbag. Grandmother then gave Jade a look that caused her to whither back into the corner of the car. "You. Are nothing."

"THAT WAS ODD," Jess said as the fancy limo pulled out into the traffic running in front of the school. "Not like I could tell her." He snorted in amusement as he looked down at the business card in his hand. "I'm sorry, ma'am, but this here school is for supernatural young 'uns and those of other supernatural folks." The card was crumpled up and tossed to the ground as he turned to walk back to the construction. "Nope. Let's get back to work."

Reno bent down to pick up the card, then stood and stared at it.

"Yeah. Odd." Whereas his brother meant it in the interaction with the old woman, Reno felt it about the girl. There was just something strange that caused both Sundown and Madness to pace mentally inside Reno's head.

I don't know. So before you start bugging the shit out of me or even asking, I have no idea. But something wasn't right about that girl. But I didn't pick up any Epsilon juju from her, the old lady, the driver, or the car —nada. Just something is really strange about that kid. Madness, as rare as it is, agrees. Doesn't know any more than I do.

Reno nodded as Sundown summarized that all three of them were in a single accord. Something about Jade Shen was different. But what? And how? And why?

"You comin'?"

Reno glanced back over his shoulder at Jess as he shoved the card into his jeans pocket. "Yeah, I'm coming."

3

She does not know how wrong she is, Jade.

Jade sat on her bed with a book resting on her drawn-up knees. Earbuds were pumping P!nk from Spotify with the volume at max. It did nothing to drown out the voice trying to assure her, as the words often tried to do, that Jade was not worthless.

Because it was in her head.

Jade had begun hearing it as a whisper a year or two before her parents died. At first, she had been frightened, afraid she had developed a brain tumor or some other medical reason for the anomaly. Still, the voice was always on her side, almost as if Jade had an internal cheerleader supporting her on the bad days and applauding on the good days. Jade dared not reveal it to her parents, however. They were supportive in their way, but her father worked unbelievably hard with long hours at Shen Corporation, and her mother, while a bit more loving than Jade's father or grandmother, placed more importance in Jade being the perfect little girl.

Jade was not sure if it was because her mother thought she was or wanted to prove to her grandmother that she *could* be. With the right grooming and structure, Jade Shen could be a productive, strong legacy flag bearer of the family name—even if she was a female.

Her mother became obsessed with those goals. She insisted that Jade take advanced classes. Learn from social mentors on proper behavior. Learn not only Mandarin Chinese but also Spanish, French, and Latin. That workload was on top of the school's course work Jade completed under the strict, fast-track curriculum her parents demanded that she be allowed to carry. A large donation to the private school made it then possible, of course. Her parents told Jade they believed that she could not only meet the minimum to succeed but exceed far above it. They had been right about that. The advanced lessons did not prove to be difficult, but the backlash from her fellow students upon learning the school made exceptions for Jade added to their bullying and jealous scorn.

It was after an embarrassing episode at school when the voice had first spoken to Jade. Two of the most popular girls had passed around a note for their friends to list words to describe Jade. She was not sure if it was meant ever to cross her path, but it had. Jade sat in the cafeteria with her lunch forgotten, tears coursing down her cheeks, reading what her peers thought of her.

Geek. Nerd. Bookworm. Stupid. Skinny. Brainy.

And the worse words that blurred the rest from her vision as Jade started to cry—*Jade Shen is nothing. To anyone.*

Those simple words written in perfect block handwriting had been truer than the anonymous author may have realized—because it was how Jade felt every single day. She was not the perfect daughter. Not even close to the smartest. And if her parents had ever bothered to ask Jade, she would have told them she did not want to run the business one day. She could not and did not wish to be the boy her mother had been incapable of producing.

Her grandmother often berated her father about that very fact. While divorce would be shameful in the old woman's eyes, a child created outside of wedlock would be less disgraceful if it produced a son to carry the Shen name. But Jade knew her father loved her mother. She was not, however, sure if her father cared a single bit for his own since emotions were rarely shown in the Shen household. It was a matter of control and discipline. No little girl wishing it would be different would change a generational mentality.

Her parents would never rebel against her grandmother. She was the matriarch, and she held that role with an iron fist wrapped around the purse strings of the family's fortune.

Jade just always wished she could get a hug.

Her fellow students had laughed at Jade when she ran from the cafeteria that day. Perhaps some had not been, but to her, it sounded like the entire populace of the world found her public shaming hilarious.

Finding herself once again huddled in a dusty corner of the school library, Jade had cried as silently as she could with her hoodie gathered around her head. That section of the library housed outdated encyclopedias and yellowing periodicals. It was rarely—if ever—visited, so Jade retreated there often. The mild acrid scent of deteriorating pages combined with the aging ink gave her comfort and assisted her in reaching a calmer state about a role assigned to her that she did not want to play, ashamed that she was too obedient to break free of it.

She heard the school bell ring to signal lunch had ended, but Jade remained in the dim of the only haven of comfort she found in her life. Books and stories. Tales and fantasy. She often wished she could climb inside the covers and escape. But being as smart as she was, Jade knew, even as a little girl discovering books, that their escape was not a real one. It was impossible to escape to Hogwarts. Or appear in Wonderland with a bite of cake. Wishing for something impossible only made her more sad and tired. She stopped doing it at an early age.

They are envious of you, child. They want to be you, but they can't. Only you can be you.

Jade's head snapped up, her hoodie falling back as the voice whispered. She leaned forward to look down the long aisle of bookshelves and found no one there, just the dust mites swirling in the shaft of pale sunlight penetrating the darkness at the opposite end of the row. The voice of the librarian resounded far away in the front of the place. And the voice she had heard was close. Very close. Yet Jade found no one near.

"Hello?" Jade whispered in return, blinking in confusion as she moved her hair away from her face. "Is there anyone there?"

I've been here a while. Watching you. Drawn here by them but fascinated by you, Jade. I found you unique. How they want to be you. Yet you do not want to be you. Why is that? Can you explain it to me? Why would you want to not be you? Wait, that's not correct. Why do you not want to be anyone at all?

Jade jumped to her feet quickly. Panic made her feel cold that someone, somehow, knew how she really felt. She had never voiced it to anyone. "Where are you? Who are you?" Her voice trembled. Her bottom lip and body shook with fearful bewilderment. "How do you say that? How could you know?"

Oh, child. I know how you feel because it's what has me wanting to help you feel it less. And them... I want them to feel more. Because until they do, they can't learn just how dangerous envy really is. You want them to be better people, right, Jade? Let's do that together. Would you like that?"

Jade wiped her tears and nose on her sleeve. Logic told her what occurred made zero sense. She was very obviously alone. Yet the voice was right next to her, whispering in her ear. This person? Thing? Jade wasn't sure. That, too, was rare with her mind. But either way, regardless of its form, for the first time in Jade's life, someone or something knew how she felt.

And cared that she did.

"Yes. I would."

❧

THE VOICE CALLED herself Envy and had been Jade's constant companion from that day to the present. It had been Envy who comforted her when her parents' plane crashed, comforting and consoling. Envy was also there whenever her grandmother made Jade feel like a disappointment— just from being a child and a girl and that she hadn't died with them or, maybe, instead of them. Jade sat and watched her grandmother wail and scream about how the Shen legacy had died along with her father. How it would end with him. How she and Jade would be out on the streets without a strong leader at the company.

And when Grandmother learned that her father had left everything in a trust to Jade and it couldn't be touched beyond maintaining Jade's lifestyle and needs until she turned eighteen? That grief turned into rage and abuse. And Jade had been the sole target of both.

Jade had tried to tell the woman that she did not want the company. Nor the money. It did not matter. Her father had received it from his when the elder Shen had died of cancer. And now the son was leaving it all to his child.

Even if that child was a girl.

It made no difference that Jade's grandmother was also of the same gender. Her grandmother labeled Jade as a child and ignorant. A dreamer and simple.

It had been Envy who told Jade all of that was wrong. It was Envy who Jade chose to listen to and find solace in. And that, in turn, assisted Jade in finding her own strength—with Envy assisting in creating the blocks to build it. One insult equaled one brick of fortitude. Each fit of anger equaled mortar to make it all stick and be strong.

Jade loved her grandmother—in a way. She was all Jade had left of her family. Her father had been an only child, so there were zero uncles or aunts. No cousins. Nothing. Her grandmother had a brother once, but he died during one of the wars before Jade was born. It was not wise to speak of the dead, which meant Jade was reprimanded whenever she tried to talk of her parents. She believed her grandmother mourned, and they could find that in common. To help the other get through it.

No. It was just another trigger for her grandmother's anger.

Envy got her through those incidents just as she did the rest.

"How do you know she's wrong? Why are you so sure?" Jade set the book to the side as she pulled the earbuds free and hit pause on the music. "What if she is right and you are wrong? She has known me longer. And I still don't know why you care."

A deep sigh filled the silence in Jade's head for a moment. Perhaps Envy herself did not even know. As the silence continued, Jade suddenly feared Envy had given up on her. Would leave her just as suddenly and painfully sharp as her parents did when they died.

Because I do. And how do I know she's wrong? Because deep down, you know she is. Remember, Jade, I can touch all your darkest secrets. Your most hidden personal judgments. I care because I can. I care because we both need me to.

"You need me? No one needs me, Envy. But I care about you, too." Curling back in the bed, she pulled her worn stuffed Winne the Poo bear her father had given her as a toddler. "Can you help me sleep? Like you always do?"

Envy started to hum a song in a language that Jade did not recognize. She wasn't even sure if it was one. But it was soft, beautiful, and the lullaby her soul was now in the habit of hearing to welcome in sleep.

And shut out the world.

4

"You want to grab some breakfast?"

Tyrus DeMonte did *not* want to grab some grub, and he wished the nude woman wasn't still here to ask about that meal. It was against his standard operating procedure, but he had been fucking exhausted after Grid patrol last night. But not so tired that he turned down the offer from the sexy Relay, who coaxed him to wait a few hours to sleep, but he was unable to stay awake after they had sex. Bracing his hands on the bathroom counter of his loft apartment, he looked at himself in the mirror as he stood with a towel wrapped around his waist after a shower. Dark skin and lighter colored eyes like his father. His hair was having some severe bedhead issues, and he'd probably clip it short later, but for now, he needed this woman out of his personal space.

When Tyrus walked out, she hooked a foot behind his knee with a "come hither and let's fuck" look on her makeup-smeared face. Did he really think she was hot last night? Where had *that* girl gone? Or perhaps weariness worked in the same manner as beer goggles. "What I want is for you to go." Dodging her efforts to tug the towel off, he picked up her shirt, jeans, and purse from his floor and dropped them onto the bed. He stood as he tossed a condom lying next to the bed into the waste can by the nightstand and gave her a slight smile. "As in now. If you don't mind."

Her response to his eviction was predictable, and he rolled his eyes as she ranted while she dressed. She threw a pillow at his head, which he caught, and he looked to the side as she cursed a few more times and left. The front door made a resounding slam, and he winced as the screaming tirade continued, echoing up the stairwell as she exited the building—one owned by his father, Marcus DeMonte.

As he tossed the pillow back onto the bed, he hoped that perhaps his sire and girlfriend, Alexis, were out and about already. But no, Tyrus wasn't that lucky when a sharp knock rapped against the recently slammed door.

"Shit," Tyrus mumbled as he pulled out a set of sweats from his dresser drawer. Padding to the front door on bare feet, he opened it without a word and turned to walk into the kitchen. It wasn't even eleven, and of course, his father already looked like he was prepping for a runway walk in a Tom Ford suit—sans tie. It was before noon, after all. Ties, apparently, were evening wear.

He glanced over to find Alexis had accompanied Marcus, and Tyrus held up the coffeepot. "Can we wait until I have at least one coffee in me before the lecturing starts?"

Alexis gave him a smile of comfort while his father glared at him with the predictable and often repeated interrogation. "Who was that? Anyone I should be concerned with? Civilian or Grid?"

Tyrus rested his forehead on the kitchen cabinet in front of him and closed his eyes as a pre-caffeine headache began to throb behind them. "I am going to guess the one cup reprieve is a no-go." Interrupting the brewing process, he moved the pot out of the way and slid a mug from the cabinet to catch the flow.

"Your father is just concerned as always, Tyrus."

Tyrus nodded at Alexis's summation, and after replacing the pot, he turned to lean against the granite counter and found they had both sat at the island across from him in the open kitchen. Taking a sip, he bit his bottom lip with his fangs—another inheritance from his half-demon father—and nodded. "I know. I always know. Which is why you two offered me a place in the building." He had accepted the offer willingly at the time as he recovered from being shot up and beaten by Epsilon, the son of a bitch offspring of Lucifer. Taking another sip, he sighed. "She was Grid. Human." He lifted the mug and regarded them over its rim. "Don't ask me her name." He let out a snort. "I don't believe I even asked. It may have started with a G. Or P? Or, fuck, an H?"

Alexis put a hand on Marcus's shoulder. The immortal Breaker knew her boyfriend well, as well as Tyrus did, most likely. Hell, maybe even better since she had been in Marcus's life almost as long as Tyrus had the man in his. Must have been a bitch to start fathering a full-grown man who was the baby you tossed into the Hell fires at birth. Complicated. Evolving. And as Marcus growled around his own fangs—never dull.

Especially when they also had Murder, a dark asshole power, in the family dynamic.

Was she hot? I tried to tune into your head to listen, but it was a no-go. Give me details later, kid. We have our own door—big and broody doesn't even have to know.

"Big and broody didn't need to know any of that. And thank you, Murder, for the intel about the new door." Marcus smirked as he let both Tyrus and Murder know that they did not have as tight of a secret bromance as they thought. "And you must stop bringing these strange females to our home." Marcus stood and paused by Tyrus on the way to the coffeepot. "I worry. And their screaming in the morning as you remove them from our home makes me cranky." But his father's tone had changed to a gentler one, telling Tyrus the subject was considered trivial and not worthy of further discussion. Today, anyway.

Good. That suited Tyrus just fine. "Just imagine how much they would scream if they were asked to stay." Murder chuckled in Tyrus's head, and a mental high-five was imagined. "And I'm not talking about sex." He glanced over at Alexis and then down at the floor. "I hear a broken heart can be pretty fucking painful." He refilled his mug. "And I don't believe in love, so one night is it." He grinned at Marcus. "Even as handsome, awesome, and badass as I am, it's not going to happen." Because it was something that Tyrus refused to want.

5

"Master, we had a bite at the offer."

Epsilon sat in the penthouse apartment, which also functioned as the base of his operations. The mess with his father over the Murder and Marcus situation severed the razor-thin ruse Epsilon had to make use of the ruler of Hell's funds, assistance, and turning a blind eye. That had ended, and his father had cut him off—Epsilon's finances were proof of that. The coffers of cash after securing an army and weapons were bleeding out faster than the freak Reno had the night Epsilon slaughtered him.

He glanced up from his place at the dining room table where avocado toast went untouched. "Which offer would that be?" Epsilon replied with a touch of disdain for the lack of information given. He had dozens, if not hundreds, of lines tossed out into the underbelly of the dark web among the mercenary's chat rooms and forums. It had suited him well to build his human army— trained, some of them ex-military, and willing to take high cash payment to do what was asked and ask no questions when doing it. Their numbers were complimented with demons and halflings—rejects from his father's realm or mutts that crawled out, afraid of Lucifer's wrath.

"Forgive me, Master." The demon fell to his knees. The high-level, human-appearing demon from Hell had been one of many that had left the realm in mutiny to Lucifer. Epsilon knew the real reason was that his father had begun cleaning "house" of any demonkind found or rumored to be assisting Epsilon. Even if a demon only expressed a slight sympathy for the excommunicated former prince for the throne, that would no longer be tolerated.

Epsilon once entertained reasonable hopes that Lucifer would realize how ridiculous it had been to give the title and rights to the throne to a Keeper. A host for the dark power of Madness. And Reno Sundown was not aware of how very entitled he was to the right. He was, after all, Lucifer's own son via the rape of Epsilon's wife. Twisted fuckery... every bit of it. Epsilon had enough. Between Marcus being *allowed* to be created by the dark lord *and* giving the freak Reno such power, Epsilon would not take the honor from his father even if offered to be restored. If he could not be given his birthright, he would end his father. End the freak and fucking take it. Take what was his.

Epsilon slowly slid the plate of food away and placed his arms on the table to tap fingers on the surface. He bared his fangs with a slow exhale of breath. "Speak. And off your knees. I tell you when to kneel. Or jump off the roof. Or breathe in my presence. You do not make such choices." On the other hand, the demon most likely also knew that if it had not knelt, Epsilon would have punished it for that as well. Ah, the power of keeping one's beasts and pets trained and afraid. "What bite? Which offer?"

The demon quickly rose to his feet, then approached the table, head down, and placed a sheet of paper in front of Epsilon.

Raising a brow, Epsilon waved the demon off dismissively as he read what was printed on the page.

It had been an offer to remove anyone, anywhere, from someone's life. No questions or names and cash—for a costly charge—the only acceptable form of payment for the job. Epsilon listed the price at such a large amount that only the elite of clientele would give it notice and be able to afford it. And now someone had.

Smiling, he ran his fingers over the information and said the name out loud, "Sigu Shen. Hello."

6

PRESENT DAY

The connection with Ms. Shen had been two months ago. In that time, Epsilon had not only gained ownership of a weapon's factory in Columbia via a shadow corporation but the price for the assassination of the young Jade Shen.

Or so he led her grandmother to believe.

Epsilon was quite sure the woman couldn't care less whether Epsilon carried out the request. She hadn't asked for any proof that the child had breathed her last breath, only that he orchestrated the private car driving Jade home from school to go off the Golden Gate Bridge, and the young woman thought lost as so many bodies often were when the bay claimed them. Her driver was recovered, dead, still strapped in his seatbelt when the car was discovered after a final drag of the bay. Jade's belongings were found in the back seat, the back door caved in, and the glass shattered. What a very tragic loss.

And now three months later, Jade Shen had been officially declared dead.

However—she was very much alive.

She resided in a cell built inside of a recently purchased warehouse on the docks of the same bay she hadn't plunged into. Irony. So simple. So efficient.

And yet... Jade Shen was not as easy of a toy as he had presumed. No. In fact, Jade had not come alone. How was he to have guessed that the girl, barely eighteen years old, would have been claimed by a dark power? One that was as obsessively protective of the human girl as any mother would be their child. A living human... not a host. Not dead. But as bizarre as it struck Epsilon, the girl and the power were friends.

"Dark power as a friend." He let out a snort as he walked toward the high-tech ballistic cube that held Jade Shen. Being given the small weapons factory as payment from Sigu Shen had its definite perks beyond having access to advanced ammunition and weapons. Such as the cube. It was created to test detonations and impacts during the bomb design stage of research and development. Epsilon outfitted the door with a keypad lock, and only he knew the code. Complementing the eight-by-eight container with a cot made with luxurious linens—Jade's cell was perfect for Epsilon's needs.

For the first few days, Jade had slammed herself against the walls and screamed to be set free. She had refused to eat or drink. Even bathroom trips by one of his female underlings revealed a stubbornness Epsilon found delightful—she did not relieve herself.

Epsilon had countered her protesting behavior with he cared not if she died. Don't eat? Starve. Don't drink the water? Dehydrate and die. Disobey her bladder and bowels? How inconvenient that would be for Jade, considering there was no way to clean herself within the cube. And since it had an isolated air circulation system, no one would suffer from her defecating other than her.

But the key to Jade's submission had been a simple one—die, and he would have Envy to use as he saw fit. He made it clear how delighted that would make him.

Epsilon had been informed of her cooperation the next morning. He was not entirely heartless. He then provided her a reward with fresh gourmet meals from his personal chef, clean clothes, and bottles of water. Interestingly enough, the only things Jade said thank you for were the books. Tomes from classic to current trade paperbacks. He watched as she came back from the facilities clean in her new clothing and curled up on the cot with a book, appearing both calm and resigned.

Shame. Epsilon enjoyed her outbursts and was aroused by her spirit. But a compliant toy was easier to play with than one that fought even its basic needs. But, alas, the fight was so much more fun.

He had thought that being a toy for his pleasure was Jade's only value. He would enjoy her. He would break her. And then he would throw her away as he had done so many others. Jade nor any of the others could equal to McKenzie, the Keeper of Lust. Anger spiked through his blood and caused Greed to stir with a hunger not met when he thought of McKenzie Miller. And the longer he went without obtaining the prize, the deeper the hunger gnawed at his gut like a meal of razor blades.

That is until he and Greed found a new snack to feed on.

Envy.

Reaching the door, Epsilon pressed in the code and entered. Jade sat in the corner, as usual, on the cot with a book. She smelled clean, and he glanced at her soiled clothes in the corner. Last week, her cube was moved next to the bathroom. A guard allowed her access to the restroom for privacy and escorted her back to her expensive cage whenever the girl requested.

Epsilon stood in silence. Partially amused that Jade continued her pretense of not acknowledging his existence, and he wondered if Envy whispered in the girl's mind, encouraging Jade to resist. Hold strong. Do not give in. Whereas Jade had ceased her struggles to escape, the fact he could break both her and Envy did arouse him. It caused Greed to hum in his head with agreement. And the method was beautifully simple—the truth.

"All the others that the dark powers chose are dead." He pulled up the simple chair, a recently earned addition to Jade's cage, and sat. "Did Envy not tell you that? Interesting. She should have. Perhaps you are surprised that you are *not* the only one chosen. Nor is she the only dark power."

Jade glanced up with that statement, one slender brow rising ever so slightly.

Ah, Epsilon thought, *she had not been aware.* Not surprising. Epsilon knew the powers were not only the darkest but also the most deceptive. It was their nature just as his was to put them in their place. They were deadly, yes, but he enjoyed the games—Greed thrived with the contests.

"There are several dark powers. All of which, thus far, have chosen their hosts." Epsilon pinched the crease of the tailored suit trousers and then folded his hands on his lap. "Perhaps I should begin with the proper introductions. I am Epsilon Abaddon, and my father is Lucifer." He gave her a smile as more surprise flicked across her pretty features. "Yes, that Lucifer. The Dark Master of Hell. But I am not in accord with my father. If anything, he is an adversary. I care for you and the dark powers. He, on the other hand"—he let out a dramatic mock sigh—"wants to trap the dark powers back in Hell. And that would destroy their hosts."

"Hosts?" Jade's voice was soft. Barely above a whisper. "What do you mean, *hosts*?"

"Well, have you ever seen Envy? Has she ever appeared in front of you?"

Jade's brow creased in confusion, and he wondered if she was listening to the dark power for answers. The girl shook her head. Long, dark as a raven's wing hair swung down to cover her face with the movement. She moved it out of the way, and her green gaze met his.

"No. I only hear her." Her voice went to a lower decimal. Adorable—as if she thought Envy wouldn't be able to listen to the discussion. "In my head."

Epsilon smiled. "Of course. That is due to the powers being pure energy now. It was not always the way. They once had forms like you and me. Madness, Lust, Murder, and your invisible friend, Envy. They were created as tests of humanity, to determine one's worthiness of Heaven. Or lesser value to the realm on high and, therefore, Hell was able to lay claim to the soul. Pass the test—Heaven. Fail it—Hell. It's as simple as that."

Jade's eyes widened, and she blinked in disbelief. "But I'm not evil. Or sinful. Why is a dark power talking to me? Why do you have me here?" She was on her feet, albeit standing on the cot, but she showed a dormant strength beyond her willfulness to not cooperate. "Why am I being tested? Why?" Her voice went high. Tone threaded, frantic with anxiety. "Why?"

Epsilon rose and stepped toward the cot with a hand out to touch her. She would take it since he was trying to comfort her. In truth, he wanted to feed off her emotions—drawn to the swirling feelings like a drug. "Calm down, Jade. I am here to explain it to you."

And the moment his hand touched her arm…

Everything changed.

7

The moment the man with the strange blue eyes touched her, something felt as if it burst in Jade's skull. A sizzling type of feeling that made her scream. Suddenly, a deep green mist surrounded her. The sight of it surging out of Jade's pores, a cold, slithering sensation creeping from her eyes and nose made Jade panic at the realization it came from inside of *her*. "What is happening! Stop!"

The man went flying from an invisible shove across the room. Jade knew she hadn't touched him, but there he was, hitting the glass wall opposite the cot with such force of impact that cracks appeared on the surface as he hit the floor. An alarm sounded a second before men rushed in with weapons aimed at Jade. The green fog stuff stayed around Jade like a protective cloud. The men must have known what it was because they stayed beyond its reach. When one took a step forward to pull Epsilon away, the fog surged out to stop the rescue attempt. Jade could have sworn it took the shape of a hand, but that was crazy. That was not possible. And Jade had not believed in the impossible in a very long time.

It was all too much. She collapsed to the cot, and everything went dark.

❧

Jade. Child. I need you to wake up. Come on, wake up for me.

Jade heard Envy's comforting, soft voice in her head. It pounded with a *thud, thud* like the worse migraine she had ever imagined. She had never experienced one before, but as she cracked open her eyes and the dim light in the room hurt, she had to believe she had one now. Noise was agonizing—the sound of Jade's moan too much for her head to hear. She struggled to move from a tight curl on the cot to her back and let out a gasp of pain. "What… happened?"

That bastard dared to touch you. Greed would have gobbled you up. I couldn't let that happen to you. I protected you. But now they know how much I can do. How I can help you. What we can do together. That's not a good thing. I'm sorry.

"Together?" The word alone in this situation boggled her—she hadn't wanted to throw Epsilon across the room, had she? Jade struggled to sit up and brought a hand to her forehead. "Why are you sorry? You were helping me. But, Envy." She swallowed as she struggled to form cohesive thoughts and questions. "What he was saying. About you being a dark power. About your testing. You and the other dark powers. How you test people." Tears prickled her lashes. Envy was her only friend and had been for so long. What if it was all just a trick like the man had implied? "Are you testing me? You said we were friends. Is that a lie?"

Jade brought a hand up to wipe across her eyes. "He said all dark powers lie. But you don't seem dark." Her voice cracked, and she tried not to cry, but she could not hold back. There was so much, too many emotions. "I'm scared, Envy…" she whispered as she sobbed, "you're all I have. But now I don't understand. How can you be dark like he said and be my friend?" She brought the neckline of the shirt she wore to cover her face. "Is it all a lie? Are you using me? Please, say you're not."

Envy sighed deeply in Jade's mind. She knew that now… that was where her invisible friend resided. Or at least where they were connected. Was *bond* a better word after what Jade had seen the power do? Dropping the shirt, Jade's gaze went over to the cracks in the glass wall of the cube. It had happened. Jade had not imagined it. That was reality. This place and her situation were as well. But what if…

"Envy, are you real? Or have I just gone crazy?"

No child. Open your eyes.

Jade did as Envy asked and let out a sharp gasp, her hand flying up to cover her mouth. In front of her, the green mist had returned within inches from Jade's face. It swirled in a circular shape and made a low, hushed humming.

Hello, Jade. We should have formally met before now, but I didn't want to scare you. I do not want you to think I'd ever hurt you. I want to keep you safe. Protect you. And now that the son of Satan has you, things have changed. Reach out to me, child. I won't cause you any pain. Trust me.

Jade felt paralyzed in place. Everything always changed. Her childhood changed when her father took over the company. Then changed again when she lost her parents. More when her grandmother became her guardian. And then when the woman had given her to Epsilon. The only constant in Jade's life for so long had been Envy. Her invisible friend.

Or was she an enemy? Jade was not sure about anything. Not anymore.

Jade lifted a hand as she held her breath. Her fingers trembled as her fingertips touched the swirling green mass. It was cold but felt like energy. Jade used to love to curl up next to the laundry dryer and feel the vibrating heat from the machine. Yet this was a cold sensation. But Jade could feel the energy. Different. Completely. But it was the only analogy that Jade could align with this.

The mass changed its shape to twine around her fingers, moving as she moved her digits in fascination. Her sense of overwhelming panic began to ease with each gentle stroking of the energy against her skin. A tendril curled around Jade's wrist, and she couldn't help but smile. When Jade was a small child, she was terrified of flying. Even on the private family jet. Her mother would wrap her hand over Jade's wrist, where her pulse raced, and that touch calmed her. And Envy's did the same now.

"Why are you so cold? And be energy?"

Because I have no soul, and only beings with true souls have the heat of life, which I ceased to have eons ago. I am alive but in another way. But I can feel you. I always could. And now you can feel me in return. I wish I could be warm, child. I was once. But I am as I am now.

Jade wiped her face once again and then smiled as Envy made the shape of her mother's favorite jade figurine—a dragon. "I feel you. I do. And I like the chill." It reminded Jade of her mother's cool hand on her forehead when she ran a fever. Or the wet cloth her father pressed against the nape of Jade's neck when she became scared from a bad dream. Envy's touch emulated the comfort of those memories, and Jade's tattered need to be loved held on to that for comfort.

"Is what he said true? That you test us?" Jade exhaled slowly. "Am I here because I failed? I don't understand what's going on, Envy." Her gaze trailed to the cracks in the glass. "But I trust you more than I do him. I feel like he's the evil one, not you."

Because you are a smart one, Jade—you always were. And no. I never judged you or tested you. The others that bullied you? Teased and picked on you? Oh, yes, how I found them lacking in good. But never you. They did lead me to you, that and your grandmother. Something about you made me want to stay with you. To keep you safe from them. To keep you as light as you are.

Jade frowned at that. "Light?" She brought her hand up, and yes, she was pale, but light seemed a very odd word to use for her skin tone. "What do you mean?"

Envy chuckled in Jade's head. *Your energy. Your soul. It's light and sweet. Innocent. I'm a dark power, yes. But even I crave the good. To be as close to it as I can be. To feel as I once was. Alive.*

Envy's voice took on a sad tone with each word, and Jade drew her knees up to press against her chest. "He said something about that. You used to be a person? Like everyone else?"

Envy let out another heavy sigh. *We were never human. We did take on a human shape and form, but that was taken away from us. And we were made into energy as a punishment for something very wrong that happened. But I missed being around humans. Their laughter. Their sounds. Their joy. And oh, how I loved the smallest of your kind. The children. That's what drew me to you. You were a child, but you did not often laugh. You were the saddest child I had ever come across. It pulled at the being I once was. I wanted to protect you. So I have. And so I always will.*

The words and tone of Envy were kind. And Jade could feel the sincerity behind them. She had heard very similar promises before, expressions of concern and love from her parents before every business trip. Vows met until the last trip when they weren't. Commitments from her grandmother in her aloof manner to take care of Jade—until she was given to Epsilon. Perhaps Envy really could hear her thoughts because the dark power countered the doubts with some very simple whispered words.

You trusted me before, Jade, and I have never let you down. I will not do so now. But first, we have to get you out of here. He truly is evil. And he is not to be trusted. We must escape.

Jade moved to stand, and the mist vanished, but she now knew it had not gone far. Even as it disappeared from sight, she felt its cool, calming sensation on her skin. She found both comfort and bravery in the fact Envy was truly her friend. She walked over to touch the cracks on the thick glass wall... Her friend was a powerful one.

Maybe, just maybe, Jade could be stronger, too.

"MASTER, I believe your injury requires stitches."

Epsilon batted the Healer's hand away as the woman tried to tend to his injuries. His dark blue blood dripped to the floor from the painful gash on the back of his head that he got when Envy had thrown him against the wall. *Him. Thrown. Into. A. Wall.* There was zero way the young woman Jade had that power, and the flash of green in the room right before he hit was a definitive giveaway it had been the power's doing.

But how? Jade was not dead. She had not met her mortal end. They had performed blood tests on Jade when she arrived—one had to be cautious when Lucifer and the Grid enlisted other beings in an attempt to infiltrate Epsilon's armies. It would seem laughable to think that Jade was anything other than she appeared, that Sigu Shen was more honorable than a grandmother who was willing to sell her only family member's life for selfish gain. But no, all was as it appeared. Epsilon actually felt a minuscule grain of pity for the young woman. Or perhaps it was indigestion. Either way, it passed quickly.

"It will heal in the time it takes me to change my suit." Which he would have to do as it had blood on it its pale gray silk lapels. Jerking away from the woman, he shrugged his jacket off and tossed it in the trash. Touching the back of his skull, he angled his view in the mirror and could see the dark blue oozing of blood in his white hair. "How the fuck did she do that?"

Hearing the door close and he was left alone, he narrowed his eyes as he took in his image in the mirror. Jade was unique. He had been a fool to think she was simply a human girl caught up in the web of her grandmother's deceit. "Keepers are dead, not living timid girls," he mumbled as he jerked off his tie, unbuttoned his shirt, and added it to the trash. Moving his hand down, his fingers paused on a long-ago healed scar that ran over his ribs. Its deepest point puckered below his pectoral, under his heart.

While the wound had faded to a scar—the memory of what made it had not.

❧

EONS AGO—REALM OF HELL

His father warned Epsilon to stay away from the door. The one that resided down the longest and darkest hallway in the realm. The walls leading to it were slimy slick with mold and roaches, beetles, and worms. But what his father didn't seem to realize was simple—never tell a little boy not to do something.

The first time he had ventured there, Epsilon had opened the door and learned that the Void behind it contained the dark powers. Those created to balance the light of good with the darkness of bad. Lesson learned. His father had punished his son to his chambers for weeks for allowing some that which dwelt there out. No food. No water. No sound. No light. Deep in a hole inside the palace chambers. Epsilon had begged for forgiveness then.

But Epsilon was no longer a child who now stood before the door. He was a teenager, neglected for far too long since that time. Bitterness had grown. Lucifer became stupidly sodden with affection for his general. And finding softness by allowing mutts like Marcus to be treated like a full-blooded hellspawn rather than a halfling. Lucifer was becoming a weaker master of the realm every day.

Even so, Epsilon was not strong enough, nor would he ever be, to take the throne. But just as he had not forgotten the lesson taught by his father the prior time the door opened, the whispered promises from a power unable to escape that day remained just as fresh in his recall.

"Are you there?" Epsilon pressed his palm against the door. Even with the reinforcements and layered, enchanted iron a foot thick, he could feel the immense energy of the powers contained within. "You said you could make me stronger. You said you could make it where I would no longer be his slave if I helped you to no longer be his prisoner. Are you still offering that?"

Yessss. But you have to want it. You have to want to destroy him. Destroy anything. Destroy everyone. No matter what or who gets in our way. As long as you feel that, you feed me. And I give you what you need to do all that you crave. Do you agree? I will not offer it again. You have already left me here to rot while others roam free. They, too, will pay. Agreed?

Epsilon leaned forward to rest his forehead against the grimy surface. If he did this, there would be no turning back. There would be no reconciling with his father. He had no reason to believe whichever power demanded the partnership would not make him pay for disobedience—in ways that even the son of Lucifer could not imagine.

But it wasn't like his father loved him. Or cherished him. Nor did he respect his own son.

"Yes. I agree. What do I need to do?"

It's simple. Open the door. Come inside. I'm waiting.

EPSILON OPENED HIS EYES, meeting his reflection once more as he forced his mind free of the past and its focus away from the scar from a self-inflicted wound. His greed to overtake his sire and claim the throne of the realm overtook his desire to live. He had ripped his torso open while on his knees in front of the dark power. He had regained consciousness outside the door to the Void, lying in a puddle of red blood with none of the substance left in his body and without a pulse. And Greed took residence in his head from that day forward. Epsilon had paid with his life—given willingly for the power to take over, his original purpose in life cut short so Greed could make use of it. And, in turn, for Epsilon to do the same.

The funny thing was his father had not noticed. To Lucifer, Epsilon was no more than the rest of the dead within the realm. He was given no more of the dark lord's notice than he had received prior.

But Jade still lived. "But why? And how?" He narrowed his eyes as he buttoned on a fresh shirt then slid on a jacket. "And how can I use it?" He tilted his head and smiled.

Easy. Envy would do anything to protect the girl.

"Yes, she would. But would that include letting her go to join forces with you and me, Greed?"

Only one way to find out. The girl needs to hurt. And she might just die.

"Well," Epsilon said with a deadly smile as he adjusted his jacket, "that would be such a shame."

8

"You've been really quiet, Candyman."

Reno was sitting at the end of their bed while Sophia and her little brother played in the living room. Their sounds were complemented by Eli's young service dog, Tilt, barking in the activity. Glancing back over his shoulder as Witch laid a hand on his back, Reno opened his mouth to speak but said nothing as his eyes went down to her round belly.

Turning, he moved to lie on his side, facing her and whispered to their twins, "Hi, you two. How are you doing? Getting crowded?"

Emma softly laughed as she combed her fingers through his hair.

Gosh, he loved that. Closing his eyes, Reno let out a slow exhale before rolling to his back to look up at her. Lifting a hand, he brushed her hair back. "Epsilon has been quiet. No sign of him. Nothing. For months. As much as I hate when he does show up, I hate it more when he hasn't." He smirked and moved his hand to rub his forehead and squeezed his eyes shut. "I know. It sounds silly." He opened them to meet her pretty green ones. "Does that make any sense?" He snorted. "I know I sometimes don't make *any* sense."

Emma smiled. "You almost always make sense to me, Reno. And

I agree." She bit her bottom lip as her hand instinctively went down to her baby belly. "Guess we can't hope he dropped into a deep hole in the middle of a faraway ocean, can we?"

Tell your Witch the odds are most definitely not in our fucking favor for that to have happened. So no.

"Sundown says probably not." Moving to sit next to her, Reno brought his knees up against his chest, wrapped his arms around them, rested his cheek on one, and looked over at her. "He also thinks it would be amazing, too."

"We're taking every precaution, Reno. Between you and Bounce, I can barely go to the bathroom at work without a security escort." She must have seen that sparked an idea in his head because she brought her hand up to smack his forehead playfully. "No. Do not even think of telling Bounce to add that to the list." She added a waggled finger in front of his eyes for emphasis. "No. I will stop giving you fun-in-the-bed time for the duration of the pregnancy."

"Ouch, that's really mean. I'd die without fun for six months." But he knew Witch was right. She had a dedicated combat-trained driver and an armored car to be driven anywhere. All her ob-gyn appointments were at Grid HQ medical, just as all pregnant women within its organization. Her stamp stayed online with the resources there to monitor her vitals as well as the baby. It also included her location, and she could be pinpointed instantly if the need arose.

Reno would not admit that he spent more time monitoring his wife's movements on his phone than he did any social media. Any ventures outside their home were done with Reno accompanying her. He and Sundown went on full alert, blue irises ringed by red behind shades in public as they worked in tandem to be hyperaware of threats and surroundings. It was exhausting but worth it. The trauma of Witch being attacked while pregnant with Eli had taught them all lessons.

For whatever reason, Epsilon had some severe fixations on the women and children of the Grid. It was scary. And it filled Reno with gut-twisting anxiety every minute of every day. The same could be said for Kenzie now that Lana was pregnant via a sperm donor. Heck, some days, Reno thought his fellow Keeper was *more* paranoid than he was—if that was even possible.

I still think she should have let us be the baby goo donor. I will forever protest that we weren't. I even offered to be the one to do the baby-making pounding. But noooo, can't let the dark one of you have any fun. Good thing I ain't able to eat our feelings. Our ass would be fucking huge.

"No. And don't show me your fantasies again, okay?"

Witch let out a soft chuckle. She knew her husband well, which also included knowing when Reno's split entity was being annoying in his head.

Sliding his eyes sideways to see her amusement, he gave her a sheepish smile. "He's still pissy about the sperm donor thing." Reno waved a dismissive hand. Kenzie and Reno's relationship was *beyond* complicated since their respective dark sides were once in love. Or still were? Reno wasn't sure. But Witch was a saint for trying to come to terms with it. He could only hope that time would make it easier for them all.

"Anyway," he awkwardly transitioned away from the subject as he rose to stand, "maybe he's on an extended vacation. Maybe Lucifer cutting off his money and stuff made him file some kind of weird bankruptcy. Heck, I don't know. Maybe I should just be happy that he's not around."

Emma moved off the bed to hug him from behind. Reno wrapped his hands over hers as his heart began to beat, and his skin started to warm with each thump—he *really* loved that. It would never become old how Witch and his kids could cause that strange Keeper physical behavior. Sure, they were dead, but give them someone they were destined to love, and they could feel alive with just a touch. With him, it was Witch. With Kenzie, it was Lana. And with Marcus—as much trouble as Reno had thinking of Marcus and Murder being a parent to *anyone*—it was his son, Tyrus.

"I still don't know why you don't tell the High Council about

Lucifer *helping* Epsilon rather than hunting him down as it was reported to them years ago."

Reno frowned with a nod. "I told Bounce, who was not even close to being shocked. He said not to get involved with the family dynamics, which is weird since Lucifer is family. But he did have a point. Heck, I don't even know why Lucifer told me. He said I should understand the love of a child. But uh, they don't seem to love each other. At all. I have no idea. It's all so weird." He turned to face her while remaining in the circle of her arms and sighed. "If I had to choose who I trust out of the two of them, it would be Lucifer. As odd as it is to say that the devil is a better guy than Epsilon is."

"The devil you know rather than the one you don't, right?" Emma smiled. "I know Bounce well. But perhaps he's right. Lucifer has never done anything to us. In fact, didn't he help you when you were in Heaven? And he also helped you bring Marcus back." She laid her cheek on his chest. Reno knew she loved hearing his heart, knowing she made it beat. "Epsilon, on the other hand, has made it very clear he wants to hurt you. Hurt me. And our kids." She moved to rest her chin in the spot to meet his eyes. "Lucifer, I don't trust. But at least he has some honor. If"—it was her turn to frown—"the devil can have honor."

Reno was not so sure he agreed, but with no facts to counter other than gut instincts, he kept silent on it. "Sure. I mean, he used to be an angel, right? The left hand of Omega and stuff. I would think honor would be in his DNA, uh, somewhere." As Reno thought about the statement, his eyes went right and left rapidly. They came back to Witch's gaze and found amusement. Ah, his Witch knew him really, really well. "If, uh, Lucifer and angels and demons and Omega have, uh, DNA." He gave her another sheepish grin. "I'm not sure, really. Maybe?"

Witch laughed. "They do. We healers are trained on them. Except for Omega. No one has a sample of him."

Reno chuckled as he tilted her chin up. "I know that look, Witch.

You'd love to have some Omega stuff to test. I say stuff because who knows what the creator of *everything* is made of."

She rose onto her toes to kiss him and smiled against his lips. "You betcha. But I also doubt Omega gets sick." Her brow creased in thought as her highly skilled Healer brain kicked into prominent gear. "Can you imagine how fast Omega heals? If he can actually be wounded. Sure, Keepers and Breakers are impressive with that ability but the Omega? I would love to..."

But Reno didn't give her a chance to run full speed with that tangent as he claimed her mouth with his in a deep kiss. She sighed and leaned against him, and her arms went around him. Savoring the intimacy for several minutes, Reno pushed his anxiety and worry away once again.

For now.

BETH DANIELS-BAILEY PRIDED herself in adapting to changes in the law enforcement world, and that ability had assisted her in rising from a beat cop to a detective on her time frame rather than the normal. When she became aware of the world her Cowboy existed in, she had been grateful she had those flexible abilities—to learn about Breakers, demons, immortals, and supernatural beings.

Chewing on the cap of her pen, she stared at the blank report due to both her sergeant and Evan O'Brien at Grid headquarters. She had been the most obvious choice for liaison between her world of the San Francisco police department and the secret army of the Grid, so Jess had suggested she apply for the position. It kept her busy, and with her homicide detective duties on top, she went to bed exhausted but pleased in her work more days than not.

But lately, it had changed. This would be the second week of nothing to report on the form. Evan coordinated the muni relays planted within the department with the Breakers doing their nightly patrols in hunting down the Eater demons. Those were then transmitted to Beth in a summary report via Grid's private VPN system. Last week, she thought the system had a glitch. There had been zero activity. But this week, the same thing. Other than random run-ins with Eaters as they posed as humans in the city, there had been no organized ambushes or coordinated offensive attacks. Zero. None.

And as much as Beth would have liked to think that was a good sign, she could not. Sure, she would have loved to believe Jess and the others had caused a turn in the war, but she was well versed in the ways of terrorist warfare—a zealous sect never simply stopped and surrendered. No, the bloodiest and most brutal fights occurred at the end. An escalation in violence as one side or the other came to the determination that they were facing defeat. It had always reminded Beth of how a heart beats harder and faster even when it no longer had the blood to pump. A last-ditch effort to not lose. Fighting to live was all it knew. The same could be said of Epsilon's forces.

"Hey, you want to catch some lunch?"

Beth looked up at James Miller—her assigned partner but also her friend. She, as did the other females at the station, thought he was hot. And he was, in a Henry Cavill sort of way. Tall and muscled with a Hollywood perfect chiseled jaw and features. Beth wasn't blind but had rules about dating anyone she worked with. And then an equally as tall and handsome two-hundred-year-old cowboy swaggered his way into her life a few years ago.

Her eyes went to Miller's right hand, where a small dark tattoo had been penned in the webbing between his thumb and finger. Beth had noticed it when she met him, but it wasn't until she had met Cowboy and learned of the Grid that she learned the purpose. It identified him and other munis within the city's governing sectors as working with the Grid. The marks were called stamps and electronically connected to the Grid. Beth now had her own on her collarbone, which was fused to her husband and made them connected in more ways than human or "normal" couples ever could be. Sheesh, *normal* did not even mean the same thing to her now. "Sure. Give me a few minutes."

Miller bent down to see what she was working on and lowered his voice, "I thought that was due yesterday. Need some help?" He glanced over at her and smiled. "You're not getting a case of baby brain already, are you, Bailey?"

Beth rolled her eyes. "I don't think I get that since we're using a surrogate." She sat back and glanced around to ensure no one could overhear as she pointed to the report on the computer screen. "It's week number two of no upticks in activity. No real attacks on humans or the Grid. I've read all the reports, even with the weekly summary. And I scanned the history. There has never been a lull like this. I keep thinking I'm missing something. But no, things have gone to right above a standstill." Her eyes darted sideways to Miller. "And while that should give me comfort, it doesn't. Not in the slightest."

Miller pulled a chair up to look at the reports as Beth clicked through them. "Yeah, you know what we say here in homicide. It's not that someone wasn't killed."

They mumbled in unison, "We just haven't found the body yet."

9

"Why are you doing this!" Jade had been roughly moved from her space in the cube to a room with a single chair. Food and water hadn't been brought for days, and no one had cared to inform her what she had done. What had changed? Was it because Envy had harmed Epsilon?

Pacing the room, Jade felt angry, and she slammed her fists against the door of the grimy concrete wall of the cell. "Hey! Can you hear me? Hello?"

But just as before, no response. For all Jade knew, she had been dumped there to die, and whatever place this was could be vacant beyond this room. Sliding down the door, Jade wrapped her arms around her drawn-up legs and tried her best not to cry. She was well-trained to contain her emotions, but anger, fear, and desperation were eating away at her restraint. Wiping her eyes on her hand, she lifted her head to bring her gaze to the ceiling where the swirling mist of Envy hovered. "Envy, can you feel anyone out there? Hear something?"

No, child. I cannot. I think they have some way of jamming us. I'm sorry. But stay strong, little one. We have to stay strong.

"I am trying, Envy. But let's not attack anyone again, okay?" She ran the cuffs of the sweatshirt over her face and tugged her hair back. She never wanted a hair tie more than she did right then.

Envy hissed in Jade's head, but she felt like Envy agreed. Pushing up to stand, she had taken one step away from the door when it flew open. The force of it sent Jade sprawling onto the floor. She attempted to twist and scramble away as her ankle was grasped to jerk her backward. Envy lunged down, but in a blink, Jade was against Epsilon's chest with a gun pointed against her temple.

"Hello, Envy. Greed sends his greetings. Make one move, and I will put a bullet in your lovely little human's brain."

Jade's eyes went from staring in horror at the gun to Envy. The power halted within a foot of them, swirling, and a loud hissing was heard in the room instead of in Jade's head. So were the words that followed.

You do that, and I will rip you and your men apart. Tell Greed to fuck off.

Jade went rigid in shock at hearing Envy speak out loud rather than their private connection. And while the voice was the same, the tone was completely different. Jade had never heard Envy so cold and threatening. But then again, she had never had a weapon aimed at her. Nor been kidnapped. "Envy, please..." Jade pleaded.

"Are you seriously being controlled by a child, Envy?" Epsilon began to laugh—a cold, evil sound. It caused the hairs to rise on Jade's arms and the back of her neck, where the man's breath tickled against her skin. "A human calls the shots with a dark power? One who hasn't even provided you a host body? That's both laughable and a shame. And since you and she are not bound, and I have you contained here, tell me, Envy, just why do I need to keep her alive?"

Jade gasped, and Envy became agitated, her shade of green growing darker in color. Keep Envy trapped here? With this monster? No. She could not let that happen. Jade had never fought in her life. Her upbringing had been about classical music and books, proper manners, and control of her public persona. Impressions were everything. Somewhere, deep inside her, a fire felt like it had been run along an abrasive strip and had lit. She felt hot and strong.

The impact of the back of her skull into Epsilon's face not only surprised him but Jade, as well. The man loosened his hold, and Jade let out a yell as she pulled away and spun around. Lunging at him, growling like a feral animal, she clawed at his face. He stumbled back, and the gun went off wildly. The shot hit the wall to the side. The struggle hit and closed the door, and Epsilon's back hit it with a loud thud.

Jade did not slow her attack. She continued at a furious pace, and as he tried to shove her away and bring the gun around, she continued to scratch at him and wrapped her legs around the man's waist. She was screaming in a continual sound, with barely a break to breathe. Perhaps it was the years of being told how to be, ordered on how to behave. Never show weakness but always appear meek and compliant—an impossible line to walk. Even the focus of her assault had thought of her as a nothing, just a simple weak human girl. No threat, at all.

Epsilon was able to fire another wild round, but this one hit something in a panel over the door. Sparks flew out, and the lights blinked out a second later. A red glow lit up the area, and Jade assumed this place had a system similar to her school's when the power went out to light the way to the exits on some power source independent from the rest. That thought, however, distracted Jade for a split second.

Epsilon used it to pull her free and throw her across the room. Jade went airborne and hit the chair, followed by the wall before crashing to the floor. Pain shot through her, but she paid it no mind as she rose to her feet, another of those strange snarls passing her lips. Epsilon had recovered, and the gun now pointed at her with a sure aim. "Stupid girl." The gun fired.

Jade felt the impact more than pain. Blinking, she stared in dumbfounded shock as crimson red spread through the material of the sweatshirt over her stomach. Trembling, she lifted her chin even as her legs gave out to sit on the floor. "Do not call me stupid. I'm not the one who just pissed *us* off."

The room filled with that hissing sound, but now it sounded like it had meshed with Jade's screams. Envy struck fast, attacking Epsilon's face where deep gouges from Jade's nails had dug into the flesh. The man yelled in alarm, trying to grab the green mist of Envy, and came away from the door. It swung open, and a contingent of Epsilon's men swarmed the space. Envy did not spare them as part of her essence pulled free from the main portion to attack them at the same time. Jade sat there, fascinated as each man turned their weapons on each other.

Shots filled the space, and bodies hit the floor. Jade scurried back weakly to avoid them and tried not to freak at the large puddle of her blood pooling around her. Bringing her hands up to cover her ears from all the nightmarish sounds, she found her fingers covered in Epsilon's blood.

And it was blue.

10

Mark Gibson, Relay at the Grid, had a girlfriend. Not only a *girlfriend* but a hot one. And not only a *hot girlfriend* but a vampire one. It was every video game and fan fiction dream come true. Her name was Ember Nightly, and she was the very first *le stagiaire* of her gender on the Vampire Legacy Council. Yeah, he had to ask what that meant, and Ember was amused to call herself an apprentice. Mark was proud of his girl, even if she had to stay in New Orleans while he was in San Francisco.

They spent any free time between the two cities whenever possible—which were rare. Texting, Skyping, and Facetime sufficed, though woefully, the rest of the time. Both of them dreamed of the, hopefully, near future. Talks were underway of moving vampire families from New Orleans to San Francisco. The vampires and Bounce were in the progress of negotiating a treaty. Still, Ember's father, Lassiter, was extraordinarily old-fashioned and afraid of their way of life vanishing in modern times. Ember believed the opposite and stubbornly insisted on being a part of the talks.

Sitting at his console in the comms room at Grid HQ, he was texting Ember when Bella, a fellow Relay, paused at his desk. "What is that?"

Mark glanced up at the monitor and cocked his head to the side. "Oh. Wait, shoot!" Sending Ember a text he had to go, he tossed his phone to the counter and tapped the unmute button at the same instance the blinking alarm light went out. "Crap. It may have been a glitch. Let me pull the feed."

Bella moved to sit facing him on the counter next to the keyboard. "You were sexting, weren't you? With your girlfriend? Dude, you're on duty. You better be glad it was me that busted you instead of Evan."

Mark waved a dismissive hand. "Ole stick up the butt is out to dinner." He sent Bella a proud grin. "I can monitor his movements as much as anyone else's. I am not that much of a dumbass..." But words hung in his throat when he reached the moment in the monitoring feed of the alarm.

"What was that you were saying about *not* being that much of a dumbass, Marky-Mark?" She braced her hands on the console as they both moved their faces closer to watch the readouts. "Is that a dark energy alert?"

Mark shook his head. "It can't be. Look. Here's Reno with Emma. Here's Marcus at home. And Kenzie, well, she never leaves Lana with her being all preggo, but they are at their apartment. None of them are anywhere close to this location." He reached out to tap his finger against the monitor as if it would correct what it had read. The Grid had sensors spread out all over the city to pick up dark energy. It was also fine-tuned to a specific power algorithm, such as the Keepers transmitted. "It can't be. We only have three." He shook his head again in bafflement. "Madness. Lust. Murder. So who the hell is this one?"

He reran the feed while Bella pulled up a chair to help. She looked over at him. "It was only there for what, a minute? Two? Was it long enough to pinpoint the location?"

Mark shrugged but continued working frantically to pull up code and change the parameters of the sensors. None were failing. Each one came back with a one hundred percent healthy functioning state. "It wasn't long enough. Nor was it a glitch." He swallowed and sat back to regard Bella. "It was a power. It just wasn't one we know about."

"WHAT ARE YOU TELLING ME, and why do you *not* have a location of the dark energy ping?" Bounce had Mark, Bella, and Reno Sundown closed up in his office at HQ along with Evan. He had been in talks with the Vampire Council of New Orleans when the alert came through his stamp that a new dark power had been sensed in his city of San Francisco. He had blurred back to HQ immediately, barking out demands to be briefed immediately.

"Uh. Well, um…" Mark raked his fingers through his hair as he slumped down in his chair. "I was distracted."

Bounce raised a brow and was about to demand what could have possibly distracted the Relay from his *job* when Bella added additional details.

"Dude, come on." She rolled her eyes. "He was talking to Ember. She's worried about the treaty talks. He was trying to help."

Mark's jaw dropped as he whipped his head over to stare at Bella —at first—but then appeared more surprised with her cover for him. An obviously bad one, at that.

Bounce blew out a frustrated breath. "Never mind. I'm sure that Ember is never unsure of herself. No more texting, chatting, or cybersex while on duty. Let's focus on what we know."

"Very little. We know it did not come from one of our known Keepers and their powers. We didn't get a location, but we did get a general area." Evan stepped up to Bounce's desk, typed in a few commands on a tablet, and the area over the boss's workspace lit up with a holographic map. "The warehouse district. We believe this two-block radius would be the most likely area. We ran it through the normal queries for Epsilon's shell companies but received a zero match. All legitimate businesses and most are freighter shipping companies or contracts with the same." Evan stood upright and crossed his arms tensely. "So much for hoping it would have been that easy." He smirked and glanced over at Mark. "If someone had been paying attention, we would have had a better chance. Otherwise, we can start doing a search from building to building, but that will take some time. And since we have zero proof Epsilon or one of his paid idiots are involved, we'd have to coordinate with the San Fran PD—which, as you know, adds additional time. Even with Bailey's wife's assistance."

Mark slumped down even lower into his chair and mumbled, "If someone could finally get laid, he wouldn't be so grumpy."

Bounce hit end on the tablet, and the holo-map disappeared. "Enough. And I'm going to hope that was directed at E, Mark. My sex life is not something I want in your head." Inclining his chin toward Reno in the corner, it had not gone unnoticed the Keeper, the first one of the beings, had remained silent. "What about you, Reno. Anything from the other Keepers? Their powers? Do they sense a newcomer? An escapee from the Void that we need to alert the High Council and Lucifer to?"

Reno's head was turned to the side, and one would think the Keeper was not paying attention. Bounce could tell by the deep creases in the man's brow that he was in communication with both Sundown and their dark power, Madness. The others knew it as well. They all waited in heavy silence for the input from the three beings in the one head.

The silence continued, and it was Evan who chose to step over to Reno and touch the man's arm. "Reno. Can we get your input for a few?"

Reno blinked and looked around the room as if startled awake from a dream. Or, in his case, brought back to the outside world from the inside of his mental space. Bounce gave him an encouraging smile. He could not imagine how difficult it must be for Reno to keep it all straight and not go as utterly insane as the dark power animating him. "You three can continue, but we'd like some information, if available, from Sundown. Or Madness. Did Sundown sense a new power? Did Madness feel a crack in the void?"

Reno shook his head. "No. They didn't feel a thing. Which is weird because we've been, like, super vigilant with everything so quiet and stuff." He moved across the office to stand behind Bella's chair and braced his hands on the back of it. Bounce could now see the stress lines on the man's features, a weariness in his stance. He knew Reno was hyper-paranoid now that Emma was pregnant again—none of them wanted a repeat of what went down when she had been carrying Eliam.

Bounce could also presume that having Kenzie's mate, Lana, also pregnant, the Keepers were burning their supernatural candles at both ends to keep everyone safe, healthy, and alive. Epsilon had a sick fixation on slaughtering the little souls of the Grid. Bounce had learned that personally when he lost his Tanya and their unborn child decades ago.

"Would a few minutes be long enough for Sundown to sense this new power? For any of you to know that one had come to the city?" Evan asked.

As Reno sat, his head went down, and his hands clasped between his knees. "I don't know. When Epsilon turned Kenzie, we didn't have enough info to have the sensors built like we do now. Murder and Marcus, well, I had a hand in it. The sensors registered the dark energy here at HQ. But we're sealed from the rest of the city. So they couldn't then. " He sat back and raked his fingers through his wavy brown hair. "We set up the sensors to help monitor our powers and hoped it would be able to detect any others. We have never had the opportunity to test it. But if it's a new one to the city, yeah, the others and Sundown should have picked up on *something*."

Reno shrugged and spread his hands apart. "I wish I had better news. But I'm just not sure. I wish I were. Sorry."

They all had a collective sigh, and Bounce was just as sure they said, "Shit," mentally. Nodding, he turned to Evan. "Increase patrols in that area. *Anything* out of the norm, I want to be informed immediately. I don't care if a rat sneezes, and it sounds odd, report it. And send out all crews with the scanners. If the city-wide sensors aren't working as we hoped, the scanners at ground level should read something if there's power residue. And what type. Perhaps it's a new demon soldier Epsilon has recruited we haven't come across, though I doubt it. The last I heard, Lucifer vaporized any Epsilon sympathizers instead of increasing Epsilon's forces, but nothing is beyond the realm of possibility."

Evan gave a single head nod and logged in via his stamp to update patrol orders as he headed out of the office. Bella followed, and Mark mumbled, "Sorry," as he, too, left Bounce's office.

"Reno, hold up a moment, please?"

Reno had been within steps of the door and paused. When the man turned around, Bounce took a moment to give him intense scrutiny. Tired. Exhausted. Worry was woven into the ordinarily light and carefree features of the Keeper. Tapping his fingers on the desk, Bounce said softly, "I want you off duty for a few days." Reno's mouth opened to protest, but Bounce cut him off by slicing his hand through the air. "You're tired and stressed. And I am more worried about you than I am a possible threat we know close to nothing of."

Bounce moved around the desk to stand in front of him. "Take a few days with Emma and the kids. Give Sundown a break and stay at home if you must. Minimize the threat. We'll post some Wires at the house. Switch them over each twelve-hour shift. You can handpick them since you are over your brother's squad now. But I can't have you go down. You are too important to our forces. And you're a friend." He reached out to clap a hand on the man's shoulder. "I will, of course, alert you the moment we find anything out. I promise. And it's time Marcus stepped up to do more. You don't have to do it all alone."

Reno snorted. "Yeah, I was going to say Kenzie is useless. She's acting crazier about Lana's pregnancy than I am Witch's." He must have seen Bounce's doubtful amusement. "Okay, maybe the same.

But yeah, I'm pretty sure Marcus can and would do more. I am just, uh, well…"

Reno didn't need to explain. Bounce knew all too well how hard the Keeper had worked to have the Keepers accepted as good guys on the Grid. There were many, his former best friend Evan included, who did not think that was possible. Bounce admired Reno's resolve in proving the Keepers' worth, but Bounce also believed it had been achieved. "It's fine. Marcus can reach you as well as I can if assistance is needed. Go home. Give Emmagail and the children a hug from Uncle Bounce for me. Go. I order it."

Reno released a slow exhale, and Bounce could feel the tension ease a small amount under his hand before he moved it from Reno's shoulder. "That's a good idea, Boss." Reno gave him a slight smile. "I would like to veg out totally for a few days. But, uh, can you make me a promise?"

The man's brilliant blue eyes moved to Bounce's. "If you find a person with a new dark power, I don't want them treated like Kenzie was. A prisoner. Or a threat. That was bad how we handled that. We know more about Keepers now. We need to consider their feelings and well-being *first* if there is a new one. Not their level of threat. Okay?"

"Ah, yes. Of course." Reno had valid reasoning for the request, and Bounce would agree. Keepers had proven to be an asset, and if a new one was discovered, they should be treated as such. "They will still need to be contained. To ensure they can control their powers, but they will be kept in comfort and care. Not as a prison sentence. I still feel some guilt for how we handled McKenzie. It will not happen again." He smiled at Reno. "I promise."

Reno nodded. "Okay. I have one stop to make, and then I'm heading home and going offline."

❧

Reno had not been to the high-security containment cells since they housed Kenzie there years ago. He could still remember when he made his existence as a Keeper known to the Grid when they captured her. It had been amazing to find another person like him. Containing a dark power and trying to have a life still. They had both come a long way. He had his Witch. They were expecting their twins, and Kenzie had found her heartbeat in Lana. They, too, were expecting a child.

Marcus had been an act of desperation, sure. But it had paid off in the end. Reno's daughter, Sophia, got her wish of a best friend brought back, and another Keeper was added to the ranks. Now, Marcus had his son, Tyrus, and was in a relationship with Alexis, a beautiful kind Breaker, who was giving the big man the kind of life Marcus may not have dreamed of having. That, too, was a common thread they all shared. Life was so much better and richer after death. As odd as that was.

Pressing his palm over a biometric security pad, he looked down the long hall as one overhead light after the other lit up the area. This level lay two floors below the surface, under the famous Alcatraz prison, which was made to house humans. The secret underground floor below it was to hold supernatural beings. And deeper still, where Reno stood now, was adapted to hold the deadliest of their world—Keepers and high-level demons. Sure, it had never held someone like Lucifer, but as Reno walked to the very last cell, he hoped it would someday very soon hold the son of the devil.

Epsilon.

Reno told no one how deeply he craved for all of this to end. He had nightmares most nights and dreams of victory the rest of taking Epsilon down. Of ridding the world of the bastard once and for all. And not just because he believed that would be the beginning of the end of the war. The threat of Epsilon, at times, crushed Reno's fractured soul and split spirit more often than he could calculate. Even Witch sometimes sensed his mind had gone somewhere and thought it was just him communing with Sundown and Madness. Yeah, sometimes it was.

But other times, it was him searching for a memory that was there yet hidden. Like a prophecy whispered in his ear that he wasn't allowed to hear. And when he thought about the war ending, it filled him with such hope…

And so much dread. Sickening. Could cry like a baby dread.

"I make no sense," he mumbled to himself as he keyed in a code, and the last cell powered up. He had personally supervised its overhaul over the years. He would have liked Evan's input—no one knew security better than Bounce's right-hand man—but E would most assuredly ask why Reno needed such a place. Any new Keepers would be contained in the medical room renovated for the purpose. More human and decent, as per Reno's demands.

This cell had the most current security and air infiltration system. All built secretly over the years by Reno, using the cover of orders to upgrade it. He had no such order, but no one questioned him, either. They assumed what it was for, and he never said anything to change that. A dedicated power grid backed up with both solar and battery that would keep it secure for weeks. Complete with a contained water cycling system turning gray water and waste into drinkable water—it was self-sustaining and secure. Finished off with layers of ballistic glass harder than steel and reinforced with alloys so hardened Superman would have had a hard time making a crack—it was the perfect cell.

For a Keeper. For the son of the devil. For the devil himself. Heck, even Bounce. It hadn't been tested, and Reno hoped it never would be.

But that nagging dread that curled and twisted deep in his gut…

He knew, somehow knew, that wasn't going to be the case.

11

"Do you ever wish I could give you a baby?"

Jess was sprawled across the bed with Beth lying on his chest, both of them slicked with sweat after making love. The pillows were tossed to the floor, and the sheets bunched over the end of the bed. The house could have broken out in flames, and he would have stalled moving in his sated, languid state. Beth's fingers teased the damp hairs on his chest, and he had been about ready to doze off when she asked the question. She had asked it more than once, which told Jess no answer would ever make it go away.

Inhaling slowly, the movement lifting her a bit, he let it out even slower as he answered. "Of course. I done told you, Detective. But it doesn't change a damn thing."

Beth rested her chin in an upraised hand and met his eyes. "I know. You'd still love me. You'd still want to be married to me. But I see you with Sophia, and I just feel like shit for not giving you a baby you can be there for. For all of it." She lay back down as her palm moved over and up to rest over his heart. "What if we don't find a surrogate? Even with you running the school, we don't have what one would call a stable, calm life."

Jess brought his arm up to stroke his fingertips along her back, folding the other under his head. "Darlin', first we're using Grid resources to find a surrogate. They are in this world. Hell, now that I'm retired, I'm probably more borin' than ever. And you're a cop. They'll know our baby is going to be the safest tiny person that could ever be a baby." He gave her a soft smile. "And that baby is going to be loved like crazy. You're gonna be an amazin' mama. And me a daddy. Hell, yes. I was made for that."

Beth opened her mouth to agree with him, but Jess knew how she would counter it at the same time. They'd had this same conversation a dozen times since they got married.

"I said I was made to be a daddy. I didn't say I was made to be a daddy to a baby we made together. Any baby would be *damn* lucky and blessed to have us as parents. To be a Bailey and part of this family." Hooking an arm around her waist, he brought her up to kiss but paused right before he did. "We're going to have our baby, whether it's a surrogate or an adopted baby. It doesn't matter. Things happen for a reason. A blessing doesn't always make itself real clear at first. Hell, look at Reno. He was a blessing that was muddy as a Texas river bottom but look how all that turned out."

Jess moved his lips closer to hers to kiss her. "Stop worrying that pretty and sharp head of yours, Detective. Trust in fate and destiny. It'll happen. And I'm going to love seein' the woman I love holding my baby in her arms." He cracked a huge, fanged grin. "That's you, by the way, Detective."

Beth punched him hard in the pectoral but beat him to the kiss as she claimed his mouth to cut off the laughter she knew was coming.

And that was just fine with him.

"THIS IS NICE."

Reno smiled as Witch sat in front of him in the bathtub. They had watched a movie, gave Sophia and Eli a bubble bath, and then took one of their own. Brushing her wet hair to the side, he kissed the side of her neck. "Thank Bounce. Otherwise, I'd be at work. He's super smart, knowing I needed a break."

Emma snorted and angled her head back to meet his eyes. "Oh, Bounce tells you to take it easy and relax, and you listen. Your Witch tells you to, and you give me a million excuses why you will soon but not yet." She put a dab of bubbles on the end of his nose with a smile. "I see how you are, Candyman."

Snickering, he rolled his eyes but knew she was right. Bending his head down, he lightly bit her shoulder with his fangs as his hands moved to spread over her rounding stomach. "I know. I'm sorry. I am going to try to do better. I really am. I'd promise, but we both know I forget the promises, and then I break them, and then I feel bad. And then…"

"Hush, Reno, and kiss your Witch."

He smiled and did as he was told. Water sloshed out the side of the tub as she moved to straddle him. Oh, yeah, he really needed this time off. As Witch settled over him, Reno even thought about sending Bounce a thank-you card.

That was until just as he and Witch got started, his head crackled and filled with noisy pain.

"Reno!" Witch said in loud alarm as he carefully pushed her away and stumbled out of the tub.

Groaning, he brought both hands up to his forehead and tried to lock whatever caused it away.

"Sundown! What is that? Do something!" He tugged his robe off the door and wrapped it around him as he left the bathroom.

I'm trying. It's the others. Madness, Murder, and Lust are going nuts to get everyone's attention. Madness is having a huge fit in here. I'm trying to calm his ass down, but he's beyond that in some kind of meltdown mode.

Witch followed Reno in concern as he reached the bedroom and touched his stamp. "Kenzie… can you hear me?"

"YOU KNOW, Snap, you can't keep us locked in our apartment for the next six months."

Kenzie lay on her side in bed with Lana and caressed her rounded baby bumped stomach. She shifted her lavender gaze upward and found Lana on the brink of laughing. She often did in the face of Kenzie's attitude. "Bullshit. I'll keep you locked up here as long and as much as I want. I'm Mama number two. It's my right," she mumbled with amusement as she cuddled against her heartbeat. "And we are *really* going to have to work on what my title is in all this."

Lana did not restrain her laughter at that. "You can be Mommy Poop. Being number two and all."

Kenzie snorted and lifted up to kiss Lana. Before their lips touched, her head filled with static and then pain. Lana reached out, but Kenzie was blinded with the intensity of it. "Lust! Are you okay?"

The dark power was screaming as if she, too, were in pain—which was close to impossible since she had no real receptors to feel anything. "Lust! Talk to me. What's going on?"

Lana had moved off the bed, and Kenzie reached out to steady her.

You have to help us, sugar! We need help now! By the Omega, we're going to be too late!

"Snap, what's going on?"

Kenzie darted her eyes over to her mate and shrugged. "I don't know. She's in pain." Moving out of the room, holding on to the wall in case the pain surged again, Kenzie picked up her tablet to see if she had any alerts. Reno's voice made it through the chaos in her head via the stamp as she logged in. "Yeah. I'm here. What the fuck is going on?"

ALEXIS HAD WORKED the evening shift, and Marcus had been placed on the overnight one without notice. He was in the bedroom, sleeping to prepare for being up all night. Bounce had said he ordered Reno to take a few days off, and according to Marcus, the man had been a nervous wreck lately, so apparently, the time was warranted.

She took a sip of her wine to help wind down from an uneventful patrol and stood to put the bottle away with plans to cuddle with her Keeper before he left for work. She had just set the glass in the sink of their apartment when she heard a thud followed by a yell. Running into the bedroom, she found Marcus on his hands and knees, sweat breaking out across his dark skin and obviously in pain. His fangs were bared, and his breathing was ragged as she knelt in front of him.

"Marcus. What's happening?"

He lifted his head, and those intense tawny eyes met hers. "I do not know. Murder is raging. Something about the others."

Raging! I'm fucking pissed! Stop standing around and fucking do something! Hurry! Fast, you big lumbering flesh bag! Move!

With her help, Marcus was able to stand, and Alexis pressed a palm against his cheek. "What does that mean? Has it happened before?"

Marcus shook his head. "Not since I've been one. I am not sure."

Suddenly, his head shot up as he touched his stamp. "I hear you, Reno. What the fuck is happening?"

❧

"COWBOY. COWBOY!" Jess sat up fast as Beth's voice roused him from a deep sleep. He dove out of instinct toward his gun in its custom holster designed in the headboard, but Beth caught his wrist before he reached it. "No. Your phone. It's going off like crazy. I saw it when I went to the bathroom."

Grunting, half asleep, he plucked the damn device in question off the nightstand and frowned. "It's an alert from the Grid."

Swinging his legs off the bed, he widened his eyes to try to wake up fully. Opening the text alerts, he frowned as he stood. "Something has happened at the school. Bounce needs to see me right away." Moving quickly, he had his jeans on, and a shirt swung in place as Beth got dressed, too. He stepped into his boots and put on a worn ball cap over his bed head as she called Wanda to come down from the guest house to stay with Charlotte. The moment the caregiver came in the back door, Jess took Beth's hand, and they ran to the truck.

❧

"WHAT DO you mean I can't go there? If something has happened, you can be *damn sure* I'm goin'. It's my school. I started it. I've worked my ass off to get it ready to open. We're opening in three weeks!" Jess was within an inch of Bounce's face when he spat out the words. That would teach them to have him come straight here rather than where he wanted to be if it wasn't his bed.

And without coffee.

Beth had asked the obvious question as Jess drove at breakneck speeds to reach Grid HQ. Why were they going there instead of Edge Academy? Jess didn't have an answer. The alert had simply said that Bounce needed to speak to him about an urgent issue at the school. Come to HQ immediately. Do not go to the Academy.

It was four in the morning. If Beth had not been with him, Jess would have disobeyed that command and gone straight to the renovated property, regardless of the danger that awaited there. But he would not risk his wife, which meant he stood here going toe-to-toe with Bounce.

"Calm down, and I'll explain. I just do not want to do it more than once," Bounce countered in a tone meant to de-escalate, but Jess also found hints of dark orange in the Grid boss's everchanging mood ring-ish eyes, which betrayed the alarm behind his calm façade—that was not good. Not even a little.

The door behind them opened, and Jess turned to face Reno, Marcus, and Kenzie. Narrowing his eyes at the Keepers, he slowly turned his head to regard Bounce once more. "Why do I think ain't none of this good."

"Because it's not," Reno answered as he moved over to join them. "We had a spike of dark power the other day. And tonight, something happened that's never happened before." Reno looked back at the other Keepers—all of them looking as dire as Jess had ever seen them. "An SOS from our powers. An urgent one. For one of their own."

Bounce put his hand on Jess's arm. "We ran a scan, and it's coming from the school."

Jess blinked and shrugged Bounce's hand off as he looked from one to the other. "What is coming from my school? Someone better dumb this up real quick, or I'm going to go in there loaded for bear and hopin' I ain't a rabbit in the trap." Beth moved to try to calm him, but he was starting to fear Edge Academy was the next Grid building to be turned to rubble by Epsilon's forces. "Damn it, I'll just go find out my damn self," he growled in frustration as he turned on his boots to go.

Reno moved in front of Jess to stop him from leaving. "The dark power that spiked the other day. We couldn't find it because it happened so quickly. We found it tonight because it's not going anywhere. And it's staying put. It's at your school. A dark power we've never seen or known about is there. And it's in distress. It's calling out for the others to help. And it's at your school."

Jess blinked at his brother. "Shit..."

Marcus moved past the three of them to pick up a tablet from Bounce's desk. The moment he pulled up the roster, he squeezed his eyes shut. "And my son is on security detail there."

12

"This is bullshit." Tyrus had likely said those exact words more than a dozen times since receiving his new Grid assignment. Security at a school. One that was not even open yet, so there was jack shit to do—walk empty halls, sign for deliveries after they went through a security scan and checkpoint, and, apart from that, do nothing. He had wanted to ask Marcus if he used some sort of Keeper pull to have his son appointed to the roster of the Edge Academy detail, but he let it go. He and Marcus were getting along better than ever. Tyrus valued that more than his wounded pride at his new job duties. The days were busy, and he minded those less. But the night shifts, like the one he was bullshitting about once again, he hated them. There was zero to do except listen to other patrols via his stamp as others found Eaters and slaughtered. And his updates?

Boxes of chalk haven't done a damn thing. Dust bunnies were nowhere to be found, and the whiteboards weren't talking. "Bullshit."

The halls were set to low illumination, along with the gym with its swimming pool under the floor. Otherwise, the place stood unlit at night. Tyrus had just finished an interior check and was headed for an exterior one when suddenly his stamp went to static. Frowning, he touched it, and in the next instant, all the lights went out. "HQ. Hey, can anyone hear me?"

Rubbing his palm over the stamp on his right forearm, he only received more static. "Shit." Pulling out his cell phone, he frowned in bewilderment to see it had zero signal—it worked earlier. He had watched baby goat videos via YouTube on the device during his break less than an hour ago. Hitting the power button in hopes a reboot would fix it, he shoved it in his pocket and unholstered his gun. Pressing his thumb over the biometric safety, he was relieved to see that at least *that* worked. Slowly walking heel to toe down the hall, he would have to presume that Cowboy had rigged the security system to function even if the place had a power outage. Tyrus went into a lower stance as he moved in, hoping to hear something, see something. The lights flickered twice more, had a brown, and then went out again.

It was during the latter that he saw something move near the corner up ahead before vanishing around it. "Hey! Stop."

Was it a rat? Nah, odds were against that. Bailey had this place gutted and remodeled to fancy, pristine condition. And the snack machine nor the cafeteria were stocked yet, so no food to attract rodents. Tyrus had spent a large number of hours studying rats and other vermin when he had been a homeless kid on the streets. Rats, he knew. As he continued down the marble-tiled floors, his combat booted feet made no sound as he reached the corner.

Slowly inhaling, he touched his stamp once again, but it was still a no go. Static and nothing else. Tyrus let his breath out, squeezed his eyes shut, and turned around the corner. And found... nothing.

"What the hell! Now I'm losing my mind." He pivoted on his heel to go outside and see if he could get a signal there when the air filled with a strange hiss. Pausing, Tyrus narrowed his eyes as he looked over his shoulder and found he had been right. It most definitely was *not* a rat.

The dark green mist rushed supernaturally fast down the dark hall before Tyrus could move. It reached him, and he scrambled back until a wall stopped his movement. The cloud swirled inches from his face, and he knew the gun was useless. He had seen Murder's manifested energy a few times now—amber in color and filling the air with power. Tyrus knew that Madness was black, and Lust was purple. But as far as he knew, those were the only powers running around in *peopleland*. The rest were contained in prison deep within Hell. Marcus had described the place as nothing but infinite space—the Void.

Tyrus put his hands out to the side, finger moving off the reader to switch the weapon to safe mode, and he swallowed. "Okay. Okay. Don't attack. I'm not going to hurt you." Like that was fucking possible. The powers could crush, slaughter, rip and infect. And while he was a half-Hellspawn demon, he was also half-human. Even so, his life could be snapped out in a blink if a power wanted to. Murder filled the room with wicked energy, and this one had the air around them crackling like a live wire freed from its transformer. Tyrus didn't know why it seemed more powerful, but that was how it appeared. The power swirled and snapped in a way that struck him as frantic and distressed.

Help her.

The words were within the hissing, but it sounded as clear in Tyrus's head as Murder did when the dark power was being an asshole. This voice, however, was female. "Who? Who do you need me to help?"

Her! Help her!

The power retreated, swirled, and moved away from him, pausing to ensure Tyrus followed. Nodding, he holstered his weapon and did so. The power increased in speed to the point where Tyrus had to run to keep up. They turned through the maze of halls, speeding past the empty doors of classrooms until the power made a fast right to one with an opened door.

Reaching the doorway, Tyrus continued to trail behind the power as they moved past the long bar-height work tables of what looked like the chemistry lab, complete with glass beakers and other instruments waiting to be put away. The moon shone brightly on this side of the school, even through the triple-layered ballistic glassed windows. And that was when Tyrus could see the large drops of blood marring the gray slated floor.

Pulling up as the power stopped in a corner, Tyrus saw a young woman curled up there. He was able to see streaks of blood where the woman crawled to the corner. A window had been left open that led to a contractor's chute attached to a dumpster—the point of entry, apparently.

Tyrus rushed forward to aid the injured woman, but the power rose in front of him to prevent him from reaching her with a threatening hiss.

"You want me to help her, right? Then move the fuck out of the way so I can."

The power came in closer. Tyrus jerked upright, stiffening as it touched his skin.

Murder...

He frowned that it could tell that. Did he smell like the power? Was that a thing with the dark powers? As more of the green mist moved closer, he wanted to step back, but he refused to back down. His eyes jerked to the girl and met pain-filled eyes.

You. Need them. To help her.

"Wait, what do you..." But before Tyrus could finish the sentence, pain blasted through his brain as chaotic noise filled it, and the floor was the last thing he saw as it came up to meet him.

"A'RIGHT. SO, HOLD UP A MINUTE." He, together with Beth, had arrived at Edge Academy a moment before the Keepers pulled up in a black, unmarked Grid van. A squad of Recons had discreetly blocked the street leading up to the place, and San Fran PD had been alerted to a possible threat and battle at the freshly accredited school. It had once been an affluent family's mansion, long since seized by the bank after probate court battles ended when the last remaining members of the family passed away. It was three rambling stories of elegance left to rot and deteriorate. However, property was not cheap in the Bay area, and he had to counter bid against more than a few developers wanting to raze the place to make some apartment complex or high rise. It wasn't that Jess didn't have the money. Living for two centuries and getting paid really well all that time had its advantages.

Piles of cash later, the place—along with the second building on the property, which once served as servant and groundskeeper housing—was updated, renovated, and scheduled to open in less than a month. State-of-the-art security installed. The best teachers and education professionals from across the globe were in line to start helping the youngest on the Grid to grow, to thrive. And to not hide their supernatural gifts while getting an A++ rated education.

Unless, of course, it was about to become rubble.

Jess stepped in front of Reno, who was focused on checking the customized tactical gear all three Keepers wore. Marcus had a Velcro closure pouch for dog treats. Yeah, like you'd give a pet. Except Marcus's pets were in the form of hellhounds, manifested by Murder to sniff out a killer. And Marcus held the figurative leash with his mind with Murder contained within.

Kenzie's was made more feminine and sexier—for lack of better words. Lust had insisted on it, and whereas Jess knew McKenzie hated the look, being personally anti-sexy and anti-men, Lust used it to their advantage to seduce and distract. Lust manifested in vines of snapdragons with their bizarre skull seed pods and deadly foliage with a scent of nightshade and seduction.

And Reno's? Well, it was pretty much like any Breaker's with one big exception—it had flaps designed on the back that would open and close whenever the man's wings were needed. Those, too, were manifestations of the man's power and a recent "upgrade" when he became more tapped into the powers granted to a Prince of Hell.

"Reno, I said hold up." He reached out to put a hand on his brother's Kevlar covered chest. "I know you gotta do what you gotta do in there. To find out what is causing the whole dark energy spike and all. But that place is my dream. Sure, I have dumped a few truckloads of my big ole Ford worth of cash into it. But it's more than that."

Reno lifted his head to meet Jess's gaze, and already, Jess could see rings of red starting to swirl around the blue of his brother's eyes.

"It's my dream. That place is everything I've dreamed of giving back to the world. To our world. To the kids of it. Hell, our daughter, Sophia. I ain't ever felt so passionate..." He paused to look over at Beth. "Well, a different kind of passion. But anyway"—Jess swung his focus back to his brother—"please don't destroy the school. Sure, you might need to take out a few walls. I can deal with that. Hell, I'd be fine buying all new furniture. But the building itself. Can we not have it end up like a big ole, money pit and dream death crater, please?"

Kenzie snorted as she leaned against the van. "Does anyone else find it strange and funny as fuck that the big, bad, hero of heroes, Cowboy outlaw wanted to be a school principal? I mean, come on." She pushed off to look at the rest with a huge, snarky fanged smile on her face. "I can*not* be the only one that finds it the strangest factoid *ever*."

Marcus glanced up from checking the load in his gun's magazine. "I believe we should allow Cowboy to go inside with us. To ensure we do not destroy his school. To assist us in not tearing apart his dream." He was worried about Tyrus, yes, but even he could not pass up on the chiding of Bailey. "He may be immune to whatever power inhabits the facility. It should be tested as it was with Murder." Marcus holstered his gun with a raised brow and a slight smile. "We could see if it, too, can throw him around like a stupid, Stetson-wearing western rag doll." Marcus smirked. "Actually,

Academy protection be damned. I want him to go for that reason now. Last time I did not get to watch."

"Stop it. Get ready." Reno's tone was tense and shared no hint of humor. "Look, I get it. You want us not to tear up the place. But until we know who or what this is—other than it's causing the power to cut out and scrambling all our systems—I can't say what's going to happen. So"—he glanced over at the others—"since all personnel has been moved away, we go in full Keeper form. Powers at the ready and handle it." His eyes went left and then right, his brow furrowing. "Even Sundown can't get a read on this. And that should worry us all. He can't even give us odds on if we'll survive because we don't know anything. Put the jokes away, get in sync with your powers, and let's get this over with."

Reno twisted to regard Beth before bringing his eyes back to Jess. "Are you sure you want her here? A fuse is not the same as her being a Breaker. She's still human. And she still breaks—really easy. Even if she does get to use your healing powers."

Beth stepped up and lifted her chin. "If your brother is here, I'm here. I can handle myself. And I'm also coordinating with the department." She tightened the straps of her tactical vest. "Just tell your three body sharing powers to not chew on the resident cop, sound good?"

"Whatever," Reno said with a snarl and turned to walk toward the school.

Kenzie let out a whistle as she and Marcus followed. "You know what's as weird as you wanting a school, Cowboy?" She paused to speak to Jess as she passed. "Him being that serious." She then continued toward the school. "School looks nice, by the way. It's going to make a pretty pile of dust."

Marcus let out a bark of laughter.

Jess sighed, watching them enter the place, and felt Beth's comforting palm on his arm. "Come on, Cowboy. Focus on taking care of whatever is chewing on your dream."

He rolled his head to narrow his eyes at her. "Not you, too,

Detective. But you're right." Walking over to his truck, he threw open the driver's door and hit a switch under the dash. The bench seat slid up to expose a padded weapons storage. Pulling a sawed-off shotgun free, he started loading the barrel magazine before clipping it to the loader. Tossing Beth a semiautomatic AK-15, he held out a box of ammo. After hitting the control, the seat slid back in place to hide the weaponry once again.

They both turned and took their positions in the courtyard in the middle of the circle drive in front of the Academy. Jess glanced over at his wife and shook his head. "Damn, remind me later to bring up how hot you look all ready to kill and protect." He even let a grunt and sucked air through his fangs in appreciation. "Maybe you need to come armed to bed tonight." He pulled off a small grin. "I already come to bed with my weapon fully loaded and hot."

Beth smirked as she settled into a firing stance, her eyes fixed on the building. "Sure, Cowboy. I'll remind you. Maybe it will distract you from crying about your school getting destroyed."

13

"Stay alert. But remember, if this is another Keeper, it's up to us not to treat them as a threat. Even if they think we are one." Reno glanced back at Kenzie and Marcus. "Remember how you felt when you first came back. Keep that in mind."

Kenzie moved to stand next to him, and even though they weren't touching, that hum of need they both felt when their powers sensed the other started. "How do you know it's one of the powers and not something else?" She gave him a sideways glance full of worry. "How do we know it's not a fucking trap? I have a baby coming, Reno. This better not be a *fucking* trap."

Reno swallowed. "I don't know." And that was messing with his head—big time.

Marcus moved ahead to the annex on the right, and amber wisps swirled out to form his hounds. "Remember, my son is here. Anyone harms him, no one survives. New power or not."

Kenzie rubbed Reno's arm before she started down another hallway that led to the left, purple vines of snapdragons starting to form and curl along the floor ahead of her. "Be safe. No one kills anything. See you two on the other side of this place."

Reno watched them go and faced the main hallway. Dread curled in his stomach. The same sensation that gnawed at him when he thought about the outcome of the war. No time for that. They had to figure out this latest twist. He shook off the feeling, and his wings shot out from his back. Black wisps spun out of his skin and became etched with dark markings of a language long lost. His black. Marcus a yellow-orange and Kenzie's purple.

"Time to fly." And with a thought, his wings formed as he flew up to the shadows of the old mansion's ornate ceiling to hunt or save.

Or both. Gosh, he wished he knew.

MARCUS ORDERED the hellhounds to begin searching for Tyrus. They ran several feet ahead of him, noses to the floor as they prowled through the dark halls. It was easy to discern all the labor Bailey had put into the place while preserving the past of the structure, but with the strangeness of the evening's events, the darkness and the silence, it felt like a very expensive tomb to him. He turned on the flashlight affixed to his vest, which he did not need to see in the dark, but it helped with the feel of the place being so oppressive. The light bounced off the glowing amber of the hellhounds as they neared the end of the annex's hallway without a clue or sign of Tyrus.

He was on the verge of ordering the hellhounds to head back when one of them started barking and took off running. The second took pursuit as well as Marcus. When they reached the first one, the hound was sniffing at something dark on the floor. Blood. Big drops of it. The hound whined at the scent—it was that of a victim and not a murderer. If it had been a murderer, the hounds would have lapped it up. Depending on how dark the deed, the hound might have rolled in it like a dog delighted in finding a disgusting fresh animal scat in a yard.

Shining the light down the hall, Marcus called out to Tyrus as he touched the blood. It was not his son's. Tyrus was his heartbeat, and since they had a family bond, Marcus would have immediately known if it had been his son that bled. And the hounds would have gone crazed as well—Murder, after all, loved Tyrus in his own way.

It's in there. Whatever the fuck this is, it's in there.

Marcus nodded. He could smell the source of the blood as well. Human. More relief flooded through him as he stood. "And what is it? Can you tell," he said in a whisper to Murder.

No. It's a power. Which one? Like us? No idea. It's shielded or different. Or fuck, I don't know. But it's definitely whatever sent out the SOS to us for help. And two others. One is the kid. The other, a human. I think. But everything is scrambled. Be careful. And do not get one of my hounds killed. I have zero problem with kicking the ass that keeps me.

Marcus could understand the last request, at least. The hounds were formed of Murder's essence. Killing one of them meant that not only did Murder feel the pain and death, but Marcus did, as well. And with Keepers, the less essence they had, the weaker they became. The wisps, as they all called it, were an extension of their powers and the fuel that animated them each.

But all Marcus needed to know to fuel the advance into the unknown danger was his son existed within. "I will be damned back to Hell if I lose my son after finding him after so long," he hissed under his breath, and Murder agreed. "I'm going in. Send one of the hounds to bring the others."

No sooner had Marcus said the order than one of the hounds spun around and ran back the way they had come to find Reno with Madness, and Kenzie with Lust. The other hound moved to bristle and snarl at Marcus's side as he pushed the door open fully with the toe of his boot. The room was dark, but as Marcus entered, the flashlight swept over the space.

"Over here!"

Hearing Tyrus's voice, Marcus ran to the back of the room and pulled up at the sight before him. There was a swirling dark green mass of power. Murder purred in his head, but Marcus's attention was too focused on Tyrus to pay attention to his dark power's response.

Tyrus was applying pressure with his hand to a wound in the woman's stomach, and the power was staying too close to him for Marcus's comfort. "Remove yourself from my son," he growled out the words as Murder surged out to get between him and it.

Do not harm her.

Marcus had thought his dark power was protecting *him,* but no, it was protecting the girl. Or the other power? He was not sure. But he had to get to Tyrus. Pushing past both swarms of energy, he dropped to his knees next to Tyrus, and after quick scrutiny, he found his son unharmed. "Who is she?"

Tyrus shook his head. "I have no idea. She and…" He looked up at the power mass that had returned to hover over them. "That power brought her here, I think. It needed help and found me." He darted his eyes over to Pops. "And then it, I think, used me to call out to all of you. I'm guessing it worked because here you are."

Reno and Kenzie rushed into the room, and their powers reacted to the new one in the room. Lust recoiled for some reason, the purple mist around Kenzie jerking in surprise. Madness was not as subtle as a giggle filled the room for them all to hear.

"Who is that?" Both Reno and Kenzie asked as they came over to stand close.

Marcus shrugged. "They broke in apparently. Tyrus is assisting. And it"—Marcus pointed at the green power with his chin—"used him to call us."

Tyrus nodded but kept his attention on the girl. "Yeah, she sensed the link to Murder and used it. Hurt like fuck but efficient, I guess."

"Stop. Stop!" Reno rushed forward to haul Tyrus away from the girl—who, in turn, went unresponsive on the floor.

Marcus watched in shock as Reno slammed Tyrus against the wall.

"What are you doing?!" Marcus roared as he rose to his feet and jerked Reno away from his son. "How dare you touch my son." Anger surged through him, and the two of them were chest to chest. "What has gotten into you, Madness? He is trying to save her!"

Kenzie attempted to pull the two of them apart, and Tyrus slipped away to go back to the dying girl.

Reno's face came in close, red-rimmed eyes to amber ones. "That's a power that has her. It's waiting for her to die. We can't interfere if she's been chosen. Destiny. Remember?"

Marcus frowned in confusion. "What?"

"She's dying! We not supposed to do anything?" Tyrus yelled in desperation. "Why are you standing there and not helping!"

Marcus looked back over his shoulder at his son's plea.

Tyrus pointed to the power. "She came to get me to save her. For you to fucking save her. Not to let her die!"

Reno jerked away from Marcus and squatted down to address Tyrus. "I know. Look, I interfered with your dad"—he turned his head to regard the Keeper of Murder—"and am I the only one who remembers how pissed you were, Marcus? And Kenzie, it was forced on you, remember? By Epsilon. I've learned my lesson. If she's going to die, she'll die. And if the power, whichever power this is, chooses to bring her back, fine. We'll help. But we can't interfere." He stood and hated all of this—but they had to know he was right.

"Reno, I know why you're saying all this. But we can't stand here and do *nothing.*" Kenzie's voice was understanding, but her words countered the truth. She moved to stand in front of him.

Meeting her eyes, he swallowed, and his markings faded the moment she got close. "What if you're wrong? What if we stop this, and it was supposed to go another way? How can we know?"

Kenzie stepped in closer and cupped his face in her hands. "We can't. But we can't let her just die. We have to try and hope that's in whatever plan destiny has." She kissed his forehead, and he blew out a ragged breath.

"Okay. Yeah... Sorry." He turned to see Marcus help Tyrus pick up the girl, an alarming amount of blood on her, the floor, and now

Tyrus. "Let's get her out of here. Maybe we can reach Grid EMT outside." He regarded the power as it tried to trail after the girl. "And you, whoever you are, stay here."

The power filled the air with tangible agitation.

Reno stepped closer to it, snarling and baring his fangs as his markings reappeared stark on his skin. "We need to help her. We can't do it here. Didn't you call us to do that?" That didn't solve the problem they had of having a loose power in the city. His eyes slid right and left in thought. "How about you wait here? And then the three of us can come back, and you can tell us what you need. You're going to have to trust us. You don't have another choice. Or you can go back to the Void."

The power snarled and snapped around him at the threat. His own powers flew out to defend, and the green power shrank back with a whimper.

Help her. Please. Help her.

Reno gave the power a quick nod. "We are. I promise."

"No. Not without... Envy. I... won't... leave her. We have to stay... together."

Reno and Kenzie pivoted to see the girl had awoken, her face and eyes awash with pain as she spoke. Her skin was ghastly white. It was obvious they were running out of time. At the name of the power, Madness got giddy, and the tension eased in the space. Even the power looked less intense at being claimed by name. He would think how weird it was later that a living human girl had. Reno cocked his head to the side with a soft smile. "Hi, Envy. Let us take of her, okay?"

Tyrus had begun to leave the room with the girl in his arms when he yelled, "No, no, no!" He moved the young woman to one of the chemistry tables, sweeping the glassware off the top as he stretched her out. "She's not breathing." He looked at them in a panic. *"She's not breathing!"*

They all moved to her in a rush to help. Marcus was trying to calm Tyrus as he checked her pulse. Everything appeared to slow down as Sundown started calculating what was about to happen, all the possible scenarios and outcomes. Reno watched as Kenzie moved closer to assist. As the girl's hand fell limp and lifeless to the side, his eyes followed the slo-mo drop of blood as it dripped off her slender fingers to splat on the floor. He frowned as it spread out in a splatter. And then everything spun back to normal time as the mental calculations in his head came to a horrifying sum.

"No! Wait..."

But the reality math wasn't done fast enough. When Tyrus covered the girl's mouth to give the kiss of life and start CPR, Reno couldn't stop him from that touch.

Envy reacted with a burst of energy that sent all the supplies crashing. The reinforced window glass cracked, and blinds splintered to the floor. Tyrus let out a roar as he grabbed the marble top of the table to protect the girl with his own body. The impact sent the three Keepers off their feet from the blast. Reno hit a chemistry table while Kenzie went flying into a desk. Marcus hit the wall so hard the windows rattled. The air crackled with power as the three —no, four now powers reacted at once.

Well, I think we're all about to shit our panties.

And Reno had no choice but to agree.

14

"Let me see if I understand."

Jess watched the Grid boss pace the breakroom at HQ. Bounce was hot, as in pissed off and worried at the same time. While the man's tone was flat, his eyes were dark orange—not a good sign but appropriate considering the tits-up drama of the day.

They were standing in HQ medical with the girl being monitored in one room and Tyrus in another. Both were alive but unconscious since the Envy freak-out. Reno was in a dark room, having a little chitchat with Madness, who was picked to be the power to commune with Envy. Marcus was in with Tyrus, and Kenzie waited in the hall to give support to the girl if she woke up. That left Jess to try to explain this Keeper drama.

Glancing at Beth as she stood next to him, Jess cleared his throat to say something, but Bounce's hand flew up, pointing at Jess and cueing Jess's mouth to snap closed.

"A dark power was found in the school—unfettered, unattached, and babysitting a young human female, one that was gravely injured and being aided by Tyrus. There was a discussion on what to do next, and then the girl expired. But did not due to CPR being started, and that caused the energy of Envy to lose her"—he narrowed his eyes with a crease appearing between them as he pointed at Jess again—"as you so eloquently stated, shit. And then we were called in with medical. Now remind me once again where this raw power of Envy is?"

Jess looked to the side sheepishly as he said quietly, "In the YETI cooler in my truck." He turned his head to regard Bounce with a shrug. "It was the logical place. We didn't want to leave her at the school, and she insisted on staying close to this girl. Apparently, they've bonded. Or somethin'. Reno is trying to fill in the gaps. But the crew couldn't move in with a dark power just having a fit of worry, so I offered…" He swallowed again as he realized *now* how stupid all of this sounded. "I, uh, had the cooler in my office. Beth has perfected making the best damn sandwiches, so I would bring in a load for the construction crew and it…" Bounce's eyes went to a dark red, and Jess swallowed again. "None of that is important, I guess. But yeah, Envy is curled up in a big ole energy ball in the YETI cooler… in my truck."

Beth squeezed his shoulder, and Jess wondered if she was strong enough in that hold to stop him from flying through a wall when Bounce tossed him. He gave the man a nervous smile. "That's pretty much all I know. And, uh, about the damage at my school..." Bounce's red eyes flashed back his way, and Jess shut his mouth again after mumbling, "Never mind. I'll handle it."

RENO SAT IN A CHAIR, his head pounding from not only hitting a wall hours earlier but speaking with Envy through Madness. Rubbing a hand on his forehead, he let out a slow exhale as Witch rubbed his back. Usually, his heart beating and warm skin gave him comfort, but there was little chance of that happening after last night. She still wore surgical scrubs spotted with the girl's blood after they had worked on the gunshot and other injuries to stabilize her.

Jess and Beth were in the room, and Bounce sat in a chair opposite him, waiting for whatever he had learned. Looking down at his palm as he slowly twisted his wedding band, Reno kept his voice low. Why? Because as much as they tried at HQ to keep it locked up tight with intel, things seem to get out anyway.

"She's been out for centuries, maybe since when the Void was breached the first time when Madness got out. She doesn't know. Just that for a few moments, the door was open, and she escaped. But, unlike Madness, who found me in Jess"—he glanced up at his brother—"she never settled on anyone. Never found a host. Or even tried." Sitting back, he pulled Witch close with an arm around her waist. "She has barely fed. Just enough to stay alive but never enough to be detected. Constantly starving yet never harmed any human. She didn't want to, just took what she needed. She never stopped moving and was afraid of being brought back. Afraid of Lucifer finding her. And whenever she detected a hint of another power, she would stay away. Apparently, Envy came across the girl when she was just a baby. The family was full of envy. But the girl… something about her made Envy want to protect her. Keep her safe. Envy didn't know there were other dark powers in San Fran until the school."

Jess frowned in confusion. "What do you mean until the school? Until she broke in? I don't get it."

Reno pressed his lips together in a stressed line. "She's the girl. Remember a few months ago when that rich lady stopped by? It's the same girl. Envy sensed Madness in me when I got in the car with the girl." He frowned and rubbed the back of his neck. "I felt something weird about her. Something odd. I just didn't know it was because a dark power had picked the girl as a bestie."

"Really? Ah, damn. I remember her. Saddest damn thing. Jade, yeah, that was her name. What was her last name?" Jess snapped his fingers. "Shen. Her grandmother was named Sigu Shen. I tossed her card since we aren't a school open to the public, but I couldn't very well tell granny that. We need to call her and let her know the kid is alive."

"That's a bad idea. It seems like granny sold her granddaughter to Epsilon. Envy didn't know what the price was or why. But he's the one who hurt her, has had her for a few months. And it's not the girl Epsilon is wanting. He wants Envy. It was when he went to kill and dispose of Jade that Envy was able to get them out of there. According to Envy"—he glanced up at Witch—"Jade put up one hell of a fight and attacked Epsilon on her own. Then Envy took out the rest. She had to get Jade help and remembered feeling Madness at the school, so..." He shrugged. "And then when she touched Tyrus, she felt the connection there, and that's how she did the cry for help. It just got scrambled due to them being contained in us. Fleshy hosts. She had never dealt with that."

Shaking his head slowly, Reno curled his fingers into fists. "She's not attached to anyone. Or anything. She chose to be with Jade. And Jade chose to be with her. Without dying."

"And my son?"

They all turned to see Marcus had joined them with Alexis at his side.

Reno sighed. "I don't know. He was there, touching Jade at her last heartbeat. And Envy tried to stop that heart from stopping or maybe—I don't know. I wish I did. Sundown had a scenario that if Tyrus and Envy were both touching Jade with the last breath, it would be messy. And complicated. But even that had fifty-fifty odds. There's so much we don't know about Keepers and how powers work. I'm sorry, Marcus. But I'm pretty sure he'll be okay. Just, the blast of Envy's desperation hit us all hard." He gave his friend a look of sympathy. "Sorry, we need to wait and see."

"She's awake. She's asking for Envy. And"—Kenzie raised a brow as she leaned in the doorway to join them—"the man who saved her."

15

Her head hurt, pounded majorly with each breath. Or was that the *thud-thud* of her heartbeat in her head? Jade wasn't sure. Raising a palm to press on her forehead, she cracked her eyes open to see an IV taped to her wrist. As her thoughts started to clear, she realized what she did not feel in her head, "Envy?"

"She's right here."

Jade turned her head—even that simple movement hurt—to see the man, William Bailey, from the school standing by the door with other people. He held a cooler? Yeah, it was one of those expensive ones. "You put her in a box?"

No, child. They think they put me in the box. Let them think they got me. It's safer for us both that way. But I'm right here. Don't you worry. I said I'd never leave. Just try to be calm and get well.

Jade felt relief that her friend was okay. Envy hiding was no surprise—Jade knew she had done that for survival for a very long time. And after the events with Epsilon, it was more important than ever. Moving her eyes from the man to the others, she squeezed her eyes shut to recall what had happened, but only one face swam through the haze, and he was not among them. His handsome face with eyes full of concern and worry. She didn't even know his name. As she became more mentally clear, she also remembered him protecting her. His body over hers. And did he kiss her? But why did she remember it all from above him? And above her own body? "Where is the man? The one who was trying to help?"

"My son. You're asking for my son, Tyrus. I am Marcus DeMonte."

Jade heard an elegant voice with a strange accent and saw a large, dark-skinned man step through the others. At his side, he led by the hand a beautiful woman who gave Jade a soft smile.

"This is my girlfriend, Alexis. Tyrus is not awake yet. He is in the room next to yours."

Jade rolled the man's name around in her mind. It was a nice name. She whispered, "Tyrus." She frowned and examined the man's features intensely. Well, as intense as she could with the killer headache in the way. "You don't look like him. Hello."

The man smiled and took a seat on the end of the hospital bed. "Hello. And he looks like his mother. If you were to ask him, he's glad for that." Marcus motioned to the others. "I believe you know the cowboy, Jess Bailey. And his brother, Reno Sundown."

Mr. Bailey still held the ice chest at arm's length like it was going to burst into flames. Mr. Sundown stayed behind the others and looked more serious than the rest. His head was even turned to the side—like he was having a conversation with the doorframe. He even moved his mouth a few times oddly in silence. But he had been odd the first time she met him too.

"I'm Kenzie." A tall, thin woman stepped into the room. She had the tough girl image down perfectly, complete with a leather jacket, bangles, and incredible purple hair. And the coolest thing—it matched her eyes. "And ignore Cowboy. He's an idiot. And his brother..." Jade noticed the woman's face softened when she looked back at Mr. Sundown. "He's also an idiot, but..." She approached the bed and crossed her arms. "He's talking to his friend. Like you do to Envy." Kenzie pointed to Marcus, Mr. Sundown, and herself. "We all have them. Those invisible friends that help us, talk to us, and take care of us." Kenzie smiled. "We are who Envy called to help you. And we're really glad she did."

"Reno."

Jade and the others turned to look at him when he spoke up. He had a look like he had just come out of a dream or had been distracted, but Jade understood. She had been like that with Envy sometimes. He stepped forward and gave her a slight smile.

"Reno. You keep thinking of me as Mr. Sundown."

Jade gasped, and he chuckled.

"Telepathic. We all have our own special things. I could hear your thoughts. So call me Reno. Mr. Sundown sounds weird."

"Special gifts?" Jade sat back and rubbed her forehead once again. "So, you know about Envy?" She dropped her hand and felt tears tickle her lashes. "She's my friend. He was going to hurt her. Use her. We got away together." She sniffed, and Kenzie handed her a tissue. "She saved me right back. She's all I have."

"Not correct."

A new voice entered the room, and she found the most gorgeous man she had ever seen entering the room. He was tall, they all were, but he was different. There was something completely off the charts in how the energy changed in the room, how the others stepped back to let him approach the bed. His skin was olive in tone, dark black hair, and a face as handsome as a male model. But it was his eyes that fixated Jade's. They were the softest shade of blue-green she had ever seen, like faded denim—soft and comforting. She darted her gaze to the others, and they smiled at her.

"Who are you?"

The man moved to stand next to her bed. "I am called Bounce. And all of this is under my command. You are safe here. You and Envy." He smiled, stepped over to Mr. Bailey, and took the ice chest. Opening the lid, he smirked as he tossed it back. "It's empty, by the way."

Mr. Bailey caught it like it still contained a danger or was, indeed, on fire.

Jade bit her bottom lip. "She let you think she was there. She says it's okay to tell you that. She just wanted to say she'd do it so you would help me." She couldn't help the smile that touched her lips. "She says thank you. We both do."

Bounce gave her a smile. "You are very welcome. Now, I need you to tell us everything you know. And everything you recall. I will not allow Epsilon to reach you or Envy. But we need your help to learn where you were held so we can stop him."

"That's going to wait." A pretty brunette entered the room, and Jade saw her take Reno's hand. He softened, and for the briefest of moments, their eyes met, and their foreheads touched before she approached Jade's bed. "I'm Emma Sundown." She reached up to check Jade's monitors before pressing her hand over hers. "Yes, Reno's wife. You can call me Emma."

"I call her Witch. It's our thing," Reno responded as he moved to stand at the foot of the bed. His tone was full of affection and the look of love he gave his wife showed openly.

That was how real love must look like, Jade thought. Her parents never once looked at each other that way. Jade had only imagined it could be a real thing in the fairy tales and books she had read.

"I'm also head Healer here at Grid medical. And, Bounce"—Emma gave the tall man a stern look. Unlike the others, his power and authority did not seem to intimidate her—"Jade needs more rest. She's had surgery and is still recovering. She also needs fluids and rest. As well as a good meal." Emma gave Jade a warm smile. "Do you like noodle soup? What about In-N-Out Burger? Get some sleep, and I bet you'll be starving." She brought a palm up to place gently on Jade's forehead. "We have potions that can help with your headache. And Envy will find comfort if you do. She can feel your pain. How you are. It's important to all of us that we make you two feel healthy and safe. Okay?"

The woman's words reminded Jade what Kenzie had said about

the others having friends like Envy. She wanted to ask more, but the Healer's palm on her forehead felt like it grew warmer and calming in its warmth. Like it was wrapping Jade's mind in an old sweater. It made the exhaustion impossible to keep at bay. Jade felt her eyes grow heavy, and she fell asleep with Envy humming a lullaby.

❧

"WHAT DO WE KNOW?" Bounce said as he spun a dry-erase marker in his fingers as if they were having a regular daily debriefing.

They had all gathered in the break room to form a plan on how to keep Jade and Envy safe and how to deal with the fact that a living girl was now bonded with a dark power. A power that had been among mankind for longer than was thought and starving itself to stay hidden.

Reno sat back with his sneakers resting on the edge of the table —once again fidgeting with his wedding band as he listened. "She's not crazy. Not even a little bit. Madness picked up zero. She's stable and not even slightly off after what that bastard has done." He rolled his head back to regard Kenzie. "Did you pick up anything? Did he, uh"—he swallowed and stopped himself short of saying what did not really need to be said—"well, you know?"

Kenzie sat on the corner of the table on the opposite end. It was easier for them both if they kept some distance, and Reno appreciated the effort. "No. He didn't touch her in that way, which is a first for the sick fucker. But it's not only that. Lust didn't pick up any desire or anything from her. I don't think she's even had a school crush. She's as pure as an eighteen-year-old can be. What about you, big guy?"

Marcus had taken up a place by the door. He still waited on an update, via his stamp, for news of Tyrus waking up or his son's condition changing. "No, which is remarkable, considering she is aware of her grandmother selling her. She does not even wish that woman to be killed." He looked down at his nails. "Unlike Murder and me. The woman should pay for what she has done."

"She's stable. Vital signs are good even though she needs time to heal. And while she's not doing it at a full Keeper rate, she's doing it far faster than a simple human would. And there's this." Witch walked over to the white erase board and hung printouts from a brain scan. "There's a similar secondary brain pattern as with you three Keepers. But it's different. See how it is right above Jade's yet not intertwined?" She circled the area she indicated. "With you three, it's woven together. But with Jade, it's not. They are separate. Unlike Keepers." Witch turned to face them. "They are choosing to be bonded. But Jade doesn't need Envy to live. And Envy doesn't need Jade to be a host. They are completely unconnected in their function."

Reno frowned. "Wait, hold on. So what you're saying is..." He stood and moved in front of the scans. "She's a Keeper of choice? She has Envy inside of her but not animating her? Not like us. Without hosting our powers, we're corpses. But Jade is alive and bonded because she offered to be?"

"That's fucking messed up. How come we didn't know there was an option A or an option B?" Kenzie said with a smirk. She picked up a bundle of post-it notes and threw it at Reno's head. "I am doing my best not to be jealous of the kid, but damn, I am."

Reno caught the pad without looking at her and curled it in his hand, still facing the board. "It's not like there's training or a book about Keepers. Heck, even the High Council were told it had failed when making me. It took a few centuries for that to be proven untrue." He brought the fist holding the notes up to press against his forehead. "I can't imagine Envy starving all this time. Afraid and staying hidden for so long. Alone." He sighed. "I mean, she could have wreaked havoc being unfiltered without a host. No void attachment." He looked down at the pad as his voice lowered. "How scary that must have been. For so long." Reno knew that fear. He had been a secret in Jess's head for hundreds of years. In the dark and the cold for some of the time so as not to be revealed.

Feeling Witch's hand on his back, he looked over at her, and as always, just feeling her touch and seeing her face brought his mind back from the dark places it would sometimes take him. "Sorry. Anyway, uh, okay. So she's a new kind of Keeper. We'll adapt and adjust."

"What about my son?"

Turning to face Marcus, Reno shrugged. "I still don't know, man. I really don't."

Emma pulled out more sheets of test results from a folder. "He's stable. His vitals are all good. From what we can tell, the blast and resisting it caused his current state of unconsciousness. Blast trauma. But there is something odd." She brought up more printouts of scans and put them on the board next to Jade's. "He has something new, too. See this readout here? It's new. And if you look at Jade's," she paused as everyone joined Marcus and her at the board. "It's exactly the same as hers. The one we presume is Envy."

"Infected?" Marcus said in an alarmed tone.

"No. That's blood. And both Tyrus and Jade have normal blood. No, this is at a cerebral level. It's like Envy is in them both." She angled her body to face Marcus fully, putting what Reno assumed was meant to be a comforting touch on Marcus's arm. Reno could bet it was beginning to grow warm to offer her healing gift of calm, as well. It worked. The tension in the big man's shoulder eased a bit. "It may be transient, a side-effect of what happened. It may be long term. We have no idea. And it's not as strong of a connection as it is with Jade." She pointed back at the scan. "See the space in his? It's like a flash residue on his synapsis."

"Flash residue?" Reno asked as he plucked the scans from the board. He could see what she was talking about, but he wasn't sure if it would comfort Marcus much. The man was crazy obsessed with making things right for his son. That included being both overprotective and overbearing lately. "What is that, Witch?"

She bit her bottom lip in thought for a few seconds before answering. "Do you know how, when a bright light, like a flash on a phone, goes off on your face?"

"Like a flash grenade?" Marcus countered.

"Yes, exactly. How, when you close your eyes, even after it's gone, you can still see the burst of it behind your eyelids? How it takes a while to fade? Like that." Witch leaned against the board and put her hands over her baby bump. "But again, I don't know. We'll just have to monitor him and find out. But I don't think Envy is harming him. It's just a coincidence of timing. Envy and him touching Jade at the same time during her life and death moment. I wish I could say or explain, but this is all brand new."

Bounce had gone silent and now sat at the table. "Monitoring..." He was on his feet and touched his stamp. "Send Evan in here. Right now." Getting a response from the Relay on duty, they all looked at the door as it opened, and Evan entered.

Reno stepped up to Bounce. "Wait a minute. We talked about this. We aren't treating the girl as an enemy. Envy has been more than cooperative!"

Bounce met his attitude with a raised hand and then placed it on Reno's chest. "And that hasn't changed. Bear with me." Bounce stood and turned toward Evan. "Were there any alerts when Jade was brought in? Any alarms since we placed her in the room?"

Evan, never questioning his boss, pulled up the required reports on his ever-present tablet. "None. Why?"

Bounce looked over at them. "Because there should have been. She came in with Envy. Those alarms are designed to register dark power."

Evan checked again. "But they are triggered by a Keeper's body status. No heartbeat. No body heat. The girl has both, right?"

"Yeah, she does." Reno moved to stand next to Evan, his curiosity overriding his demands about Jade's treatment. It helped to guess that Bounce was no longer headed in the direction anyway. "So have we put the sensors on since?"

Evan shook his head. "No. We didn't. Do you want me to?" Evan looked over at Bounce and waited for orders.

Bounce frowned, his forehead creasing hard in deep thought. "The girl acts as a shield. Didn't you three say she was innocent? Pure of any deep sins or dark?"

Reno nodded along with Kenzie and Marcus. "Barely eighteen. She told me that at the school. Yeah. Oh, crap." He glanced over at the other two Keepers. "She's an innocent. Heck, according to Lust, she's a virgin." Reno became alarmed for an entirely different reason now. "What is the High Council going to do when they find out an innocent, living human girl is now a... a Keeper? A new kind or not?"

Bounce combed his fingers through his hair. "They are going to disapprove. And they are going to call the Keeper's purpose and existence into question. She is still linked to a mortal purpose. Keepers are to exist *only* after that has been severed by death."

"Then we can't let them know. I mean, they stay out of things usually, right? And Envy and Jade have kept their bond secret and hidden up to now. We keep that." Reno thought and lifted his shoulders in speculation. "This is all new. But if her innocence and light is keeping Envy undercover and safe, we have to protect both of them. Make sure she stays that way." He blew out a breath. "At least until this war is over." There was that gut-twisting sensation in his stomach again. It sent a cold-as-ice feeling down his spine when he thought of the end of the war.

"But what about the fucker Epsilon?" Kenzie pulled out a purple handled butterfly knife to fidget with, opening and closing it with a fast click as she sat on the corner of the table. "He's going to want Envy. More than ever if he's figured out—like we have—that she can attach herself to anyone. Living or dead. Not to mention, she's pure, raw power. Like Madness was." Kenzie bared her fangs and stabbed the knife into the tabletop next to her. "He's going to want the power hard core even if it means killing Jade. He's already tried once."

Marcus growled. "He's already obsessed with obtaining Tyrus. Now he'll add the girl and Envy to that vendetta. The disgraced Prince Epsilon will not stop until he has obtained what he believes is his."

Reno cut his eyes over to Kenzie with Marcus's last statement. They both knew what Epsilon wanted more than Tyrus. Her. Kenzie met his eyes, and he could tell her mind had gone there too, which spawned an idea in Reno's. "What if she's dead?"

They all turned to look at him, and he angled his head up to regard the ceiling. "What if we make him believe Jade is dead. She didn't survive the surgery. That Envy is somewhere out there. And not here." He turned to see all of their reactions—yeah, about what he would have guessed. They thought he was crazy. Again. "We know he's going to come for her. We just know that. He's predictable. So, if he is convinced that Jade is dead, he has no reason to come here. Right?"

They were all still staring at Reno like he was as crazy as his power. Maybe he was, but he also knew this plan could work.

You got eighty percent of a chance of this working. Tell them. Remind them of Greed.

"Oh, yeah." His eyes darted to the others, and Witch tried to hide a smile. She knew that wasn't meant for them. "As if all this isn't bad enough. Envy also felt something else in Epsilon." He blew out a heavy breath.

"Envy's not the only new power we have to deal with. Seems like Epsilon has a bond with Greed. Which can explain a lot but is not *good* news. And with that in the mix, Sundown says it's got a high chance of working eighty percent. I'm going to guess Epsilon won't be able to back down unless he knows there is nothing for him to get. Otherwise, we're going to have to prep even more for a daily attack." He braced his hands on the table, feeling sure his face showed just how determined he was about this. "I'm telling you. It can work. She didn't survive. We just have to make sure that's known, figure a mole will let him know. And done." He looked over at Witch as she gave him an encouraging smile and more back rubbing. "We then just have to get her and Envy out of here."

Emma smiled. "I have an idea about who can help with that." She met Reno's eyes. "Lily. Who better than her to help Jade start over."

Bounce narrowed his eyes, crossing his arms. "Fine. I guess the Grid will be organizing a witness protection plan, of sorts." He took Evan's tablet from him. "Now, let's schedule a fake body cremation."

16

Tyrus woke up in the dim light of a Grid medical room. He knew the place well—after all, he had spent a few weeks there when Epsilon almost killed him a little more than a year ago. Looking over at the monitors, he grimaced slightly at a dull ache in his head before removing the tab pressed over his stamp, hitting silent on the damn machine before it beeped at the sensor's removal. He learned that trick from a Healer he had sex with when he had been laid up here before. Even shot up and healing, that ole DeMonte libido could "rise" up to the occasion. Moving his legs off the bed to sit on the side, he braced the mattress in his fingers and did a quick self-check before risking getting to his feet. Dressed in sweatpants and a patient scrub top, he went to the door and found the hallway empty.

He needed to see the girl. It was a need so strong it bordered on an intense obsession. Why? No fucking idea, just that he did. And while he should have zero ideas if she survived her injuries or where she was located, he knew she had and exactly where to go. It was a feeling, an instinct, and although it was bizarre, he let it lead him. Moving to the room next to his, he found the door open and her small form curled up under the covers. Envy swirled slowly above her but flickered in color when it saw him.

Thank you for saving her, boy.

Tyrus inclined his head to let the power know he heard it as he continued to enter the room. Seeing a chair by the bed, he dropped down in it to stare at the girl. Her face was soft in sleep with long dark lashes curling over her pale cheeks. But not near as pale white as they had been when he found her. No, there was a slight blush of health, and he slowly exhaled in relief that she had made it. His eyes went to the IV and the monitors. A heartbeat. Body heat. He lifted his eyes to Envy and became confused. He remembered the girl dying, had seen and felt her breathing stop. It had been his fingers that touched her neck for a pulse and found none. Tyrus had started CPR—that was clear in his head. But what happened after? It was all blur.

"Hello."

The girl's soft voice brought his focus back to find big, luminous green eyes meeting his. "Hey." She tried to sit up, and he reached out to help her. "Are you in pain? Want me to get one of the healers?"

She shook her head and gave him a slight smile as she sat back against the raised head of the bed. "No. It's funny. I've never been shot before, but it really doesn't hurt very much. Almost no pain at all."

Tyrus snorted. "First time being shot, huh? Wish I could say that." He smirked and folded his arms on the bed to take in the details of her features—something he couldn't do before due to the urgency of their meeting. She was pretty. No. She was fucking beautiful, hair dark as night and lips as pink as a sweetheart candy. And her skin was like porcelain. He tried to recall how soft it was. He couldn't, but he itched to find out. He curled his fingers into a fist to fight the urge to do it.

"Your name is Tyrus. Right? I met your father." She put a hand on her chest. "I'm Jade. Jade Shen. I need to thank you for what you did for me." She lifted her eyes to Envy. "For us."

Tyrus had always had a problem with compliments and gratitude. Maybe it was due to the fact he had grown up and became an adult without learning to accept them. "Yeah, I was just doing my job. I'm security at the school."

Jade wrinkled up her nose. "Your job says you are supposed to try to save a person who breaks in with a power and then give her CPR?" She did a small laugh. "Hope they pay you really good for that."

Tyrus chuckled as he let his head drop to rest on his arms. "Ah, shit, you remember all that, huh?"

"I do."

Tyrus moved his chin to look up and meet her eyes. "Yeah, we'll call all of that extra. But you were the first girl I've ever found bleeding there. Guess they'll need to update my duties from this point forward in case it happens again." He cracked a smile. "Let's not have it be you again, deal?"

Jade let out the most adorable giggle and held her hand out. "Deal, Mr. DeMonte."

Tyrus took her offered hand to shake and was hit with the strangest of sensations. Her eyes widened in startlement as they met his—she felt it, too. A quiet humming ran through his mind, and he opened his mouth to speak, but disorientation made it impossible. It was Jade who broke the contact, and Tyrus frowned. "Did you feel, I mean, hear that?"

Jade nodded. "It was Envy. But usually, I just hear it. And feel it. No one has ever shared that with me. Or vice versa." She wrapped her arms around herself, suddenly appearing unsure and shy to Tyrus. "But I'm told there are others. Like me." She met his eyes again. "Your father has a power too, right? Marcus?"

Tyrus nodded, still dumbfounded at what had just occurred. "Yeah. Right. Murder. His power is murder. Uh, there's also Lust and Madness." His eyes cast upward. "You have Envy. All dark powers."

Jade frowned in confusion. "Dark? As in bad? No, no. Envy isn't bad. She's never hurt anyone. She's only taken care of me, been my best friend."

Tyrus closed one eye and lifted a finger. "That's not true. It can't be. They have to feed on the dark deeds of mankind. Sure, they aren't allowed to kill. But still, well." He stood and walked away before turning back to face her. "Bad is the wrong fucking word to use. They are necessary. A balance to the good. Mankind needs them as much as the light side of life." He cocked his head to the side. "And I'm glad you had her as her friend. Just like I'm glad she came to find me. I guess that makes her good. And good for you. That's all that really matters."

Jade looked angry that he dared to accuse her best friend of anything other than righteous behavior. She huffed, crossed her arms, and faced away from him. But Tyrus knew this must all be new to her—and if he gave it more thought, the powers of the others were always good to their hosts. Hell, Murder had become Tyrus friend like Envy was hers.

He internally cursed himself for pissing her off—mainly because he enjoyed looking at her beautiful face, watching how her eyes showed her emotions so openly. And he wanted to see how much more lovely she was when she smiled.

What the fuck is wrong with you, kid? You sound like a romantic sop like the Madness Keeper. I think you should go back to your bed. You must have a fever. Or a fucking knot on your head. Damn delicate, fragile fleshbags.

Tyrus rolled his head and was about to tell Murder to shut up, but before he could, the second voice of Envy did the job for him.

You hush, Murder. Leave them be. You do not understand the ways of love. You never did. You are partly to blame for us losing our human form, you meathead power.

The two powers began arguing in his skull. Tyrus brought a hand up to press the heel of his hand against his forehead. "Do you hear both of them, too?" He now had one eye closed due to the throbbing pain of the bickering fest taking place behind it.

Jade was blinking at him. "Hear who?" She swung her legs off the edge of the bed, and Tyrus wished he was able to open both eyes to fully appreciate the new view given by the shorts and tee. He did note that the dark bruises she had sported yesterday were already yellowish and faded. "Are you okay?"

She touched his arm in concern, and instantly, the two powers were silenced. Like her touch had hit some internal mute button. Meeting her eyes, Tyrus let out a slow exhale of held breath. It was nice. "Yeah, I think so. But maybe I overdid it. And you're supposed to still be in bed."

Taking her slender wrist in his hand, he led her back to bed. She obeyed, and as she climbed in, Tyrus got a look at a taut stomach where a bandage was taped down. He arranged the IV line beside her and then the blankets around her. "I need to let you rest. I'm right next door if you need anything." He smiled and pointed with a finger overhead to Envy. "Have your friend come get me if you do. Or knock on the wall." He reached above her head to do that very thing. "I'll hear you. And I'll do the same."

Jade smiled. "Okay. Goodnight, Tyrus."

He nodded. "Goodnight, Jade. Sleep tight."

JADE LAY IN BED, staring at the activity around her. It was like no hospital she had ever seen. All the men were tall and big, and she knew some of them had fangs. How many of them were human? How many were supernatural? And three of the people in this place understood her, didn't find her friendship with Envy odd. It was strange. She had spent her whole life feeling unnoticed and misunderstood, but in the matter of a day, that had changed. Jade felt more accepted by strangers here than she had ever felt with her school mates or family.

He's a good boy. That Tyrus, child. A good heart. Hard to believe he's any part of Murder. But still, a good boy.

Jade smiled and whispered as Envy came down to settle inside her for the night. "He's handsome, too. Has a very nice smile." She yawned and tugged the blanket up to her chin.

He does. He saved us, child. I'm going to make sure to take care of him, too. We need him, child. And I think he needs us, as well.

Yawning once more, Jade shifted her gaze to the wall behind the head of her bed. Smiling, she rapped on the wall with her knuckles. "I think so, too, Envy. I really do."

And she fell asleep with the same smile on her lips after a soft knock sounded in return.

17

"But I don't want to change my name." It had been four days since she woke up at the Grid headquarters, four days of long-overdue sleep and healing. Tyrus had visited her several times, and they played tic-tac-toe and competed in completing crosswords in the well-worn books of puzzles from the breakroom. She had eaten stale doughnuts from the vending machines and thought they were amazing. She was learning to smile with ease and laugh without worrying about being judged, and not a single person had been cruel or bullied her. It had all been amazing until Bounce came by to explain the plan to her today.

"Jade, I understand how upsetting this can be. I think I can personally say how important it is for one to keep their sense of identity, who they were and are. But your safety is far more important to me than anything else. By killing, so to speak, your past, we are going to ensure you have as good of a future as you can here at the Grid. But I need to stress to you how very dangerous Epsilon can be." He took a seat at the end of her hospital bed and gave her a gentle smile. "And he's even more so when he loses something he considered to belong to him."

She knew they cared about her well-being, and it meant more

than Jade could say, but this was asking too much. Looking down at legs crossed under her, she picked at a loose thread on her socks. "I don't belong to anyone. Neither does Envy." She lifted her chin stubbornly and met Bounce's strange eyes. "I have lost everything. I lost my parents. My name is all I have left of them and myself. If I am going to have a future here, I can't—won't lose who I am." She exhaled in a fast burst. "And it's the only thing I have left from parents, my name. You can't ask me to give it up. Because I won't."

"Maybe she can keep the name?" Reno stood by the door and smiled at her. "I mean, sure, it's not as cool as Reno Sundown"—he winked at Jade—"but still, it can't be that uncommon that there aren't other Jade Shen's in the world. Or heck, even San Francisco."

Bounce glanced back at Reno and gave it thought. Jade held her breath, and when the boss smiled at her with a nod, she wanted to throw her arms around him to hug in gratitude. But she was not sure if the leader of her new world was a hugger, so she settled for bouncing in place.

"Thank you. Now, what do we do next."

Bounce winced and cleared his throat as he stood. "That is a bit more tasking. I'm afraid it involves a body bag."

Jade's eyes went wide with shock as her jaw dropped.

Reno snorted with a laugh. "Don't worry. I've done them. It's not so bad."

LILY DEVENMORE HAD the damage from the break-in at the school repaired without a trace in two days. Cowboy's no-limit black American Express was getting quite the workout. As she signed off on the final repair invoice, she noticed Bounce's classic ride—a vintage Volkswagen Thing—pull up. It was painted a seafoam blue, and every time Lily saw the man remove himself from the interior of the small convertible, it made her giggle.

Walking down the steps, she greeted him halfway and hugged

him. He had been the one to take in the four Devenmore children when their parents died, after all. He was also the one to help them bury their brother, Ben, several years after that. "Hey, Bounce. What brings you here? Did Jess actually get you to reimburse him for the latest repairs?"

Bounce snorted as they walked back inside the place. "No. Of course not. But what I need to discuss with you involves the recent events here that caused the damage."

Lily crossed her arms and motioned to the stairwell for them to take a seat. "I heard it was a girl. That's it. Information was locked down pretty fast." She smiled at Bounce. "Yeah, I could have asked my big sister, your head Healer, for all the details, but I know the rules. And I figured it was a need-to-know situation, so I didn't." She was curious about how it now involved her. "What do you need?"

Bounce sat next to her and turned his head sideways to meet her eyes. "When I took you children in, I felt like I had to. No"—he smiled sadly—"I needed to because your parents were my friends, and you kids needed someone to look out for you. To help you find your way alone and to adjust to reality without them. Not once did I ask for anything in return. Just to grow up as happy, independent, and as strong a person as you could. And consider the Grid as your place to do that."

He faced forward, and Lily leaned to be able to see his expression. Bounce was not the type to talk about the past, nor did he wax sentimental, so she was even more curious about what this was about now. "We did, and we know you didn't expect anything for it. We wanted to be Grid. Our parents were, and Ben died fighting for it. It was already home before it officially became the only one we had." She reached out to put her hand on Bounce's knee. "So ask, Bounce. I'm pretty sure whatever you need, I want to give."

Bounce faced her once more. "It's the girl, the one who was found here. She has nowhere to go. She has no one. And I'd like you to help her grow, be happy, independent, and strong. And show her how to find her way on the Grid as you, Emma, Rose, and Ben did."

Lily stared at him as if she had not heard him right. Whereas her sisters had both married and now had children, Lily had not been that lucky. Or, if she was honest with herself, she chose not to go that path. The Grid was a dangerous place, and if she fell in love, it would become even more dangerous—because she would be putting her heart at risk. She wasn't sure if it could recover, which she didn't believe it had ever done so after her parents and then her brother. It was easier to see her sisters happy, bask in their joy, and spoil her nieces and nephews like crazy. But love and children for herself?

It scared the shit out of her.

Standing, she ran her palms down her shirt as they broke out in a sweat. "You want me to take in the girl?" She turned to face him. "How old?"

"Barely eighteen." He pressed his lips together. "Her parents were killed. And her grandmother sold her to Epsilon."

Lily's nostrils flared in anger, and her chin lifted. "That fucker. Okay. So she's an adult, then why do you need me?"

Bounce stood and took both her hands in his. "It's a bit more complicated than it seems."

And then he told her everything, and Lily felt her heart crack open just a little bit. She could only hope the pain she was letting in with it would be small, too.

18

"You want me to get in that?"

Jade gawked at Bounce, Reno, and Evan in horrified disbelief. They'd entered her room with a gurney and stretched out on that was a thick black zippered bag. She swung her head down to stare at the bag—a body bag. She had never seen one except on television. The three men had informed Jade of their plan. She had to appear to be dead to everyone in their facility. They explained that as hard as they tried, some persons who worked here were moles—bringing Epsilon information due to either working for him on the side or being paid for betraying their duty. Jade questioned that if Epsilon already knew about her survival, then the plan was both unwarranted and useless. Bounce assured Jade that access to her condition had been restricted to the Keepers, Emma, Bounce, and Evan.

"And Tyrus," she said and quickly wished she hadn't. She was doing her best to hide her feelings about the man who saved her. A man she barely knew. It was not helping that Envy encouraged her to find out more about him. The last thing Tyrus would want, Jade was sure, was an insecure eighteen-year-old girl having a crush on him.

Reno darted his eyes over to the others before smiling and lowering his head to nod. "Yeah, sure. Tyrus. But he's sorta Team Keeper." He looked up and gave Jade a wide, friendly smile. "He's like our mascot. And since you're on the team now, you can trust him and all of us."

He stepped up to the body bag and held it open. "It won't be more than a few minutes. Maybe five. We're going to act out a scene in the hallway for everyone to hear. We'll make it *very* clear that you didn't survive. I'll act like an idiot—"

"He has a great volume of skill doing that. Could win an Academy Award for the most idiot acting person ever known in the history of acting like an idiot," said Evan as he interrupted Reno and gave her an encouraging smile. Reno, in turn, elbowed the man hard in the side. Jade could tell they were friends. "No need to be worried. After this, the rumor mill will be abuzz with your unfortunate demise. We can get you out of here and someplace more like a home."

"You can do it, princess."

Jade and the others turned to see Tyrus standing in the doorway. He wasn't smiling, but Jade could not help the one that formed on her lips and the feeling in her stomach when he then gave her one in return. She tilted her head. "Princess?"

He entered the room, and Envy purred in her head—growing louder with each step he took to close the distance.

Did he hear it, too, Jade wondered.

When he reached her, with the horrible bag on its gurney between them, he reached out to lightly press his hand over her fist as it curled on top of the bag.

"That Disney movie. Mulan." He rolled his eyes and gave her a sheepish look. How a guy could look so hot doing that expression, Jade had no idea, but he did. "And before anyone says I'm being all stereotypical and bullshit, that's not it, at all."

His eyes looked into hers, and Jade felt warmth swirl up her spine. It felt like the others have vanished. The bag did not exist, and it was just the two of them.

"She's a young woman whose family didn't believe in her. Hell, she wasn't even sure if she believed in herself. But she learned to. She learned to fight. And then she became a warrior. A legend, right?"

Jade felt the heat of blush climbing up her neck and into her cheeks. She lowered her head down, and her dark hair swept forward. "Mulan wasn't a princess."

"Yeah, well, you're not Mulan, either. You're Jade." Tyrus's hand moved from hers, and he tapped his fingers on the body bag. "I'm calling you *Princess*. Deal with it. Come on, Princess. Got to trust us. And I know you can do this."

Does that make him our prince? Oh, Jade, I think he needs to be.

Ignoring Envy, Jade *really* hoped Tyrus hadn't heard that. Nodding, she climbed into the bag with the men's help and swallowed down her anxiety. "Okay. Just five minutes or less, right? And uh, will I be able to breathe?"

Reno smiled. "Yep." He put his fingers into the side of it through slits in the fabric, and Jade felt the cold tips of his touch against her side. "We made sure of it. And it won't be more than a few minutes." He came in close and tapped her nose. "Just, when the bag opens, we need you to lay there perfectly still. Hold your breath. Can you do that..." He glanced up at Tyrus, and Jade knew he was about to call her by the newly given nickname. She glanced over to see Tyrus curl a lip and show fangs—oh, he was claiming it exclusively. That made Jade giddy, and she smiled.

Reno must have noticed that reaction, too, and looked back down at her. "Jade. Ready?"

She nodded and sucked in a deep breath to help calm herself as she felt and heard the rasping of the zipper as it slid up. "Envy?" she whispered, fear clawing its way up as the bag began to close over her face.

I'm right here, child. I always will be.

As the opening closed over her, Envy started humming their lullaby, and it helped.

A little bit.

❧

"You could have done more!" Reno shouted in Bounce's face and tossed in a shove with his hand against the boss's chest. "Why do you all treat Keepers like we're the plague or something?"

They stood in the hallway outside the patient rooms where a dozen or so Grid staff worked and milled around. The gurney sat to the side where Evan stood guard over it along with two heavily armed Recons. Gosh, Reno wished he had the man's skills to keep a nonplussed expression. However, Reno did have Sundown, who was helping fuel a rage—even if it was fake.

"Calm down, Keeper. We couldn't have a power loose nor the human it chose to host itself in. The girl died, and I am sorry for that. It happens. But I have to keep all the others on the Grid safe and secure. Now we need to focus on finding the power. It's running loose in my city once again." Bounce, on the other hand, always acted cool and calm. Dude had no need to act. "Perhaps, if you and the other Keepers had let us know there was a new power, we could have found it and her host sooner."

"We believe the power has already left the area. The sensors on the edge of the city tripped on its exit," Evan stated as he moved to grasp the handles on the gurney. Reno guessed the discreet hand pressed to the bag was to reassure Jade inside of it. "Now, if you don't mind, I need to take this to the incinerator in case traces of the power exist. The room is already being scrubbed down using Keeper protocol."

Reno strode over to stop him. "Wait. I want *both* of you to see her! To see what you allowed to happen by your stupid fear of the powers." Grasping the zipper fob, he jerked it down to show Jade's face. Sure, she didn't look dead, but no one else was close enough to see the color in her cheeks—it helped she was still pale and healing, too. It was enough for the others to see she was contained in the bag. And her chest, with her held breath, didn't even tremble. "Look! Take a real good look."

Bounce looked away as if he really did feel guilty. Gosh, he was good.

Evan jerked his hand away and said in a warning tone, "Stop it. Respect the dead." He then closed the bag and secured the zipper.

Reno let out a dry laugh and gawked at the man angrily. "Oh, sure. Respect the dead. How about you respect the dead that are not..." Okay, he probably should have rehearsed this but too late for that now. "You know what I mean. Keepers." He stepped away and paused by Bounce. "I won't forget this. And I better be told if you find the power, too."

They held a tense eye lock, but Reno could see the light blue hue of Bounce's eyes. Amusement big time.

"I will consider it, Keeper. Go home. I'm signing you out for the day. Get your shit together."

Reno snarled with bared fangs and turned on his heel to leave. Evan went the opposite direction, rolling the gurney through double doors where the two Recons took up guard. Reno even added throwing open a door to the act. The knob dented the wall and everything. He internally winced. Bet that was coming out of his paycheck.

LILY HAD BEEN UP for two days to prepare for her new guest. Tyrus had arrived an hour earlier, and she drafted him to unwrap decorative objects, carry furniture up the stairs, and shove it into every possible position in the room. Its former purpose had been her reading room, and it had been set up by her parents previously for the children to gather and do homework. The built-in shelves were packed with books from her childhood, as well as her favorites now.

The desk and file cabinet, as well as a craft table, were stored in the remaining part of the attic, but Lily didn't have the heart to move the well-worn comfy couch in the corner. The throw her mother had made out of all her children's baby onesies and blankets still draped over the back of it. The room had three windows with two large ones overlooking the backyard, which ancient live oaks shaded. A new bed now rested between the two shelves on the wall with its peaked roof. Adorning the bed was a soft duvet and sheets done in pastel colors, and throw pillows completed the look.

Lily stood in the middle of the comfy room and looked sideways at Tyrus. "What do you think? Will she like it?"

Tyrus looked at his watch and then back up. "I would say yes. But you need more green. Envy will want green in the room." He stepped over to the third window facing the driveway. "They should be here any minute."

Even though Lily's parents' house was as secure as any residence of a Grid member, Tyrus had insisted on checking the setup before Jade arrived. His stance at the window was tense and on full alert. Lily could even see his fingers often twitch to his sidearms. She did not know Tyrus very well—just that he was Marcus's long-lost son, able to access his father's power of Murder, and had worked really hard to move beyond his personal history of being Epsilon's right-hand man. That must have been hard. Lily was pretty sure some people still didn't accept him. But from what she could tell thus far—he was a good man. And he was trying to do better.

"What's she like?"

Tyrus turned his head to look back at her, and Lily only noticed then how much his eyes were like Marcus's, that tawny, light brown color, bordering on orange. She always thought that was due to Murder inside of Marcus—but maybe not. He narrowed those eyes and faced the window again to scan the street. "She's sweet. Timid and quiet. She's a killer at crosswords, and I honestly don't think there's a book she hasn't read." He skirted his focus to the bookshelves before taking it back to the window. "But I think she's stronger than she's been made to believe."

He turned away from the window and faced her. Lily could hear the status of Jade's transport in her stamp. She knew Tyrus would have heard it, too, yet it wasn't enough for him. Interesting.

He crossed his arms, and a slight smile curved his lips. "She's beautiful. I don't think she knows that, either." He looked up at Lily as his lips evolved into a snarl with fangs bared. "Her fucking bitch of a grandmother sold her to Epsilon. What kind of person does that?" He snorted. "Forget I brought that up. Shit, my pops threw me into a fire. Guess family is fucked up all over."

Lily took a seat on the bed and smoothed out the wrinkles in the new bed covers under her palms. "Well, I'm not the best to ask about that." She looked up to see Tyrus wince, guilt obvious on his features.

"Sorry. I forgot about your parents. I'm still learning all the histories beyond my own."

Lily smiled at him. "It's okay. They are still here. My folks. Just in a different form." She could tell he fought the need to recheck the street. "You like her—Jade, right?"

He blinked and gave into the need to face the window once more. But Lily was intuitive when it came to people. His grunt and back to her told her all she needed to know. Tyrus did like Jade—but in what way? She'd have to find out. For now, they just needed to get Jade Shen under her roof. She'd hope her mama gear kicked in later. Emma would be so proud that her sister was even willing to try. Lily just hoped she *came* with such a gear like her sisters. Auntie was different. And this might as well be, too—Jade was eighteen and not a child. Especially considering everything the girl had been put through in the last few months.

"They're coming up the block."

Tyrus's statement brought Lily out of her musings, and she followed him down the stairs. The SUV's approach was detailed via their stamps as Evan let them know they were entering the driveway. She and Tyrus stood in the garage as the black vehicle backed into the space with the garage door closing behind it. Lily felt nervous at meeting Jade, which was silly. She wanted the girl to like her and feel a sense of home. Sure, Jade had a power attached to her, but she was used to that with her brother-in-law Reno.

Lily smiled when the rear passenger door opened of the car driven by a Relay, but it faded when Evan stepped out. Of course, the man didn't give her any notice. The man had a stick shoved up his butt so high, and Lily was sure that unless she had a bullet hole or was giving one, she was not worth his focus. The man was hardcore dedicated to his job, but damn, did he ever just lighten up?

The rear hatch of the SUV popped up to reveal Jade sitting in the back—unseen behind the dark-tinted windows. The same windows that protected Evan from the sunlight. Dang, it took some balls to do what he was doing in broad daylight. Lily's smile grew even as her nerves made her want to chew on a nail. Evan helped the girl step down on steady legs. Lily would have thought Jade would still be in pain after being shot and surgery, but as a green mist moved behind her, she assumed the power had gifted Jade with superhuman healing like the other Keepers.

Stepping forward, Lily resisted laughing at how Tyrus beat her to Jade. And Jade looked more than happy that he had. Ah, so he did like her. And judging by that response, he was liked back in return.

"Hi, Jade. I'm Lily Devenmore. It's nice to meet you." She moved past the man to take Jade's hand in hers. She was a toucher. Jade was just lucky she was keeping the need to hug at bay—she rarely did. "This is my house. And I guess it's now yours, too."

"Let's get her inside." Evan rudely shouldered Lily back as he took Jade's elbow in his grasp to lead her into the house. Tyrus followed, and Lily stood there, arms crossed on her chest.

"Rude much, gentlemen?"

Both men gave her zero attention, and when they reached the living room, they stepped away from Jade to discuss security measures, leaving Jade standing there like a package dropped off rather than a person. Lily took her hand and led her to the foyer.

"Men." She snorted. "Anyway." She pressed her hands to Jade's arms and rubbed. Guess that mama gear was starting to churn—Lily's mother would do the same thing to them when they came home from a lousy day of school or a horrible date. "I'm Lily, and I'm so happy you are going to stay with me." Jade's eyes were roaming around the large Craftsman home. Envy had vanished. Lily thought perhaps the power wanted to do its own security survey. "This was my parents' home. They bought it when I was a baby. It was built in the 1940s, and they made it their own." She smiled when Jade's eyes came back to hers. "You want to see your room? You have your own floor, basically, with a bathroom, too. It used to be part of the attic, but it was renovated, as well. It's small but cozy. You'll have it all to yourself."

Lily turned to lead Jade up the stairs when the sharp sound of curtain rings on rods sounded. Pausing, she frowned as she watched Evan and Tyrus pulling all the drapes closed tight over the windows. Evan had to know the glass was not only ballistic but also had UV blocking, so there was no risk of him turning crispy in the sunlight. "Hey, stop that."

She stomped into the dining room and grabbed Evan's arm to jerk him away from the window. "What are you doing? I was told I should have the house as I always do. And that means..." She swiftly threw the curtains back open to flood the room with sunlight, and Evan stepped back from it out of habit. "It's Breaker-safe glass. There's no need to close these. I only do that at bedtime."

Evan blew out a breath as he faced her and crossed his arms. His handsome face, which Lily steeled herself to resist, held a look of irritation, and he lifted his chin. "I am aware. I am also the one who created the security protocol, Ms. Devenmore. Therefore, I can also change it." He reached to close the curtains.

"But this is my home. And I say"—she smacked his hands as they reached past her—"they stay open so that it looks like nothing is going on out of the norm." She mirrored his stance and waggled her head. "Don't like it? Ignore it. Like I do you with your blah-blah bossiness."

Jade let out a small laugh, and Lily looked back over her shoulder to see both Jade and Tyrus found this entertaining. Turning back to Evan, she smiled. "Grid approved all my security measures forever ago. And I do the routine updates and upgrades." She stepped closer to him until their crossed arms touched. "If you want to take it up with Bounce, fine. He is, after all, *your* boss, right?"

"You should be more policy-compliant like your sisters." He kept his head toward her but reached out to the side to throw one panel of curtain closed. "It would be easier on us all, Ms. Devenmore."

Lily smiled, reached out, and opened the curtain. "I am abiding by policy, Mr. O'Brien. Mine. In my house. Approved by Grid." She smacked his hand as it reached out once again. "And I am not my sisters. I'm me. And you can call me Lily."

Evan slowly exhaled and did not even try to hide his irritation from her. "Are you quite sure you are related to Emma at all? She's sweet. Kind. Respects and adapts to security needs. I find you very unlike her." His eyes moved across her face and trailed down to her sandal-wearing feet and back up. "Are you adopted?"

Lily was used to that reaction from men. Whereas she, Emma, and Rose all had the same dark hair and eyes in different hues of green, Lily was curvy and plus-size. Her sisters were lean and even a few inches shorter than her. She opened her mouth to rip Evan a new one for judging her by her looks, but he did not have an expression of judgment nor disgust. In fact, it seemed to her it was more of one of appreciation—until he hid it away, of course.

"You know very well I'm not, Evan. You're so old your immortal ass was around when I was born." She opened the remaining curtain. "And the curtains stay open." She rapped her knuckles on the glass. "It's tinted one way out. No one can see in, and it's also ballistic." She moved her hand to poke a finger into his chest. "Now, if you are done, can you go so Jade and I can get to know each other?" She turned her head to smile at the girl. "And maybe order some pizza. Do you like pizza?"

"Someone needs to stay on security detail, Ms. Devenmore. I'm not going anywhere. Curtains closed or not," Evan informed Lily.

She gawked, jaw falling open. "Are you kidding me? Why wasn't I told?" She picked up her tablet from the dining room table and opened up the Grid portal to see the latest updates. "Oh, yeah, I see that now." She winced while biting her bottom lip. "But why you? Why not Cowboy? Or Reno? Or anyone. Heck, a stranger might be more pleasant than you."

Evan smirked. "Cowboy is retired. Reno has a family and most likely being tailed until Epsilon is sure the girl is dead. He is not to come here. Others have patrols. So, it is I you get, Ms. Devenmore."

"Lily. My name is Lily. Can you at *least* call me by my first name, Evan? Or I'm just going to start calling you Sir Asshole until you do."

"I can stay." Both she and Evan angled to regard Tyrus after he volunteered. Jade's face brightened with it, and for a moment, Lily met Evan's eyes to determine if he detected the exchange—he did.

"The school has a replacement for me since I've been put on medical leave for two weeks. Place isn't opening for a while anyway. And like you said, Evan, everyone else has patrol. And I'm pretty sure your plate is full already." The man paused in his proposal and moved a hand up to motion to Lily. "That is, Ms. Devenmore if that's okay with you?" He looked sideways to Jade. "And with Princess here."

"Yes, please," Jade said excitedly, the words coming out in rapid order, and Lily smiled.

"I'm fine with that as long as Sir Asshole is."

"Oh, for Omega's sake. Fine," Evan grumbled. "As long as *Lily* approves the placement, I will approve it." He looked out the window to see the dark blue sedan parked down the block Lily had been informed of earlier. "Routine overwatch rotation will continue outside as already approved."

Lily narrowed her eyes at Evan as he even tried to "accidentally" close the curtains as he stood back to face them. "That's fine. And, Tyrus, I hope you don't mind dogs. The only room I have left to put a guest is in their space. But the futon in there is comfy. It's either that or the couch."

Tyrus gave her a nod and a tight smile. "You'd be surprised how much I'm used to hounds, Ms. Devenmore. Thank you. And, Evan, understood."

As the man spoke, Lily kept her eyes on Jade and expected the young woman to bounce on her feet and squeal with joy at her newly assigned bodyguard. But no, Jade held a perfect composed stance. Lily didn't, however, miss the smile that teased right before dark hair swung forward for Jade to hide it behind.

19

"Only eighteen? Wow."

Kenzie and Lana sat at the breakfast bar in their apartment. Kenzie was nursing a much-needed cup of coffee while Lana, not allowed the stuff, put away her favorite pregnant craving breakfast—oatmeal loaded with candy sprinkles and hot sauce. Kenzie had thought her heartbeat crazy the first time Lana prepared it. She also learned Lana thought it disgusting, too, yet she ate it the next day and every day that followed. They both had a running bet whether Lana would stomach or crave the concoction after the baby was born.

Kenzie cocked a foot on the chair and downed her coffee. "Yeah. She's a tiny girl. Pretty sure she's been sheltered her whole fucking life and then sold to Epsilon like she was a garage sale item. Can you imagine that?" She stood and placed her cup in the sink. "Talk about culture shock."

Lana was eating bites of the horrid mix as she spoke around them. The baby made her so hungry, but so far, her weight caused the doctor no concern, and her damaged leg and hip accommodated her pregnancy—so far. "And she has a power?" Lana finished the food and joined her by the sink. Kenzie wrinkled her nose. Lana snorted with a laugh and rinsed out the bowl to remove the smell. "I know. I have no idea how I can eat something that I also find so nasty. Just ugh."

Kenzie leaned over to place a kiss on Lana's cheek. "That makes two of us, Dancer." She brushed Lana's hair back, and her thumb stroked over the pulse beating in her neck. Her own heart began to beat, warmth heating her skin, and Lust let out a loud purr that made them both chuckle.

Lana's smile dropped. She turned to hug Kenzie tight, arms going around her, and buried her face against her chest. "Will he go after her? Jade?"

Kenzie tensed at the question and gauged how best to answer. The last thing she wanted was to upset Lana by discussing topics guaranteed to do so. Like the well-known fact that Epsilon still wanted to get Kenzie back in his clutches. She'd hoped that in time, it would cease, but from the intel culled from sources and words said by the man himself, that was not the case. Kenzie and Lust doubted it ever would be. If Greed functioned as they guessed, it would fixate on a want and make its host crave obsessively until obtained. Kenzie knew hunger of a dark power all too well. She was lucky that Lana fed most of it.

Unlike Epsilon, she and the other two Keepers did not kill to appease their appetites. Epsilon threw himself into it with crazed abandonment regardless of the source of the feast offered to his dark power.

Kenzie hated being his favorite "toy." Lana feared he would find a way to drag Kenzie back into his sick play, but Kenzie would choose to end rather than let it happen again. And now she had so much to lose. Lana. Their baby.

"Lana." Kenzie bent her head to look at her. She gave a sad smile when Lana's eyes met hers with tears shimmering in their depths. So much for not upsetting her. "Are you asking because you're scared Epsilon will get Jade? Or"—she cupped Lana's chin in her fingers—"are you hoping he will and then not want to come after me?"

Lana broke into a sob, and Kenzie sighed. Yeah, pregnant women were emotional as fuck, and she got that. She also understood how hoping for something awful would make Lana feel like shit. But Kenzie understood. It was an easy route for a desperate, emotional mind to travel down. Willingly or not.

"Baby." Kenzie took Lana's hand and led her to the sofa. She helped Lana sit next to her, then encircled her with both arms and legs. Resting her chin on Lana's soft hair, she whispered, "I don't think he'll ever be that simple—even if he got Jade. Or a dozen more. He thinks because he made me, he owns me. But..." She angled her head to meet Lana's eyes as she grasped the cuff of her sleeve to wipe her lover's tears. "Nothing changes. We fight to make sure he never gets me. The others are just as solid on that as we are. And we do the same hardcore efforts to make sure he doesn't get Jade, either." She gave Lana a determined nod with a raised brow. "He will not take me without going up against the wrath of all three of us and our powers. He would never be that stupid. He knows that together we can end his sorry, sick ass."

Lana sniffed and brought her hand up to press a palm against Kenzie's cheek. "Good. Because I need you, Snap." She gave a tearful smile, took Kenzie's hand in hers, and rested it on her rounded baby bump. "We need you." She let out a weak and adorable laugh. "Baby Snappet needs his or her Mommy Poop."

Kenzie rolled her eyes with a snort. "Great. We're letting *that* version stick?"

Lana giggled. "Well, poop sticks really good. You'll find out, being the one to change all the poop diapers."

Kenzie's head jerked back, and she pursed her lips together. "When did I agree to that?"

Lana smiled. "Oh, you haven't yet. Just giving you a heads up. I'm nice like that."

Kenzie added an additional eye roll for fun. However, she felt a sense of relief despite her new title as Mommy Poop. Any positive thoughts looking forward was a good thing. Kenzie would hold on to that, no matter what. "Fine. Mommy Poop, it is."

❧

"MY KEEPER IS WORRIED."

Marcus sat on the end of the bed in the apartment. Alexis had not "officially" moved in, but he had no issue with her unofficially doing the act. He enjoyed her being there when he came home, when he woke up, or, on the rare instances that their patrols aligned for them to do so, go to bed together.

Her hand smoothed over his bare head, and he lowered it.

"It's Tyrus. And the girl." He angled his head to look back at Alexis. "He's somehow now linked mentally to both her and the power of Envy. I am not sure how I feel about that." Marcus stood and started unbuttoning his shirt as he spoke. "My son is already a target that Epsilon seeks with zeal. This would solidify that quest for the bastard. He does not give up. And he revels in being the bully, believing himself to have power. It's how he validates every move he makes."

Alexis moved off the bed and slid her hands under the shirt to push it off Marcus's back, and she tossed it to the chair. "And we will do everything to make sure he doesn't get Tyrus. Nor Jade." She stepped around to stand in front of him and met his eyes. "He would be an even bigger idiot than he is now to go up against three powers and their Keepers."

"Four. There are four of us now. Albeit, Jade is untrained and unique." He thought about it all and narrowed his eyes. "Perhaps I need to view this differently. If Envy has become attached to Tyrus, perhaps that translates to her also protecting him. It's clear the power hates Epsilon as much as the rest of us."

Alexis lifted one shoulder in a shrug, her focus attuned to undoing the buckle of Marcus's belt and tugging it through the loops of his trousers. Her fingertips grazed along the waistband of the pants, and she looked up at him. "How about we stop talking about your son. And a girl. And the other powers." She gave him a seductive smile as her deft fingers unsnapped and then unzipped so she could dip her hand inside. "I would like to assist you in not thinking about those things at all."

Alexis lifted onto her toes as one arm wound around his neck while the opposite one was busy.

Marcus let out a hungry growl as she wrapped her hand around his length, her thumb taking delightful time in teasing the ridges of the shaft. Demonkind competed to mate, and the ridges and their fleshy barbs assisted the male to copulate.

And fight.

At the same time.

Can I fucking watch? I'll settle to just listening. Promise to keep my eyes—which I don't really have, by the way—closed. Come on, fleshbag I own, let me have some of this fun. Plea—

Marcus shut Murder out as he wrapped a hand around Alexis's wrist to jerk it free from the interior of his clothing. She smiled and showed her fangs as he twisted that arm behind her back. Her predatory behavior was such a turn on to him. Capturing her mouth with his in a heated, passionate kiss, their tongues clashed as lifted her with one arm while the other released her wrist to wind his fingers in her hair cruelly. Alexis let out a lustful chuckle as she bit the side of Marcus's neck, being careful not to pierce his skin and have Murder involved in a completely unwelcome way. Marcus was falling in love with his beautiful Breaker girlfriend, and the last thing he wanted was to infect her with his dark power.

"Going to let your hellspawn side out to play, lover?" She moved her head to tease the right side of his neck and took a chance to bite a little harder. "You know I can take it. And you know how much I want it."

Marcus let out a snarl as he threw her off him and onto the bed. Letting his trousers and briefs drop, he watched as Alexis loosened her robe and threw it to the floor. She moved as much like a predator as he did, and it made him so hard, he throbbed. It bounced, standing away from his body like a sexual GPS indicator to what waited at the end of this seductive journey.

Alexis looked back over her shoulder, and as she whipped her hair to the side, she crawled over the bed until she was on her hands and knees, her beautifully curved ass beckoning him, providing as much of a "welcome home" to the end of his aroused journey as any motel could.

Climbing onto the bed, Marcus let out a low, guttural sound as he rested on his knees and grasped her hips in his hands. One hand moved up her back to press firmly between her shoulder blades to force her down on the bed while his other kept her hips aligned with his. With a savage thrust, he entered the heat of her body. The sudden joining of their bodies caused both of them to cry out in pleasure. The demon rings on his shaft enhanced both their pleasure with each stroke.

Bending over her back, Marcus curved his own until his mouth found the curve where her shoulder joined her neck. Alexis mewed in need as he kissed the spot gently and smiled against her skin as she began to beg by demanding, "not that." He knew exactly what she wanted, but he did enjoy playing with his prey. Alexis writhed under him, and her arm came up to place a hand against the nape of Marcus's neck, and her fingers curled to dig her nails into his skin.

"Breaker wants some pain, does she?"

Alexis's breath was gasping as she hissed through her teeth. "You know I do. Stop with the tender bullshit and give it to me, Keeper."

Marcus let out a breathless laugh. "Most women," he said between intense thrusts, "like that sweet, romantic bullshit."

Alexis slammed her hips back against his. "Then save it for them. Give me what I want."

Who was he to deny a woman such as Alexis what she wished? He sank his fangs in, and she climaxed with a scream.

20

"How are you adjusting, Jade?"

She sat in an office within the medical wing of HQ. The nice woman sitting in the chair opposite her was a doctor by the name of Skyler Wyatt. "What kind of doctor are you?" Jade looked around at the cozy office decorated in soft hues of pastels. Furniture and décor in various textures. And Doctor Wyatt wore leggings and a long sweater. With trainers.

Wyatt smiled. "I'm a psychiatrist. With a master's degree in social work counseling, and Bounce recruited me to work here at the Grid a couple of years ago. I help those within come to terms with not only their past lives but their new ones if they are supernatural. For the humans, I help them with battle fatigue, counseling, and PTSD. And at other times, I'm just an ear that listens. With no judgment." She crossed her legs and sat back. "Anything you say here stays here. It's all private and confidential."

"But I'm not crazy. I'm not supernatural..." Jade bit her bottom lip and gave that a moment of intense thought. "I don't think so, anyway. And I don't have a past life. So why am I here?"

Doctor Wyatt tilted her head. "You're right. But I'm here to help anyone and everyone. We're a family here, and now you and Envy are part of it. We don't have to talk about anything. But you do have to meet with me. It's part of the rules. Everyone does. Now"—she sat forward, and her tone changed—"you may not have a past life, but you had a past. One that I am told you'd like to hang on to, even if it's just keeping your name. Can you explain to me why? Bounce offered you a new start. From what I can tell by the notes in your chart, it wasn't a happy life. You lost your parents. And your grandmother..." The pause was so slight, but Jade picked up on it.

"Sold me. Wanted me dead." Jade looked away and sighed. "I already told Bounce why I think she did that. She wanted everything when my grandfather died, but she didn't get it. My father did. And then, when he died, she didn't get it again." Jade brought a hand up to wipe threatening tears. "I guess now she has."

Doctor Wyatt nodded. "Do you hate her for that?"

Jade's eyes snapped to the doctor's, and she shook her head. "No. I know I probably should, but maybe something is wrong with me." She looked down and wrapped a loose thread from a rip in her jeans around her finger. "I don't think I can hate anyone. But it's hard to understand. My grandmother is just a product of a world where girls—women have little value."

"What about Epsilon?"

The thread she'd had wrapped around her finger snapped. Jade narrowed her eyes and curled her hands into fists. "I take it back. I guess I can hate, after all."

Jade heard the sound of Doctor Wyatt's chair scooting across the rug, and then a gentle hand laid on her knee.

"Good. He deserves your hate, and it is perfectly normal for you to do so. No one would blame you. You'll find everyone here shares that with you."

Jade lifted her head to meet the woman's gaze. "I've never fit in. It's weird"—she looked down—"how fast I felt like I fit in here. So quick. Maybe that's why."

Skyler let out a soft laugh. "Or maybe it's because Envy knew you needed to be with the other Keepers. What has it been like before? With her?"

Jade swung her gaze around the room, and it stopped on a framed photo of the woman with what she guessed was a family. A smiling man and a little boy. A big black shepherd. "I don't know. I didn't know she was a dark power. I just knew her as my friend." Jade brought her focus back to Doctor Wyatt. "She protected me. Kept me safe. Was and is my friend. My only one." This time, the tears could not be stopped, and she went to wipe them away when a tissue was held out. Taking it, Jade did her best to keep the sobbing at bay. "I'm so scared right now. Everyone is telling me that it's okay—that I'm safe and wanted here. But I felt like I was every time before, then people died. Or they picked on me. Or they bullied me. Or..." She wiped her eyes and then blew her nose. "They sold me. She just gave me to him. Like I was some..." Her breath caught, and the sorrow faded to anger, unlike any Jade had felt before.

"Like an object." Jade let out a pained laugh. "I don't even know the price I was bought for—if there even was one. I have to wonder since she called me worthless." She met the woman's eyes as she spat out the words through her teeth. "She said that acting like I was worth something would cover the fact I wasn't." She ground her teeth. "My name is Jade Shen. My name is all I've ever had. She had to be wrong. I know she was wrong." Jade gave into the emotions and began to cry so hard her body shook with it. Great heaves of emotions caused her to leave the chair and crash to her knees. "My name is Jade Shen! And *I* am *not worthless!*" Jade's fists hit the floor, and she knew she was screaming, but it felt so good to let her emotions have free rein. "I am Jade Shen! And I am *not* worthless!"

Doctor Wyatt's arms wrapped around Jade as the woman joined her on the floor. She rocked Jade, and it was the type of embrace she had wanted from her mother but never received. From her father, who had been too busy to do so. And from her grandmother, who only saw Jade as an end to a profitable means. Doctor Wyatt brushed her hand over Jade's hair and attempted to soothe her.

Jade's eyes came open, and through the tears, she saw herself in a mirror across the room. A green mist swam behind them, and Jade found her eyes glowed—and it didn't scare her. She would stop being scared.

And she had help to do that now. "I am Jade Shen. And I am the Keeper of the Envy of man."

21

"I would like to remind everyone that I am retired." Jess brought a finger up as he protested. "And I really do not think this is a good idea."

Reno grinned as he keyed in some code to a room that Jade had not been taken to yet. She had been part of the Grid for two weeks and been shown how to use a gun—which she thought was the coolest thing *ever*. They had tried to teach her hand-to-hand combat, but Envy would lash out and do the fighting for her, so it had been determined that it was not needed in Jade's case. She had settled in living with Lily Devenmore, and they were becoming fast friends. Lily and she would spend most of their evenings as a mini book club, having deep discussions about whichever book they each were reading and watching movies based on books. Jade was happy for the first time in a very long time.

"What's wrong, big brother? Scared of a little girl like Jade?" The door opened, and Reno motioned for her to step in first with Jess following her. It was an octagon-shaped room with padded walls and floor.

Jade looked up and blinked. "The ceiling is padded? Seriously?"

Reno leaned back and nodded. "Yeah. They put those there for me. Let's just say I needed some adjustment time to figure out how to fly. It was hitting the repair budget really hard. I've gotten better now."

"Wings? You have wings?" Jade twisted a wide band of jade she wore on her wrist. A nervous habit formed shortly after Bounce had gifted her with the dragon carved out of jade. To anyone else, it looked like jewelry, but it was actually hollow inside where Envy resided to stay close but also hidden beyond Grid and home.

While Jade had yet to go out into public, she was hoping it was soon. She asked Lily, Skyler, and the others almost every day when she could. Glancing back, she saw Tyrus stayed by the door leading from the hallway. He had become distant, and Jade thought maybe that was best. He was still assigned as her bodyguard, but he stayed outside of Lily's home and remained in the car or transport when she was brought to headquarters. They barely talked, and Envy was not happy about it. But Jade was determined not to be a gushy girl over a guy who probably only saw her as one. She needed to stay focused. She had decided that day in Doctor Wyatt's office never to be a victim again. Not a scared little girl, wanting someone to love her. She had that.

She had Envy.

"So, what do I do?"

"Yeah. He's got wings and trust me—he was pretty insufferable for weeks when he got them. And as far as what you need to do, Jade?" Jess stepped up to rub a hand on her arm. "Don't kill me," he said with a lopsided grin.

Reno laughed, and Jade watched him leave, locking the door behind him. He moved outside of the room to stand next to Skyler in what Jade guessed was a reinforced observation area. The air current reversed, setting off a beeping noise, and she looked up at the vent.

"That's just them isolatin' the airflow. This room and other Keeper protocols in HQ are engineered with systems that prevent the powers or a part of them from reaching the rest of the place.

Closed air and all. It's even got its own power circuits so as not to take down all of HQ." He shoved his hands in his jeans pockets as he rocked back on his cowboy boots. "Yeah, we take precautions and all. Don't take it personally."

Jade had grown to like Cowboy. He was easygoing and funny. And now she knew he was Reno's original home—which she still found odd to imagine Reno being anyone's bad side. But it was pretty cool to learn about. As Jess stepped up to her, Jade focused on whatever lesson she was about to be taught. He was, after all, the one who trained her on weapons. Jade could guess he had a new one to teach.

"We're going to need Envy for this, darlin'. Can you ask her to join us?" His fingers reached out to tap on the carved jade dragon bracelet. "I need you to have her try to, ah..."—his whiskey brown eyes rolled up before he snapped his fingers, apparently finding the correct words—"infect me. Get to me and try to make me do something. Say something. Anything that Envy can make a fella do." He winked at Jade. "Within decency, please. I'd like to keep this PG-13 and all."

Jade bubbled out a giggle. "I would like that, too. Thank you." Jade inhaled slowly and focused on connecting with Envy. That, too, had been lessons to be learned. The Keepers were teaching those. Kenzie and Marcus. Reno, too. Everyone wanted to help her, and they were all patient and kind about it. Jade closed her eyes, and she knew when they opened to see Jess, they glowed bright green. Even her vision had a green tint to it. "Envy, show him what we can do."

The bracelet grew cold on Jade's arm, and then the power's green mist form swirled above it. It formed a dragon shape like the bracelet and her mother's statue. Jess's chest expanded with a deep inhale of his own, and Jade could sense the air being released slowly to ease tension as Envy touched the man's hand and then wound up his arm. Jade could feel the goose bumps that followed on his skin, and she watched in fascination as Envy disappeared...

Inside of the cowboy.

"CAN you tell me where my husband is?"

The Relay on duty smiled at Beth and pulled up Jess's coordinates. Jess had sent a text letting her know his presence was requested at HQ—a frequent occurrence as he worked with the youngest, newest Keeper to become what she was now destined to be. Jess burned his figurative candle at both ends between training and running the school. Between his schedule and hers, they were passing badasses of each other, and she missed him like crazy. Today, she'd hoped she could spend the afternoon with her husband at home, but no, so Beth came to him.

Holding a bag of In-N-Out burgers with fries for them both, she thanked the Relay as he directed her to the secure area and showed her the way. He asked if she wanted him to let Jess know, but she waved off the offer. Beth wanted to surprise her husband with the visit.

Nodding and saying hello to those she knew as she walked, her stamp was scanned at the secure area entry as she snagged a few fries from the bag. Sure, she was hungry, but she craved time with her man more.

RENO BRACED his arms on the counter as Skyler monitored both Jade's and Jess's vitals. Watching through the thick ballistic glass as Envy swarmed over Jess, he tapped the intercom so Jade could hear him. "Okay, Jade. Don't worry. None of us can infect him. I don't know if you can, but chances are you can't. One of the perks of Jess once housing a dark power. Don't be scared. And don't worry. He can take it." He grinned with a chuckle. "I mean, come on, Murder threw him around in that same room when we tested before. It was kinda fun." Skyler cleared her throat in reprimand, and Reno chuckled. "So fine. No fun for you. Just infect. Don't throw. Okay?" He mumbled to Skyler with a snicker, "Spoilsport."

The door opened, and he glanced over his shoulder to see Beth enter the room. "Oh, did you bring enough food for all of us?" He reached out to snag the bag.

Beth smirked and came over to stand next to him. "You know better, brother-in-law." But she held the bag out to him anyway. "Just take his share of the fries. Leave mine alone. That's what I'm doing."

Reno laughed and snatched a handful of fries and chewed. "See, I like you more than him, Beth. Which, depending on the day, isn't saying much."

"Is this safe for him? He still has days when his back and legs bother him."

Both Reno and Skyler looked at Beth in surprise. That was news —Jess had been injured a year ago, but Reno didn't know his brother still felt the effects of the spinal blow. He met Skyler's eyes. Cowboy starting the school made a lot more sense now. "Uh. They aren't going to fight. In fact, nothing at all may happen." Reno crossed his arms on his chest. "We just want to see if he's immune to Envy like he is the others."

Beth nodded, and all three of them focused on what was happening in the space beyond. Reno had left the intercom on, and Beth heard it first.

"Is he saying something?"

Reno frowned and turned up the volume so they could try to hear what Jess mumbled. "Jess... Jade? What's going on?"

"I JUST DON'T GET it. I mean, he's a fool. Always been one. And yet *he* gets to be the top of the food chain?" Jess laughed and let out a sharp exhale. "Him. I mean, sure, he had to die and get slaughtered to become it. But the fact that Reno has all that power, just…" He snorted. "It ain't right. Not even a little bit."

Reno jerked to stand upright. His mouth fell open as Skyler put a hand on his arm. "Reno. It's Envy. She's making him say all that. You can't believe it all."

He narrowed his eyes. "Oh, yeah, you can. The powers don't make you lie. They make you speak the truth." Pushing the intercom button, he swallowed. "Okay, Jade. Enough. Have Envy shut it down. He's infected. He's not immune."

"It ain't that I want to be a Keeper. Nah." Jess laughed and started to pace. Apparently, Envy had the man so engaged in his envious thoughts, Reno's command was not heard. And in doing so, Jade was lost in obeying, as well.

Jess curled his lips off his fangs as he shook a fist in frustration at his side. "It's just… him. That, bumbling, who can't make a decision to save his soul, gets to be that kind of power!" Jess leaned in to snarl in Jade's face only for Envy to jerk him back and caused him to stumble in the sand for getting too close. "And then on top of that? He's a prince? A *prince!*" Jess's voice faltered, and his tone went to one that sounded sad. "Ain't he got enough? Ain't he enough with all of that! He got the girl. He got the life. He got it *all!*"

"Asshole," Reno mumbled as he bent over the intercom. "Jade. Listen to me. Focus on me. Not him. I really, really need you to pull Envy back. Stop it." His fist hit the intercom button as if that would increase the effectiveness of the function it already performed. "Damn it, stop it before he says…"

"And babies. He got babies."

Jess was circling Jade now. She stood there, swaying on her feet, and the lights overhead started to flicker.

Reno turned to Beth when the bag of food fell to the floor, forgotten. "Beth…" She looked pained and pale. She heard. "Get out of here. Beth." He touched her arm to lead her out gently, but she jerked out of his grasp. "Don't listen. Beth…"

"Didn't you say he can't lie. Right?" A single tear cascaded down her cheek. "Then let him say it. It's not like I don't know." She let out a shaky laugh. "Of course, I do. I know him too well. Even when he hopes I don't know about this."

Skyler reached over to turn off the intercom. The lights flickered again, and the system failed in the disconnect.

❧

JADE FELT herself start to float. At first, it was an internal sensation that pulsated inside to vibrate on the outside. She also felt incredible power. Even as her sneakers lifted off the mats and no longer touched the floor, she wasn't scared. Not even close. She felt invincible and strong. Reno's voice registered in her mind, but it sounded so far away. Jade wasn't even sure if it was real. It was the same with Cowboy's, words and sounds. But none of it mattered.

All that did was how she felt. Incredible and powerful. Safe. Envy craved to be fed. Jade longed to be safe. Together, they both achieved their needs.

"Feed us. Tell us more." In the sizzling haze, her voice sounded strange. It was as equally exhilarating as the rest Jade didn't understand. One throat. Two voices in perfect unison.

"He got the girl. And with my luck, it was Emma who could give me babies. But no, luck hates me. It gave him, the luckiest damn fool on the planet, babies. Even a boy. And what does it give me?"

Jade watched as Jess went to his knees. That move brought awareness through the static haze in her brain. She watched as his brown eyes became tinted with green. They began to glow like hers. Was she doing that? "Envy... wait..." But Jade could sense Envy driven wild with what Jade knew was the power's first full meal in a very long time. Jade wasn't even sure if she made a sound. If her words even formed. It was too chaotic. "Envy. Please. Stop!"

Jess began to sob. A heavy sadness was weighing down each word. "It gives me nothin'. Not a single baby. I'm supposed to live the rest of my miserable immortal life without ever experiencing what that idiot got *three damn times!*" Jess started to laugh as he crashed forward, his hands splayed on the mat. "He is even the reason I couldn't be here to have that with Sophia. Because he fucking had to have his *own damn life!*" Jess lifted his head to meet Jade's eyes, her vision awash in a deeper green haze. "He got everything. And I got... nothing."

❧

"CRAP!" Reno grabbed the doorknob. It didn't budge due to the systems being shorted out by Envy's raw energy. He looked over at Skyler and paused at how Beth stood there. Her face was frozen from emotion, but tears streamed from her eyes. She didn't move, fixated on the drama playing out in the other room. Emotional shock, maybe. He had no idea. But he had to stop this. Somehow. "Get by the other wall. And hold your breath. Now! Or you're going to be infected, too."

Both women just stood there.

"Do it! Doc! Beth! We are out of time. Do it, or she will feed on him until his brain is goo!"

Skyler nodded as she recovered and pulled Beth with her to the farthest corner she could reach.

"Sundown!" Receiving a huge surge of strength, the knob twisted and broke in his hand. Reno tugged the door open. He ran across the mats, grabbed Jade's arm, and spun her around. He grabbed her shoulders, shook her, and yelled, "Envy! Shut it down. Let her go!" His eyes darted to Jess. "Let them both go! Now!"

He brought his hand up to show the ring that designated him as a Prince of Hell. "Envy, do it, or I will send you back to the Void." His markings grew dark on his skin as black wisps spun out to form his wings to arch over him. Wings he knew Envy would know could and would carry her back to Hell. "Please don't make me do that. What will Jade do without you to keep her safe?"

In an instant, Jade went limp in Reno's arms. He caught her and lowered her to lay on the mat. He looked sideways at Jess to find his brother struggling to stand. Reno moved over to him to assist. "Hold on. Wait." Jess looked past him, and Reno followed his brother's line of sight to see Beth rush out of the observation room beyond as the systems came back online. "Yeah, she heard it all."

Jess pulled away, got to his feet, and went after his wife. The cowboy's gait was unsteady, swaggering like a drunk, but at least the man did not face-plant the floor. Reno was pretty sure if his brother's brain had been made into the beforementioned goo, walking would have been impossible.

Jade moaned on the floor, and he squatted down next to her. "Easy. Take it easy." He helped her to sit and reached up as dark green blood dripped from her nose. "I need to get you to medical." He scooped her up in his arms and carried her cradled against his chest.

Skyler met him in the observation room as he passed through it. "Reno, I think we need to talk when you get back."

He didn't stop walking as the doctor took stride next to him. He kept his eyes downward on Jade, who had passed out again. "No need." He turned to use his back to open the door to medical and met Skyler's eyes. "I already knew all that. I always have."

22

"Beth, damn it, woman," Jess croaked as he careened through HQ to catch up to her. He bumped into everyone and everything. He began to think he'd fail to stop her from leaving. She'd get in her car. She would drive away, and god help him if she didn't keep going. He got a lucky break. She had to stop at the exit of HQ and wait for a lift that would take her topside in Fort Point under the Golden Gate Bridge. Beth angrily alternated between stabbing her finger against the elevator button and wiping her face. Just as much anger in one move as the other.

"Darlin', listen, please," Jess begged as he reached out to touch her.

She whipped around and, in a blink, had her service pistol out and pointed at his chest. Jess froze as he lifted his arms to present himself as no threat. But if she heard all he recalled saying, the damage was already done. The target already hit.

Her.

"You said you had nothing," Beth said through her clenched teeth. Her eyes luminous with tears before they fell from her dark lashes. Each one of them felt like they fell from there to burn his heart with guilt. "You said Emma was the one to give you babies, that you were jealous. Or envious or whatever that *he* got her! And you did not!"

People had stopped to watch the show. Jess did not dare to take his complete focus off Beth; otherwise, he would have yelled and told them all to go to hell.

"Did Envy get me to tell when that was? When I felt like that?" He arched a brow and took a step toward her, his arms still held up and out to the side. "No, it didn't. I don't feel like that, not anymore. Not since this ballsy, bold, and beautiful lady cop banged my big head on the top of her cop car." He chanced another step. "Please. I felt like that before. But not now. Not since you. You fixed me in so many ways, Beth." He slid forward closer, and now the gun muzzle rested against his pectoral. "You changed me. I was unlucky once. Until you made me the luckiest damn cowboy on the planet."

His voice softened. He pressed his lips together with an exhale as he brought a palm up to press against her cheek gently. "I ain't ever lied to you, Detective. I sure as hell ain't gonna start doing it when you got a gun over my heart. But you shoot it, and I bet you'll feel the impact because you own it. It's been yours for a while." He swallowed. "So, how about you don't shoot it for both of us?"

Beth narrowed her eyes as more tears fell. The gun lowered, and Jess pulled her into his arms. He buried his face against her neck and whispered, "I am so sorry, darlin'. I don't mean any of that now. I promise you. I don't."

Beth holstered her gun. Her hands came up to fist his shirt, and he closed his eyes as he held her. She cried, and he felt the tears soak the cloth she clung to. His lady cop rarely cried. And he had made her do it one time too many today. He also knew the last thing Beth would want was to have witnesses while she did. He looked behind him to find they still had a crowd. He didn't even have to yell. He simply bared and snapped his fangs. Everyone scattered. Good. Beth would have probably shot them, too.

"WHOA, PRINCESS. GO SLOW."

Jade sat up with a start and regretted it instantly as her head pounded. She had to squint to look around and seek her bearings. She was in her room at Lily's. She gingerly turned her head with a grimace and found Tyrus sat by her bed. "Oh..." she whispered as she lowered herself back down.

"Do you remember what happened?" Tyrus spoke softly, full of tender concern.

Jade tried not to delight in the feel of his warm hand pressing over hers on top of the comforter as she slowly nodded. "I do. I attacked Cowboy. I made him say horrible things."

No, sweetie. Not you. Me. I'm sorry. I let my hunger get the best of me, child.

"Oh, good. You're awake."

Lily's voice ushered her entrance to the room, and Jade pushed to sit against the headboard. Lily came over to sit on her bed.

It did not go unnoticed from Jade that Tyrus not only jerked his hand away, but he also moved to stand across the room. "I'll go."

"No. Please, don't," Jade weakly pleaded. "I'd like you to stay." She glanced from Tyrus to Lily. "Is it okay if he stays?"

Lily scrutinized Tyrus for a moment, and Jade feared the woman would say no. She then met Jade's eyes. "If that's what you want, sweetie. Of course, he can stay." She smiled at Jade as she reached up to press a hand on Jade's forehead. "How are you feeling? Reno brought you here after medical checked you out. I heard and rushed there as fast as I could from the Academy. They wanted to isolate you." Lily smirked. "They are all about the protocols." She rolled her eyes. "I told them if they wanted to keep you away from everyone, then they could do that here." She gave Jade a small smile. "I didn't think you'd like to wake up there again."

"Thank you. And yes, you're right. I would have hated that." Jade wrapped her arms over her chest and bit her bottom lip. "I don't remember being taken to medical." She glanced over at Tyrus. He chose to stay there rather than return where Jade wanted him—at her bedside, touching her hand. After what happened, did he want nothing to do with her? Jade wouldn't blame him. "What did they say? Is Jess okay? Reno?" Guilt swam up, and her stomach churned with it. "Did I hurt anyone?"

Lily clucked her tongue. "Jess is fine. And no, you didn't hurt anyone long term. This is how tests work. They learned a great deal, and that was the point." She moved her hand down to take Jade's in hers. "You were cold, and for vitals, you registered just like a Keeper for over an hour." Jade noticed then that she had a Band-Aid on her arm and frowned. Lily must have seen. "They took your blood. It was both red and green. You and Envy combined during the test. That was new information."

Lily gave what Jade knew was meant to be encouraging smile, but it did very little to help Jade from feeling like crap about it all. However, the information was interesting—if not a little scary. "Combined? Like, she was inside me? Using me?"

"No. That's not how it works." Tyrus moved back to stand by her bed, and Jade looked up at him. He looked tired. Stubble darkened his upper lip and jaw. It was a good look for him—exhaustion aside. "The powers work *with* their Keepers, not use them. It's more like a partnership. When the powers need to feed, they come out to, ah"—his brow deepened in thought, and Jade knew he was doing his best not to scare her more—"drive. Take control. But she didn't use you. You helped her. And don't worry, Princess, the cowboy takes a beating and always comes back with some smartass summary of it all. I saw him and his woman. They left together and were holding hands. They are fine."

He squatted down next to her bed, and Jade met his eyes.

"She was hungry. Envy." Jade gave them both a desperate look. The last thing she wanted was for Envy to get in trouble. "I know that now. I know what it feels like when she gets like that. And..."—Jade looked down in shame—"I felt the other stuff when she does."

"The high? The feeling of being super strong. Everything sharpened?" His voice was knowing and sure. Jade recalled that he was linked to his father's dark power—so, of course, he would know. "That's normal, too. It's how others feel. You'll learn to use that. To know when you've gone too far."

Tyrus's hand returned to hers. Jade turned her head shyly as he did, and her dark hair swept down over her face. She hoped it would hide the emotions that such a simple touch from him made her feel. "It was"—she frowned and tried to label it—"I felt invincible, I think."

And safe, I know you did, child. I'm glad. And we'll learn. Together, we'll do it.

"Yeah, safe. Like Envy says," Tyrus repeated. Jade judged by his sheepish look that he didn't mean to do so aloud.

Jade's brow went up, and she smiled. "You can still hear her? In your head?"

Tyrus nodded. "I can, Princess. But only when I'm close to you."

"Really? Is that why you've stayed away? Close but not too close?" She looked down at his hand, still on hers. He put his pinkie finger over hers. How one small finger could make such big butterflies in Jade's stomach, she had no idea. They fluttered and hit the side of her insides—wiping away all the fear and anxiety with each brush of their wings.

Tyrus met her eyes as he reached out to brush her hair gently behind her ear. "Yeah. But I insist on being closer now. To help you. I won't let anyone put you in that position again. Test or no test." His hand took hers fully and squeezed. "You nor Envy are alone in this. I promise." He gave her a soft smile. "I got you both, Princess."

Envy purred in her head, and Jade could have sworn Tyrus wanted to kiss her. Or maybe it was Jade's imagination, one fueled by too many romance novels or movies to hope he would. The hope that had her leaning toward him to receive it.

"All right, let's let her rest."

Jade blinked, and she looked sharply over at Lily. Oh, wow! She totally forgot the woman was in the room. Tyrus cleared his throat, then stood, and his hand pulled away, leaving both Jade and Envy sighing at the loss of his warm touch. Tyrus's and Jade's eyes met for a charged moment, and the thrill of such a simple moment energized Jade. She shoved the covers off her legs.

"I don't want to rest." Her stomach let out a loud rumble, and she blushed. "And Envy fed, but I didn't." She stood and then let out a squeak to find she only wore her tee and panties. She grabbed the blanket off the bed quickly to cover herself and the hot blush, which crept from head to toe. She glanced at Lily. "Who?"

Lily laughed. "I did. Who did you think did it?" Her expression was full of humor as she leaned in close to Jade with a Cheshire cat smile. "Hmm?"

Jade did not *dare* to see Tyrus's response as she pulled the blanket higher to cover her head. To escape Epsilon only to die of embarrassment. "I'll, uh, be downstairs. Oh, ah, after I get dressed." Even Envy laughed inside of Jade's head.

Lily rushed over to shove Tyrus out of the room. Jade chanced a peek at Tyrus by lifting a corner of the blanket. It was her turn to laugh. He kept his head back and eyes directed up on the ceiling. Lily got him to the door, and Jade's laughter burst free when smacked him on the back of the head and left Jade alone.

23

Word had gotten to Marcus about what happened with Envy and Jade at HQ, which was the reason he now stood in front of Lily Devenmore's door. Knocking on it, he checked his suit and looked up when it opened. "Hello, Ms. Devenmore. May I see my son, please?"

Lily opened the door wide to allow him to enter. When she closed it behind him, she touched his arm. "Sure. But do you mind if we talk first?"

Marcus arched a brow and gave the woman a nod. After she led them into a dining room, he became more intrigued when she slid two oak pocket doors closed for privacy. "If this is about what occurred during the immunity test, I am very much aware. It is what brought me to your residence."

"I guessed that much." Lily smiled at him. "And I keep telling you, Marcus, please call me Lily. I'm Reno's family, and you are part of Reno's Keeper family. So"—she raised her palm toward the ceiling—"that makes us family. Or cousins. Or something." She motioned that hand to a chair as she took a seat at the table.

Humans and their family bullshit. Like we would dare call ourselves part of any human, fragile dynamic. Tell the bitch to go to hell. We can even show her the way.

Marcus chose not to remind Murder that he was half-human. He ignored his power and lowered himself into a chair across from Lily. "Cousins. Fine. I shall call you Lily. Noted." He flexed his fingers and splayed them on the table—his irritation scraping his patience. He had concerns about Tyrus. This woman delayed him from abating the feeling. "Now, I'd like to see my son. He is here, correct? HQ tracked his coordinates here."

Lily sat back and crossed one arm to wrap a hand around the biceps of the opposite. "He is. And I think there might be something you, as his father, need to know." Lily cocked her head to the side, and the smile she gave Marcus caused him to worry.

He knew Emma Devenmore-Sundown very well. She and Reno were, indeed, close friends. He had been, after all, her children's bodyguard. And while he and Emma's sisters had come to know each other, Marcus made a point at the time of not considering anyone a friend. All were a possible threat. His focused purpose was the protection of the Sundown children. And while that had changed since he became a Keeper, he lacked the skills to transition a relationship from a professional acquaintance to that of a friend. It, among other things in his life, was a work in progress. According to Alexis, it became a quest to teach an old hellhound new tricks. Many, many new tricks. Marcus was not entirely sure if his girlfriend referenced the actual hellhounds he could manifest or him.

"Is there something wrong with Tyrus?" He scanned the home and brought his focus back to Lily. "Has he broken a house rule? Damaged your belongings? If so, I shall speak to him." He reached into his suit jacket's inside pocket for his wallet. "I can pay for damages or make restitution." He frowned and looked up as Tyrus's recent behavior came to mind. "Please tell me my son has not entertained females in your residence. If so, I will remove him promptly and request another guard be appointed to the girl."

Lily laughed and reached over to touch Marcus's hand. "No. He has been the perfect gentleman." She smiled as her hand moved away. "He's very much like you. Tough guy and intense. His manners are impeccable." She brought a finger up to chew on a nail and pressed her lips together. "It's not that..."

Marcus became concerned and leaned forward to fold his arms on the table. "Then, I am confused. What is the issue with my son?" He rolled his eyes up, and using his connection, sensed Tyrus upstairs in the home. He detected no illness nor injury. He brought his gaze back to Lily's. "Why do you require a discussion with me?"

Lily sighed. "Jade likes him. And not in just a 'friend' way. I think she has developed a crush on him. And that has me worried." Lily stood and moved to sit on the corner of the table next to Marcus. The volume of her voice lowered. He presumed she did not want to be overheard.

"She's been through a lot, had a lion's share of heartache and tragedy. And while she's finding her way more with each day, she still has a very long way to go." Lily lowered her chin and whispered, "She reminds me of me. When I was in the shadow of Emma's strength and the glare of Rose's boldness, it took quite a while after my parents died for me to find my footing. To figure out who I was. And what I wanted to be." She let out a laugh. "I even developed a crush on a certain cowboy once. And then"—she looked over at Marcus and then back down—"my sister hooked up with him." She sliced her hand in the air, trying to dismiss it as nothing, but it was easy to see it had been painful. She looked away to prevent his seeing it.

Marcus could tell she was unsure of which information to share and what to keep hidden. "I understand that. I was bullied in Hell for being a halfling. I fully understand having an identity crisis. But Tyrus is different. He knows who and what he is. And what he wants."

"Are you so sure?"

The question blindsided Marcus. He frowned and sat back to consider his son's behavior. The random women. Working constantly. Marcus tried to think of a single friend his son had spoken about. Of seeing Tyrus joke or have fun with any of the other Breakers or Relays at HQ. Not a single instance came to mind. "Perhaps, I am not."

❧

JADE HAD EATEN breakfast with him and Lily and was ordered to rest by the latter. Tyrus stood in the hall, leaning against the wall to ensure she did as told. He checked to find Jade sleeping deeply and sensed his father was in the house as he left her room. He made his way down the stairs but slowed as he heard Marcus and Lily talking. Pausing against the wall by the dining room, their voices were muffled by the closed door, but he was still able to hear their conversation.

Tyrus frowned, crossed his arms with chin on his chest, and listened as he and Jade were discussed. She had a crush on him? Really? He brought a hand up to rub his jaw as he thought about it and felt like an idiot. It became clear to him. The way she smiled, how she relaxed when he made the simple move of touching her hand. The coy and shy looks his way.

"She's a kid," he mumbled under his breath, but the statement felt false. She was over eighteen. Yeah, but as far as life was concerned, age was just a number when it came to maturity. He was forced to be an adult long before the law designated him as one. When Epsilon recruited him, Tyrus was short of being a teen. And there, he grew up far faster with each wicked deed the man tested him with.

But Jade had been sheltered her entire life, lived in privilege with a shit ton of cash. He could guess her grandmother's home was fancy. But she had lost her parents. Been treated like a doll rather than a living, breathing person. And try as he might, the images of her when she stood in front of him wearing almost nothing had an impact, even if she wore a Sailor Moon nightshirt. Her long legs that he wanted to see more of. And those eyes—so damn green it made him hurt when she nailed them to his in a look that lasted longer than a second. Then there were her lips, which still reminded him of light, delicate-tasting candy.

Those thoughts were *not* the kind a full-grown-ass man should have for a kid. Did he consider her as anything else? She was strong and smart. He was floored with how well she handled all of this. Shit, she came close to bleeding out, and her only thoughts of concern were for Envy. Not herself. Tyrus had never met anyone kinder than Jade Shen. And really witty, though she felt unsure about being so—surprised every time she made a joke or discovered her own sarcasm as if laughter, joy, and fun were out of the scope of her life until she had landed in the world of the Grid.

It made sense from what Tyrus knew, which was very little, about her life before. Uptight bitch grandmother, though Jade never called the woman that. Parents reserved and demanded Jade be more. Perhaps she never got the chance just to be herself. To find her own life in her own way.

Tyrus would have been a complete dumbass not to see how he and Jade had been on parallel paths. He felt abandoned by his parents, and she must have felt the same way when hers died. Tyrus, trying to find favor and approval from Epsilon, someone who only showed him cruelty and disgust. Jade, a grandmother who didn't care enough—if at all. One that sold her to obtain what she had been denied. And now their paths merged.

"Tyrus?"

Tyrus heard Jade's voice on the stairwell, and he lifted his head to find she stood there with a look of concern. He was not sure if it was for him or if Envy sensed another dark power in the house. He tilted his head, then narrowed his eyes and really looked at her. Long, dark hair and a beautiful face. But the body that showed beneath her bookworm T-shirt and jeans was not of a girl. Small breasts and slender waist, which led to curved hips above those amazingly long legs. No—

Jade was a young woman trying to find her way. She was no girl.

Tyrus moved to the base of the stairs and asked softly, "Do you have a crush on me? Like me?"

Jade gasped. "I, uh…" Her mouth fell open as if it ran out of words, and puzzlement spread across her features. A soft blush flushed over her cheeks as Tyrus took the few steps up to reach her. She moved her hair down once again in an attempt to hide behind it. Tyrus knew that tactic. He took the last step between them, which left Jade one step up and the two of them eye-to-eye.

"Say it, Princess." He reached up to move her hair back. But rather than dropping his hands, he kept them in place. His thumbs tenderly caressed her cheek. Her blush felt warm beneath his palms. "Do you think of me as anything else other than your friend. Than your bodyguard?" He wished she would bring those amazing eyes to his. When she did, he looked deeply into their depths. "I need to know because what you say will determine what I do next. So say it. Come on, Princess. A brave warrior would. And we both know that's exactly what you are."

Jade remained silent. For a few weighted moments, Tyrus thought he had inserted his boot in his mouth and was able to kick his gut at its descent for buying into the bullshit going on in the dining room. Or maybe not when Jade nodded.

"At first, it was a friend and bodyguard. But I don't have a crush on you, Tyrus."

His heart thudded painfully at her words. But when he stepped back to move his hands, she reached up to stop him. He had been such a fucking idiot to think a woman like Jade would want anything to do with a guy like him. "Fuck…"

"A crush is something a kid has. What I have for you is so much more." She swallowed. "I want to be more to you." She lowered her eyes. "To be more *for* you."

Those words made Tyrus feel like the house collapsed around them. That the floor vanished, and they became suspended together in a strange place he had never been. All premise of being a badass and having to prove himself as one of the good guys vanished, as did doubting himself more than anyone else because those thoughts could not exist in this bubble with her.

"You are already more than enough, Princess." Tyrus captured her lips in a kiss. Though they did not taste like the candy he imagined, they were far sweeter. She was shy, and it made her sweeter. Tyrus had no doubt this was her first kiss. It meant everything to him.

Jade's attempt to meet his skill in the kiss caused Tyrus's need to protect her expand and encase his heart—the bonds pure and simple. And amazing. Like her.

His arms wound around her to hold her tight against him. She melted with a sigh against him, trusting him to hold her up and keep her close. When Jade's tongue sought his first and welcomed him, her breath became his. He took that air in hungrily. He wanted to keep it trapped in his chest. To always have a part of her to take with him wherever he went. To keep her so close that no one could touch her. No one would harm her. And no one or nothing changed her.

Jade Shen was the perfection to his imperfections. And he would be the strength to her weakness. No need to hide either from the other. And together, they'd both find their way. Tyrus pulled back from the kiss and gave Jade a wide smile. "Damn..."

"Damn would be correct."

Tyrus tensed with a wince and glanced back over his shoulder to find his father. And standing with him, Lily. Neither held expressions of approval. He turned to face them and shielded Jade with his body. "Hold on. Before you two start blaming shit..."

"We both want to try this. To be together," Jade said as she stepped in front of Tyrus, went down the stairs, and stood in front of Marcus and Lily, "and we don't need permission." She glanced back at him as he stood there, dumbfounded. When she held her hand back to him, he quickly recovered. He took it to stand at her side. "But your respect and opinions do matter to me—to both of us.

But we choose this. We want this. To just see what could happen." Jade looked up at him, and damn, the confidence in her smile was a booster to his own.

"Yeah. What Jade said." Tyrus met his father's eyes. "Pops, I know you and the rest look at her like she's a kid, but she's not. Fuck, she's been through so much that most kids would cave from. Give in to. Give up to. But not my princess." He looked down at Jade and smiled. "She's an adult. And yeah, a young woman, I'll give you that. But a kid." He slid his gaze to Marcus and then Lily. "She's no kid. She's a badass. And a person I care about."

Jade wrapped her arm around him to rest against his side. Yep. That boosted him even more—not counting the "boost" the kiss gave him. It had started to fade but rose back to life as she made that move. "We just want to see where it can go. And like she said, we don't need anyone's permission, but we'd like you to at least try to understand."

Lily turned her head to regard Marcus, and the two of them exchanged some look Tyrus couldn't read. "I'll take upstairs."

Marcus nodded. "I will partake of the space on your porch."

Jade looked up at Tyrus in confusion, which vaporized when Lily took her hand to lead her away, and Marcus tugged him out the front door.

24

"Pops, I know what you're going to say." Tyrus leaned against the porch rail and crossed his arms. "She's young. Inexperienced. I can pretty much recite everything you're about to say to change my mind. So let's not. And if you don't mind"—he pointed his finger at Marcus—"I'd prefer not to have a two-way convo where you and Murder gang up on my ass."

Marcus paced the width of the porch, and Tyrus couldn't tell if his sire was pissed or worried or both. "Why do you think I had this talk out here? In the sun. It is just you and I."

Tyrus noticed they were indeed in the midday sun, and he blew out a breath. "Thanks. Sorry, but this came as much a surprise to me and her as it did you and Lily." Tyrus smirked. "Not sure how I feel, being the source of you and her chitchatting, but I did overhear you. In fact, that's what made me realize the so-called crush you two were worried about was not one-sided." He shrugged. "Nor is it a crush. We really care about each other. And we'd both like to see where it can go—if it can go anywhere. But we at least deserve that chance, right?"

"Son, I am not saying you do not deserve love. Or a relationship. In fact, I welcome it. It is part of the reason why I frowned upon your nightly conquests with females with no names. But Jade?" Marcus stepped up to him and placed a hand on Tyrus's shoulder. "She has to be in an emotional tailspin coming to terms with all that has been done to her. And on top of that, adjusting to being a Keeper with Envy. She very likely is not sure what she wants. What will you do when she finds a landing? When she settles into her new life, and it is not you that she desires?" Marcus angled his head to the side. His expression and voice softened. "Or wants?"

Tyrus knew his father meant well, but each statement caused a tinge of pain as they struck. "I don't know. Neither does she. But Pops, does any couple? Are you telling me that you have zero doubts that you and Alexis won't change over the years? Damn, the centuries? No. You can't. You have no way to know that for sure. How is this any different?"

He brought a hand up to press over Marcus's on his shoulder. "But I can tell you this. If or when that happens, I'll still be there for her. Be her friend. Wish her luck and love. And still be there. Sure, it will hurt like fuck. I may have never had my heart broken yet, but I know that it caused my own father to cast me into a fire. I can guess it hurts like no other pain. But Dad..."

Tyrus moved closer and leaned toward Marcus until their foreheads touched. "Shouldn't I have the same opportunity to feel it like everyone does? That you and Mom did?" He searched Marcus's eyes and whispered, "That's all I am wanting. A chance to get my heart broken. Or not. That's all."

Marcus let out a sigh that caused his big body to tremble. "And it is my role as a father to not want your heart broken, son." A slight smile curved his lips even with worry clouding the clarity of his gaze. "And can we pause for a moment to revel in the fact you called me dad?"

Tyrus snorted. "Too late. Moment over. And don't get used to it, Pops."

❧

"THAT WAS YOUR FIRST KISS, wasn't it?"

Jade sat on her bed with knees drawn up to her chest and her chin rested on one. Lily sat on the end of the bed. "Yes. It was." She could not help the smile at the thought of it. "And I think, though I don't really know, he is a very good kisser." Dang it if she didn't blush yet again.

Lily let out a small chuckle. "Oh, I bet. Like father like son probably." Her smile faded, and she reached out to touch Jade's knee. "So you haven't ever had a boyfriend? Nothing?"

Jade simply shook her head. She could easily guess the next question. She answered it before Lily felt forced to ask it. "And yes, I'm a virgin."

Lily's smile returned. "That was pretty much a given since you haven't been kissed." She moved to sit next to Jade and wrapped an arm around her. "I have grown to really care about you, Jade. I don't have kids of my own. But I do love spoiling my nephew and nieces like crazy. But if I did have a child, I'd like to think she or he would be as amazing as you are."

While the words were stated in sincere kindness, they reflected the core issue all of them had other than Jade and Tyrus. "I am not a child. I don't think I have been for a very long time." Jade rose from the bed with a heavy sigh. "To be honest with you, Lily, I know everyone means well. I know you care, but Lily..." She turned to face her and lifted an arm to the side. "I feel like my whole life has been on hold. Waiting for something. And every time that I felt like that pause had been removed, something else would happen that made my life stop again." She moved back to bed to sit on her knees in front of Lily.

"Until all of this. Then it felt like that pause button got snapped off and thrown away, never to be found. I feel alive. I feel like I have a say-so in my life. And people care about those choices. But Lily"—Jade reached out to take Lily's hand, knowing she sounded desperate—"I also need to know my choices, the ones I can finally make for myself, are respected. That's just as important as them being heard. Does that make any sense?"

"Of course it does, sweetie. That's what everyone wants." Lily squeezed Jade's hand and brought the other up to place on her cheek. "I just worry. He's older. He's more experienced, and none of us want to see you or Tyrus hurt."

"But isn't it part of growth to hurt? To feel painful things?" She tilted her head. "I want to have all that life offers. I've had more than my share of bad. I want some good. And he makes me happy. He treats me"—she smiled—"not like a princess of an empire, nor some heiress to the fortune. But as *his* princess. And our kingdom is one that doesn't exist yet. But we want to build one together. And if we don't, it's okay. It's worth the chance to at least know we tried."

Lily smiled and brought her hand up to wipe tears. "Of course, sweetie. I'm here to help you with everything you need my help with and to stay out of those that you don't. What do you need from me?"

Jade bit her bottom lip and smiled. "Can you help me with my hair?"

"YOU CUT YOUR HAIR."

Jade had been so nervous to show off her new bob haircut. She avoided Tyrus all morning until she had reached HQ. It went unnoticed at first when they did see each other. Until Jade released a giggle, and he stumbled over words when he registered the change. She always kept it long, using it as a shield of sorts since she had been a little girl. But the woman evolving from a child no longer wanted to hide.

"I did." Jade toyed with her hairstyle and gave Tyrus a shy smile. "I like it. I really do. Do you?"

Tyrus stepped up and ran his fingers through it. "I do. It shows your face, Princess. Those amazing green eyes." He gave her a wide smile, one that Jade thrilled in—they became more often and appeared more at ease. He ran his finger down her jaw and tilted her chin up to meet his eyes. "But what I do or do not like shouldn't decide shit for you. If you like it, if something makes you happy, that is all that counts."

Jade felt those big butterflies return. They slammed against her soul in excitement at his simple touch. She stood on her toes, smiled, and pressed her lips to his. "Thank you. I like it. But I like that you do, as well."

"Hey!"

Jade stiffened, and for a moment, hers and Tyrus's eyes met in alarm. His widened before she shifted to look over her shoulder.

"Shit," he hissed and took a step back but remained close to take her hand in his.

Jade turned to find that Reno, Kenzie, and Marcus stood there. How could she have forgotten they were all meeting for training? She had been excited to see what the other Keepers could do with their powers. Thoughts of that and why she sat there had flown from her mind the moment Tyrus had joined her.

Jade cleared her throat and reached up to her hair out of habit, only to remember its security curtain no longer existed. Its absence did, while not offering a haven, remind her why it was gone. She lifted her chin as she tightened her grip with Tyrus's hand. "Hi. Are we ready to train?"

Marcus ducked his head down, and Kenzie leaned in the doorway with a smile. Jade could tell the Keeper was not at all surprised to find her kissing Tyrus. Oh, right, the woman held Lust. Reno was another story. He looked angry—his stomping steps over to her, and the tightness in his face made it simple to discern.

"I was. Until I came in here and found you two kissing." His brilliant blue eyes jerked from Jade's to Tyrus and back to her, and she was shocked at the amount of accusation in both his tone and gaze. "What are you doing? You can't be doing that!" Reno moved to the side and put a hand on Tyrus's chest to move him from her. Tyrus refused to budge. His body was tense, even his fingers intertwining with hers.

"Back off, Keeper," Tyrus growled, and Jade was afraid they were about to fight. The tension and aggression in the room tangible. She gave Tyrus a pleading look. He chose to be the one to back down.

"She's just a kid," Reno spat out, the words full of venom and disbelief.

Marcus joined them to put a hand on Reno's shoulder in an attempt to defuse the situation. "She is not. Let her explain, Prince."

"You knew about this?" Reno turned his ire on Marcus with a frustrated snort. Jade was relieved he took no further action other than to take their united front as a personal assault. "Fine. Explain." He crossed his arms on his chest with a huff. "I'll listen first. Then you need to."

"Thank you, Marcus." Jade had thought Kenzie would offer additional assistance as another female on the team. She did not. In fact, the woman seemed greatly amused. She gave Jade an encouraging smile with a thumbs up. Both seemed rather snarky to Jade, but she didn't know Kenzie well enough to know.

Right. Jade was on her own. She had become determined to make that clear to not only herself but all from this point forward. "He's my boyfriend. And it's our decision and choice. And yes, we will take it slow because neither of us wants to hurt the other." She met Reno's eyes as she stepped up to him. Other than Tyrus, Reno's belief in her was important. He was not only the leader of their team, but Jade genuinely respected the Keeper of Madness. "I need you to understand. It won't change my decision, but it matters to me that you do."

Reno's eyes narrowed, and his attention trailed from her to Tyrus. "I'm sorry. I can't, and you can't either. This can't happen. I can't let it. I get it—you have a crush. But as much as I hate to say it, Jade"—his focus swung back to her, and she saw sorrow battling with the harshness of his statements—"I can't let you do this. This stops. Here. Now."

Tyrus exploded. It happened so fast. Before Jade could respond, Tyrus's hand jerked free of hers, and he surged forward. He grabbed Reno's shirt and used it to slam him so hard against the wall, the dry-erase board with its markers skittered to the floor.

"Tyrus! No!"

He got in close to Reno, and both men bared their fangs. "You are the *last* one that has the right to say *shit* about what she can or cannot do!"

Jade rushed to stand next to Tyrus. She said his name and placed her hand on his arm, but her attempt to appeal to him went unnoticed. He was laser-focused on Reno.

"You didn't even want us to save her! You told *all* of us to let her fucking *die!*" Tyrus pulled the man away from the wall. Jade hoped it meant his hold would release, but no, he just slammed Reno back against it a second time. "Just like it's *your* fault that my father is a fucking Keeper!" Tyrus brought a hand up to point a finger an inch from Reno's face. "You got him killed! Almost got your own kids killed. You should have zero fucking say so in *anyone's* life."

As a collective shocked gasp sounded from the others, Jade became confused. Marcus tugged Tyrus away and put himself between his son and Reno. Kenzie had moved into the room and tried to speak to Jade. Reno just stood there, back against the wall. He did not move beyond lowering his head to look at the floor. His behavior screamed guilty to Jade. Was all of that true?

"You wanted me to die?' Jade frowned and stared at him. Her tone shifted from shocked disbelief to anger. She smacked her palm on Reno's chest to get a response. "Is all that true? You didn't want to save me?" Her resolve to be a new, stronger Jade crumbled with each word she slung at him. "You were just going to let me die at the school?"

She stepped back, shook her head, and brought a hand up to wipe angrily at tears. "I thought you cared? I thought you were one of the good guys."

Child. I think it's more complicated than that. Listen to me, Jade—

Before, Jade would have listened to her friend but not in this. Reno lifted his chin and opened his mouth to speak. Jade had no idea what he was about to say. Maybe it would have been reasons. Or perhaps excuses. It did not matter. Jade moved her hand fast and slapped him hard across the face. The sound of the impact echoed in the silence of the room. The force of the blow stung Jade's palm and sent Reno's head snapping sideways.

"Tyrus is right. You can't tell me what to do," Jade choked out. "Who to love. Nothing. Since you were like everyone else. I was nothing to you." She stepped back with her fists at her side, and the air started to crackle with power. Tyrus reached out to her, and she jerked from his touch. "Leave me alone. All of you just leave me alone."

Jade twisted toward the door. Before she could reach it, a hand grabbed her arm. She knew it was Reno who stopped her, or maybe her dark power sensed his. She turned her head, and he looked… why did he look like he was sad? Didn't he have everything? A wife, kids, everything!

He reached up to touch his newly split lip. Jade didn't feel even the tiniest bit of guilt that she caused it. "Jade. I have my reasons. And fine, you don't want to listen to me?" He touched the stamp on his arm to speak to someone on the other side. "Find me Bounce."

25

Jade sat in a chair in Bounce's office. She felt, once again, that she had screwed up and gotten in trouble. But this was no principal's office. The tall man who perched on the corner of the desk in front of her had far more power.

"Jade, I know none of this has been easy for you."

She looked to the side as the Grid boss spoke. She slowly inhaled before turning back to listen and reached into her training of being passive. To become expressionless—like a fine piece of art made to decorate to impress but did not dare serve any other function. "You would be correct. Are you going to tell me I'm not allowed to have Tyrus as a boyfriend, too? Remind me that I am young and not aware of what I am doing?"

Bounce smirked as he folded his hands in his lap. "No. I am not. I do not normally involve myself with personal matters or relationships, but in this, I find I must."

Jade was on her feet, her practiced composure shattered. She would be leaving those lessons behind. They were taught to hide who she really was. She must stop pulling them out of the dust of her past. "Why? I don't understand! Why is it any different for me?

In the eyes of the law, I am eighteen and a consenting adult! And yes, Tyrus is older but he's a good man. And he respects taking it slow!" She sputtered in confusion and painfully exhaled. Emotions were making it hard to breathe. Frustration attempted to block her words. "Why? Can you *please* explain to me why?" She lifted her chin in defiance. "Because if you can't, you are fooling yourself to think I want to be in the Grid. And I'll go."

Bounce moved to stand in front of her, and Jade could feel the man's power like static across her skin. "Because in order to keep you and Envy safe, we must ensure the measures put in place to keep her hidden remain, that the illusionary walls created to hide the fact you still live don't crumble. The plan of making sure Epsilon never discovers you survived. And Envy is with you and must be a priority." He brought a hand up to place on her shoulder.

"And how does Tyrus change any of that?" Jade prided herself on being intelligent, but she felt both naïve and stupid in this. "He will want all of that, too! He'll keep me safe. He'd never betray me. Or are you saying all this because he used to work for Epsilon?" She let out a desperate sound. "I know all that. I thought you and the others trusted him? Am I wrong? I do not think so."

Bounce rubbed a hand on his jaw. Jade babbled, and when she wound down, his hand dropped. She noticed his eyes had changed to a deep gray with a somber and sad hue, which reminded Jade of the rainy day when her parents were buried. Her grandmother had declined an umbrella for her and Jade. That would have interfered with the stance Jade was ordered to hold through the ceremony. Hands clasped in front of her, even though the starched black dress scratched her neck. The raindrops were making it even more so as she became soaked. She felt desperate and confused to understand how life took what she cared for away. And she felt that way now.

"The powers are very simple beings when you think of their existence." Bounce's voice took on a storyteller's tone. Jade was incredulous that he could have a story giving clarity to it all. "They are dark power, needed to counter the good energy in mankind. We call it a person's light. Both are important for balance." He faltered on how best to explain. He reached back to pick up a desk lamp to rest on his thigh and returned to sit on the desk.

"This is light." He flipped the switch and placed his palm under the pool of light. "Bright. Glaring."

Jade, not sure the direction this story was leading them, returned to the chair in front of him. "Yes. Light. What does that have to do with Tyrus and me?"

Bounce brought his hand up to cover half of the cup of the lamp surrounding the bulb. "See how it is now not as bright. How darkness has dimmed its light. Covered it up. Yet it still shines." His hand proceeded to cover the opening completely. Very little light escaped between his pressed fingers. "Darkness. You can barely see the light now. It's been covered with darkness. The light is still there, yes, but being able to shine outside no longer."

Bounce set the lamp aside and switched it off. "If you allow the darkness within you to expand, to grow and take more of your light, the dark will be seen. Not the light. At first, an equal division of both light and dark. It's the reason the Keepers are called Shadow-Keepers. They must never go too dark. Nor too light. A perfect blending of light and dark to a balanced shade of gray. However, you are different."

Bounce went to sit on his haunches, and his eyes met hers. "Your light has kept Envy hidden. She hasn't created that blend. She has not overtaken your purpose with hers. You are pure light without enough sin to dim it. Innocence that keeps it bright. And glaring. You change that..."

Jade felt tears tickle her lashes as the stark, crushing reality of his strange lamp analogy struck home. "She could be found. I couldn't hide, and neither could she." She brought a hand up to wipe the tears. "That's not fair. I don't want to be different."

Bounce pursed his lips and pressed his fingers over the pulse in her wrist. "This. Your heartbeat, which pulses within, states you already are. Unique in the fact you still live, yet you are a Keeper when you and the power need you to be."

Jade rubbed at her tears. She hated that they did not know the difference between frustration, sadness, or joy. "So, I'm being used by Envy. Is that what you are saying?" Once again, she was just an object. "I don't believe you."

Bounce lowered his head enough to make eye contact again. "I don't believe she is using you. If she truly was"—he tapped his fingers on her pulse—"you would not be alive. She would have allowed you to die and animated your body. Taken it as a host vessel as the others did their Keepers." He moved his touch from her wrist and gave her a gentle smile. "She stopped your death. She and Tyrus together did not want you to die. Perhaps, in a way, she does use you to hide. To not be found. But if I am correct, that was a role you offered, yes?"

Jade nodded with a ragged breath. "She asked. I said yes. So, I guess I'm not being used." She used the heels of her palms to wipe away the last of those traitorous tears. "Tyrus said Reno wanted me to die. That he didn't help. Is that true? Does he even want me here?"

Bounce sat back. Jade could see he was conflicted about how best to answer. It not only showed on his model-perfect face but his eyes—a kaleidoscope of different hues of gray and blue—as he considered. "That is complicated, as is Reno. But I assure you, the last thing Reno would want is anyone good and kind to die."

He rose to his feet and lowered his head as his tone softened. "Reno is rather infamous for his bad decision abilities. That aside, he has a big heart and has fought very hard to prove both himself and the Keepers are heroes." He brought his head up and focused on the wall behind them. "He knows better than most how destiny and fate must have their time. Their dues must be paid when demanded. Knowing him as well as I do, he must have been tormented not to assist you. But he also knows the ripples an action can cause when a consequence is thrown into the flow of destiny."

Bounce smiled and took his former position in front of her. "He's had others hate him for interfering in their lives. And others their deaths. He's had others blame him for everything going forward. It has a long-lasting impact. But you can be assured that he would have hated himself if you died, and he had stopped the others from saving you. Just like he is immensely concerned about what is going to happen to you next now that they did."

Jade listened and could not imagine that much pressure on any one person. How Reno could remain so open and friendly was amazing. To have to consider someone's fate beyond his own, and then felt guilty if he failed to make the right choice. "I didn't know. That must have been really hard for him."

"Yes, it must have been. If you look at it in the way you should, he cared about you before he even knew you. And that included the ways one choice could impact everything." He stood. "I'm sure Sundown helped him in that. I, personally, am glad you are with us and not dead." He gave her a wink and moved back behind the desk. "Now, about your relationship with Tyrus."

Jade jumped to her feet and resisted the instinct to stomp—that was what little girl Jade did. She was no longer her. "Not you, too. We will be careful. We…" The rest of the protest caught in her throat. Her eyes landed on the lamp. "Oh, it's bigger than that."

"Yes, it is. If you wish to continue to give Envy a haven, to stay hidden"—Bounce laced his hands together on the desk—"you must keep your light as bright as you can. And as awkward as this is to state, your virginity is the brightest light. The innocence of the young."

Jade shook her head slowly as new tears began to form—these knew their role. Sadness. "That is not fair. There has to be another way!" She met Bounce's eyes. The awful truth clear for her to see. She dropped down to sag into the chair. It felt like her heart was breaking before it had a chance to grow and bloom. "There just has to be."

Bounce sighed. "Yes, there is. We lock you away in a shielded and jammed containment area until the war and the threat of Epsilon is eradicated. Or," his voice changed to a harder tone, one Jade had no problem hearing as a general leading his army, "you can ask Envy to set you free. And it is her we contain. Her freedom will be gone. And you can have yours."

"What!" Jade shook her head in horror. "I can't let you do that!"

"I know. And there's more. There is a High Council. It governs us all and allows the Grid to be. It supports our cause. If they find out that you hold a dark power that *can* be unrestrained rather than being in a host, they will insist on it us restraining it. And they will return Envy to the Void. Not to mention, they will sense you are as innocent as we have. There are prices to pay for what Epsilon did to you. And they will add that to the long list of crimes he has performed. But"—he sighed—"they will also blame us for allowing you to witness all that is the Grid. And they may very well not agree with you being saved and interfering with destiny."

Jade stared at him. She began to tremble as she whispered, "No, you mean..." She blinked through her tears. "Bounce... you can't mean..."

He sighed. "I do. And, as I said, it's complicated."

JADE EXITED Bounce's office some blurry time later to find Tyrus leaning against the wall opposite of the door and Reno doing the same next to it.

"Princess?"

Jade tried to focus on Tyrus. He sounded so worried, and she hated that. But he would have to wait for a little while longer. She moved to Reno instead. His brow rose, and his mouth opened, but Jade halted him from speaking as she wrapped her arms around him in a hug.

He was chilled beneath his clothes, a coolness that reminded Jade of all he had given up and what she still had. She laid her cheek on his chest and heard only silence beneath it—another hard slice of reality of the choices made for her. "I'm sorry. But thank you for caring about me and my destiny. I know it could not have been easy."

Reno stood there unmoving. Jade was not sure if she should have touched him at all. Did Keepers have rules about that? Jade had so much to learn. After a weighted moment, one of his arms came up to return the hug. She felt his chest rise and fall with a deep exhale. "You're welcome," he said, voice edged with emotion as he rubbed her back with a hand.

Jade lifted her head and looked up at him. "It's okay. Bounce explained." She stepped out of the hug and nodded. "Since you're my boss, is it okay if I take the day off?" She motioned a hand toward Tyrus. She avoided looking at him, or she would start crying again. Her resolve would weaken. "And can you arrange for him to have it off, too?"

Reno's eyes followed her motion, and he frowned. Doubt washed through his expression. Worry still hazed his eyes, but he nodded. "Yeah, I can arrange that. And cover for him. Go. I got it." He cupped her chin in his fingers to tilt her face upward as their eyes locked. "For what it's worth, I'm thrilled no one listened to me. I am glad you and Envy are with us. But yeah, get used to me being all over the place on, like, every decision." He gave her a slight smile. "It happens. All the time. A lot, *a lot*." He chuckled. "Imagine my wife trying to nail down dinner plans with me." The wink that followed told Jade that it wasn't as bad as he joked.

"Thank you." She turned to Tyrus, and when he reached out to take her hand, she refused it. She wrapped her arms around herself, and he gave her a hard stare as she looked to the side. "We need to talk."

26

Child, are you sure? You giving him up for me?

Jade watched the city of San Francisco as it slid past the car window. She was being driven from HQ to home. She had asked Tyrus to meet her there. He could tell she was upset and asked if he should ride with her. The obvious hurt on his face when she said she needed to be alone and would meet him there drowned Jade with guilt. Envy had tried to soothe, but Jade asked her power to stop that as well. Her head was all over the place. And her heart? Jade wasn't sure where it would land very soon. Or if it would even survive. But if she didn't do this now, she doubted it would later.

Lily opened the door to her house before Jade made it halfway inside of the garage. Tyrus pulled up on his motorcycle, and it was not hard to see him both angry and bewildered. Jade achingly craved to wrap herself around him. To soak up his warmth. Listen to his heart. But she used the time in the car to cry. To come to terms and prepare herself for what she must do, and the commute home offered that.

"I heard about the argument." Lily wrapped Jade in a hug. "Grid is a huge rumor mill, remember?" Jade nodded and took the embrace gratefully. Lily stepped back. "What do you need from me?" She looked beyond to Tyrus, where he stood awkwardly in the interior of the garage. "If anything."

Jade sighed. "I've got it. Can you just leave us alone for a little bit?" She lifted her gaze to Lily's and found sorrow mixed with understanding. "Please?"

Lily nodded and kissed her forehead. "Of course. I'm going to make some lunch. Maybe some coffee. Maybe add some bourbon to both." She moved into the house and closed the door behind her.

"Jade, what's going on? What did Bounce say?" Tyrus set his helmet on his bike seat before reaching out to take both her hands in his. "You're fucking freaking me out, Princess."

Jade told herself she was not going to cry in front of Tyrus. She would not fall apart and lose it. Reno, Bounce, the whole Grid had taken incredible measures to ensure her safety—hers and Envy's. Jade had zero doubt none of it had been easy. Not without risks. This the least she could do to make sure those efforts were worth it.

She lowered her forehead to Tyrus's chest. She brought a hand up to spread over his heart and felt its strong beat. He was always so warm. She knew that it was due to him being part hellspawn—their body temperatures were higher than that of humans. The contrast between him and Reno's chill served as another reminder of what could have been and what could not be. "We can't be together. It's too dangerous. And we need to end it before it hurts us more than it does is now."

Tyrus palmed the back of her hand. She felt him stiffen as she continued. "Princess, what are you talking about?" She started to cry despite steeling herself not to. Her tears quickly soaked into his shirt as she fisted it in her hand. His voice held such tenderness. And such worry. "Hey, talk to me, Jade. What did Bounce say? Why are you doing this?"

Jade slowly shook her head. "It's too dangerous. I need you to understand. I want this. I want a chance for us to be together. But it's bigger than my wanting something. It's bigger than both of us."

Tyrus frowned as he searched her eyes. Could he see how much this agonized her through the tears? "Wait. Not here." Still holding her hands, he led her over to the motorcycle and offered her the helmet.

"What are we doing? Tyrus, we need to talk." He took the helmet and pressed it over her head. Jade could not tell what he was thinking, and he skirted his eyes from hers as he fastened the chin strap.

"I know. And we will." He swung his leg over the bike to mount and started it up. Jade sniffed behind the face shield of the helmet, but confusion helped keep more crying at bay. She hopped onto the seat behind Tyrus, and he took her arms to wrap around him.

"Just hold on tight, Princess. And when I move, just move with me. It's like dancing. Together. Okay?"

She opened her mouth to ask once again where they were going. What were they doing? The look on his face and the turmoil of emotions in his eyes silenced any words. She nodded and did as she was told.

The garage door opened, and they took off into the early evening. Riding on the motorcycle both thrilled and scared Jade, but Tyrus operated the machine as if it were a part of him. His hand came up to wrap around her arms, and Jade closed her eyes at feeling him against her—knowing it might be the last time she did.

The motorcycle climbed up the Pacific highway. Jade could see the fog thickening around the Golden Gate and below, where it crossed over the bay. The setting sun made both glow gold. It was utterly breathtaking, and any other time, Jade would have found beauty at the sight, but all she felt was sadness. Resigned to a life without love. Without dating. Children. Alone and longing to take more motorcycle rides with Tyrus.

When the bike slowed down, Jade lifted her head as Tyrus maneuvered it to one of the scenic overlooks. She waited while he kicked the stand down, and when he dismounted, she followed. Jade removed the helmet and stood quietly. She sought to muster the small strength she felt earlier to do this but felt betrayed when it was nowhere to be found.

"Now, we talk. You tell me what the fuck Bounce said. Why are you ending us before we even got a decent start." He prowled up to her, but his touch gentle. He lifted her chin to meet his eyes. "Princess. Jade. Whatever it is, we can deal with it. Is it the bullshit Reno spewed? Fuck him. He's made more screwups than anyone."

"No. Tyrus, listen to me." But he kept going, and she spurted out the words she planned on not saying, that had started to claw at her thoughts mentally. "Can you be with me and not have sex?"

That brought his verbal tirade to an abrupt halt, and he blinked. "What? Is it because you're a virgin? Sweetheart, I already told you we'd take our time. As long as you needed to be ready."

Jade balled up her fists and rested them against his chest. "No. It's not that I will want it or not. It's that…" She exhaled a quick, shaky breath. "I owe Envy. She needs me to keep her safe. To give her a haven." She moved a hand to spread her fingers over her heart. "In me. I'm her shelter, but because of how she and I are together, I have to make sure I stay as light as possible. Otherwise…"

"She'll be found. Detected. Felt. By Epsilon." Tyrus put his head back with an agonized groan. "Shit. So that means your innocence."

Jade nodded, relieved he understood. It was hard enough to say what she had already. "Which, beyond a child, is some of the brightest light there is. I have to avoid..." She let out a pained breath. "Heart break that could make me dark. Sex that could make me less light. And then there's the High Council." He had paced away from her, and she reached out to grasp the sleeve of his motorcycle jacket. "They can't know I'm a Keeper not linked to Envy. That she can be apart from me, and I can survive! They'll put her back in the Void. And Bounce and the others can get in trouble for interfering in what might have been my destiny."

"That was me! I interfered. No one else! And I did it because…" Tyrus turned to face her. "He slaughtered so many people. And I did *nothing* to stop it. You have no idea how it made me sick. I turned my back on the bodies as he dropped them, one after the other. And I did nothing. I found a way to avoid being there when he raped, and when he played with the victims before passing them on to his paid killers to use. He called them his fucking toy. And when he was done, he had no problem either killing them or giving them away. If there was anything left to do that."

His head went down, and he curled and uncurled his fingers. Jade was sure if there had been a wall close, it would have felt his wrath. "And when I found you, when I smelled that fucking stink of him on you, I could *not* just let you die. You, I could do something about, Princess. And now that I know you, I'd do it million times again if it meant I have you."

Jade silently cried, her heart cracking with each horrifying declaration. She let the tears fall without care. Her grandmother would have been so ashamed. "But you can't have me and not have everything! Tyrus, I can't have sex with you! I can't give you everything you'd want to have in a girlfriend! In a lover! Are you seriously going to be okay with that?" She swallowed and tried to catch her breath. "I know you're experienced. Even Lily said so. I saw how the nurses and others look at you. I can't..."

She grabbed at him, and he was there. Like he had been since they met. She laid her forehead on his chest again. "It's not fair. And it hurts, but it's the truth." She sobbed as she clutched the leather under her hands. "Not while this war is going on. I can't ask you to go without what you need for years." Jade began hiccupping, and she could not care less of her composure. Not with Tyrus. "For all we know, it could be decades. I care about you too much to ask you to do that."

"This fucking war. It's taken so much away." Tyrus growled out the words. He wrapped his arms around her, and a hand came up to comb fingers through her hair. "Epsilon, the bastard, needs to be ended."

A thought manifested in her head. It could not be that simple. Jade had been on a fast track and one huge learning curve since landing in this new world. "Ended. That's it. Tyrus"—she pulled away from him and began to pace—"what if he were caught? Or ended? What would that do to the war?"

Tyrus sat against his bike as he crossed his arms. "Without Epsilon to lead it? It would end pretty quickly. The demons and mercs he has working for him are pretty much ball-less idiots following him like lemmings. His forces would fall apart. They'd be easy to track down and destroy. Or imprison. If they didn't just drag their sorry asses back to Hell." He narrowed his eyes and angled his finger toward her. "What are you thinking?"

She wiped her tears and found enough hope to smile. "So if we can catch and contain *him,* the war would end sooner. And then, it wouldn't matter. The High Council wouldn't care because we caught Epsilon. We ended all of this in a win for the Grid. Epsilon wouldn't be able to get to Envy, and the war would end. We could be together, right?"

Tyrus raised a brow and let out a bark of laughter. "That all sounds amazing, Princess. But we've had that goal for years, from the get-go most likely. Catch the sonofabitch and end all this fighting. It seems black and white, an easy thing, Jade, but it's not. He's smart. He's greedy. And he always seems two steps ahead of us."

Child. No. I know where your mind is taking you. You have risked enough. We have risked enough. I will not let you put yourself in danger, Jade.

"Trust me, Envy. Please. I need you." She looked at Tyrus. "But I need him, too." Jade squeezed her eyes shut and whispered, "I need you both."

Envy hissed in her head but granted her silence. Jade became a little giddy with the plan, the more she considered it. She moved back to stand in front of Tyrus. "No, you're not seeing it, Tyrus! We have something he wants." She put a hand against his cheek. "Me. What if we trap him?"

Tyrus growled and bared his fangs. "No. We are *not* using you as fucking bait. That is *not* happening!"

Jade pushed up on her toes and put her forehead against his, leaving him no choice but to look deeply into each other's eyes. "You promised you would keep me safe. That you would protect me. This can work." She gave him a tearful smile and wrapped her arms around his neck. "So help me plan. Let's end the war by getting Epsilon." She pressed her lips against his to say against them. "So we can be together."

27

"I can get the door, Candyman."

Emma stood in front of the door of their home, intending to open it. That was before Reno pressed a hand on the thing by her head to stop her.

"You shouldn't be answering the door." He met her eyes, and his tone softened. He put a hand protectively on her stomach. "I don't care if the fancy security stuff and the monitor shows it's Jade. And Tyrus." He frowned in puzzlement to look at the video monitor by the door. "Why *are* they at our door? At ten o'clock at night?"

Emma smiled and tilted her head with a smirk. "That's what I was going to open the door to find out about."

Okay, she had a point, but Witch usually did. Reno smirked and moved his hand away, and Witch swung the door open. Jade and Tyrus stood there, and he closed one eye. "Are you coming to get in another fight, Tyrus? Because if you are, it's a real dumbass and fatal move to do it at my house." Popping his eye open, Reno gave a wide smile and showed his fangs. "We can do it the yard, though. The grass is really soft."

"Oh, hush. Hi, you two. Come in."

Reno gawked at Witch. She just let them walk in as if the day's events hadn't taken place. She knew about them—the Grid rumor mill gave her a summary, and when he had arrived home, he had filled in the details. Tyrus had gone all crazy boyfriend after getting caught doing kissy face with Jade.

And the two of them looked close to falling back into kissy facing as they stood in his living room, arm in arm. He pointed to them both. "I thought things were clear after the talk with Bounce." He narrowed his eyes. "Or maybe you don't get it. I thought you were a smart one, Jade." He smirked as he rolled his gaze to Tyrus. "You, well, are you."

Jade looked over at Tyrus—Reno guessed for support—before returning to him and Witch. "We understand that we can't be together completely as a couple until the war is over. Or until Epsilon is caught. So"—Jade gave Tyrus another glance—"we have a plan. To catch him. So the war can end, and we can be together."

"What?" Reno broke out in laughter. "You have to be kidding, right? I mean, come on. What do you think we've been trying to do for like, I don't know"—he lifted both his hands and shoulders in a shrug—"forever? Or well, as long as I can remember, which is a really long time. We've been trying to catch him." His hands dropped. "What did you think we were doing? Having tea parties and playing Uno? No. We all have scars to show differently." He crossed his arms. "But I have been known to do a tea party or two." He waggled his head. "Okay, and Uno is my favorite game." He sputtered and regained his seriousness. "But anyway, you know what I mean."

"Reno, listen to them." Witch put a hand on his arm before she addressed Tyrus and Jade. "What's your plan?"

"IT'S CRAZY. I mean, it can work. But it's crazy." Reno looked back at Witch where she lay in their bed. Jade and Tyrus had told them their plan. He had to admit it was simple yet brilliant. "And I thought she was the Keeper of Envy. Not Madness. But still, if it could end all this..."

Witch moved to wrap her arms around him from behind and pressed against his back. "But dangerous. For Jade. For Tyrus. For you. For all the Keepers." He glanced over his shoulder to meet her eyes. They were full of worry and stress. Reno also knew it was not just because of the plan presented hours before.

Witch worried as much about the future as he did. For their children. Both born and unborn.

Reno sighed and brought his fingers up to graze over her jaw. "I know. But so is him being out there, a constant threat, always wondering when he's going to show up and do bad things. Come into our home and..." Reno closed his eyes and moved them both back to lay on the bed. Witch cuddled up as he put an arm around her. His eyes went upward to the ceiling. "He invaded our home. He tried to kill Rugrat and Eli. He *did* kill Marcus. In. Our. Home."

"I know," she said softly. Her hand stroked on his chest over a now beating heart. Reno knew Witch knew the danger more than most. Epsilon and the war had been behind her parents and brother being killed. "But Reno, Jade barely survived Epsilon. Kenzie and Lana. Lana is having an at-risk pregnancy from what he did. I bet if you asked Marcus, he might tell you he has nightmares about what Epsilon did to him. Not to mention what he's told us about when he was in Hell with the bastard." She lifted her eyes to his. "Imagine if Epsilon's cornered. What if this doesn't work? Are you really able to use Jade as bait? And not worry about how bad it can go?"

"No, I'm worried. Big time. A lot, *a lot*." He carefully pulled free from her and rolled off the bed to pace beside it. "But I have to agree with them that it could work. That we could *finally* see the end of the war in sight." When she struggled to rise from the bed, he took her elbow in his hand to gently help her up. He took advantage of the move by curling his arm around her. He brushed her hair back and rubbed noses with her. "When was the last time we had this good a chance, Witch?"

Emma sighed. Reno knew she had to agree with him. How could she not? "I know, Candyman. I do, I promise I do. But I'm scared for her. And for you. If anything happened to her, you would eat yourself alive with guilt. And according to you, Tyrus was angry today. Imagine how he'll be if Jade gets hurt. Or worse." She rubbed noses back. "Is it really worth the risk?"

Reno thought about it. His eyes shifted left. Then they slid right. He waited for some clue from Sundown. A statistic. The odds of success. But Sundown was silent. Great, he was on his own. Again. That usually indicated his dark half knew this was a bad idea—but no way would Sundown attempt to talk him out of it. What would be the fun in that?

As his focus returned to Witch, Reno let out a frustrated sigh. "And if we don't say we'll do it, what's to stop the two of them doing it anyway? Without backup. Alone without us to help?"

Emma bit her bottom lip. "You're right. They did seem pretty determined." Her forehead creased in thought. "Okay. So you ask the others, Team Keeper. Get everyone together, and let's discuss. And if everyone agrees it's worth the danger, then take it to Bounce. That's all I'm going to ask." She brought a hand up to brush her knuckles across the scruff on his jaw. "Please. For me."

Reno slanted his face more against her touch and closed his eyes to soak it in. "Good idea." He opened them to look down at her and smiled. "You know. The kids are asleep, and I may or may not be facing danger soon." He wiggled a brow. He had no need to explain further. Witch pushed him back on the bed with a wicked smile.

Gosh, how he loved when she took charge... And the fact her boobs were so very nice all preggo made it very easy to do.

KENZIE'S BOOT heel tapped a fast staccato on the floor of Ms. Woo's noodle shop. For whatever reason, Reno had sent all the Keepers a discreet message via text that they needed to meet. The fact he used a traditional cell phone to send it rather than their stamps made one thing clear—Keepers only. No other Grid. Despite the bowl of steaming noodles sitting in front of her, she also knew this meeting wasn't just for lunch. If that had been the case, she would not have been shown to the private room in the back. She kept her head down, focusing on the security camera of her and Lana's flat linked to her phone. She watched her heartbeat sleep. Lana knew about the security. A measure Kenzie took whenever she had to leave her alone. The baby being due any time now triggered every paranoia Kenzie had to keep her safe.

Hearing the bell of the shop ring beyond the room, Lust sensed Murder before the big man entered the space. "Hey. Do you know why he wanted us here?"

Marcus acknowledged Kenzie with a bob of his chin. "I do not know. I was told to be here by Reno's text. No more info than that. It is strange." He arched a brow. "I also called Tyrus, and he was with Jade. No additional information and declined to be forthcoming when I pushed for it. They are headed here as well." Marcus smirked and took a seat across from her in the booth. "That, too, seemed strange."

Murder and Lust snipped at each other from the moment Marcus walked into the place. They were not the best of friends. To be honest, they were a thin line above enemies. They would start growling and insulting each other whenever they were in the room together. Kenzie wondered if it gave Marcus as much of an annoying headache as it did her. The answer came within seconds.

"You two, stop it," Marcus growled.

Kenzie snorted and then felt an entirely different sensation. That strange warm, mind-blurring feeling. She knew Reno had arrived. Whereas Lust and Murder disliked each other, Lust and Madness were another story. The two powers had been in love once. Their Keepers dealt with the residual effects of it. Kenzie didn't need to turn to look at the entrance of the room to know Reno entered. They could and most likely always would sense each other. A soft purring would start in their heads, along with a need to touch, which they both fought.

And it was awkward as fuck.

Glancing over her shoulder, Lust had not, however, registered Jade with him along with Tyrus. That would take some getting used to—Jade becoming a Keeper like them while not being the same. The three of them could not feel Envy inside of the girl any more than the sensors programmed to pick up on dark energy. Kenzie slid her gaze past Reno's. Not looking into those fucking blue eyes helped with the weirdness. Kenzie instead chose to meet Jade's to give her a smile. "Hey, kid." She addressed Tyrus. "And Murder's kid."

Marcus scoffed with a snort, and Kenzie chuckled as he nudged her leg with his under the table.

"Sorry, I still think it has some joke mileage left. I'm going to ride it like a bitch until it runs out." She sat against the wall and crossed her ankles as she stretched out in the booth seat. "So why are we here? You know Lana is close to popping. The last place I want to be is away from her. So this had better be good, Madness."

"It is. These two"—Reno indicated toward Tyrus and Jade hanging by the entrance with his thumb—"have a plan to end the war. Or at least, shorten it."

Kenzie lifted her brows in interest and intensified her focus on the youngsters. Lust did a soft laugh in her head when Tyrus took Jade's hand in his, and she leaned against him.

Someone is falling in love. That's sweet, sugar. Look at them.

Kenzie had to agree with Lust—it was sweet. Not completely unexpected considering the guy had saved Jade's life. He was also hot. But them being together had to be unwise. "They have a plan? And"—Kenzie swung her gaze to Reno—"I going to guess since we're discussing it here and not HQ, Bounce isn't in on this plan?"

"Not yet," Jade spoke up and stepped forward. "Tyrus and I came up with it. We told Reno last night. And it's a good plan. But he won't help unless we're all in agreeance. As a team."

"Yep. I told her and Tyrus, either we all agree to do it, or none of us do it." Reno sat in a booth opposite Kenzie and Marcus. He stretched out his legs on the seat, mimicking her position as he settled. "It's a good plan. It can work. But it's going to take all of us." He smirked. "Four Keepers are badass. We just have to work together."

Ms. Woo entered the room. The ancient woman brought more bowls of noodle soup and a tray of soda. Kenzie smiled at the old woman and chuckled when she smacked the top of Reno's head. It was done, she knew, in love. The shop was affiliated with the Grid and often a hangout for those on it. Ms. Woo was a retired Relay—made immortal as a gift for actually surviving to retire. Kenzie had no idea how old the woman was. But her soup was fucking fantastic. She could be trusted more than a devout priest during confession. And she had a love-hate kind of affection for Reno—which the rest of them found highly entertaining. "Okay, so what's this plan?"

"I want to trap Epsilon. We have the bait," Jade replied and put a hand on her chest. "We know what he wants."

Jade stated the words so plainly. Like she read off a line of a homework assignment. But the impact was mind-blowing.

Marcus barked out, "What?"

Kenzie absorbed the statements like a series of punches to the gut. She slid to the end of the booth seat, incredulous that she heard Jade correctly and stared hard at Reno. "Are you fucking serious right now?

"Kenz, listen. Before you freak out, just listen." Kenzie knew Reno softened his tone to give comfort, but Kenzie found zero in any of this.

"No. You can't trap Epsilon. And to offer up *yourself* as bait?" Kenzie rose to her feet and stepped in front of Jade. "Let me tell you something, little girl. You got *lucky* he didn't do to you what he does to others."

What Epsilon had done to us...

The slightest opening of the past always caused Kenzie's

stomach to stir. The memories and flashbacks to swim to the surface of her mind. Lust attempted to wrap around them to keep them in the depths away from her day-to-day. The weeks of torture and rape at Epsilon's hands. Followed by her slaughter. The sick bastard loved it, got off on it. Kenzie still had nightmares about it. "No. I am not on board with this plan." Kenzie stood upright stiffly as she wrapped her arms around herself. "We didn't go through all the bullshit of making you look dead for you to find him and wave hello. Say to him, 'hi, I'm alive. Want a second chance to rape me?'"

"Lust, sit down, and calm down." Marcus reached out to touch Kenzie's arm, but she jerked from it. Marcus glared at her before addressing his son. "Tyrus, surely you do not agree with your girlfriend."

Kenzie's head whipped to the side to regard Tyrus, and she snorted. "You'd be a really shitty boyfriend if you did."

Tyrus bared his fangs at her, and Marcus was on his feet next. "Let's all calm down, shall we?"

Kenzie flipped Tyrus off and returned to sit in the booth. "Fine. So explain. What is the whole plan?"

Tyrus exhaled, and Jade moved to stand next to him. "No, we do not use Jade for bait. But Epsilon wants me, and he wants Envy. The power is the bait. I go to him and tell him I want back in." Jade looked down, and Kenzie could tell the girl feared for her man. "And I offer him the power as restitution. The moment I know where he's located, we move in. We take him down. Envy will help." Tyrus looked over at Jade with a look of a man losing his heart and happy about the loss. "She is kept away. And as far as he's concerned, I'll make sure he knows she didn't survive. That Grid captured Envy when Jade died, and I stole it."

He turned to sneer at Kenzie and volleyed the finger her way. "So no, I am not putting my girlfriend at risk. And fuck you for thinking I would."

Reno added more to this crazy plan from his place in the booth. "Envy can reach out to us. She can tell us where Epsilon is located in the place. We hit it at the same time, all four powers with us three Keepers. Jade will be kept safe. But Epsilon doesn't stand a chance."

"We've thought that before, Reno, that we could outsmart him. We can't, I..." Reno rose, and Kenzie met his eyes when he stepped in front of her. That purring started in her head. It grew louder when he pressed a palm against her cheek. "You know he's evil, Reno." She ground her fangs. "You *know* that." She knew her voice held an edge of pleading, a tone full of fear. Her brain spazzed as both fight and flight fought for control. Her fear fed both. "Are you sure about this? Because I'm fucking not."

Reno transferred his hand to press against the nape of Kenzie's neck and brought their foreheads together. His blue eyes met hers, and she sought red in those depths because this must have taken root from insanity, spawned from Madness rather than rationality. But no, they were clear. She dealt with all Reno.

"I know. And it's the best chance we have." He sighed. "He's killing kids. She was a kid." He pointed a finger toward Jade. "He has to be stopped. For our kids. For Rugrat. Eli. My twins. Your baby. He's just going to get worse, so we have to do this."

"Bounce is never going to let us do this." Her eyes widened as a strange look passed over Reno's features. "But you know that. Sundown ran the odds. We're not going to tell him..." She shook her head in disbelief. "We're going outlaw on this?" Kenzie bared her fangs and lifted her chin but did not break the lock of his gaze. "And what does Sundown say? The odds without him. Of us pulling this shit off. I want to know."

Reno pulled back from her and smiled. "Eighty percent we take the bastard down. Less if we involved the Grid. And more people would get hurt." He turned to the others. "We know there are moles at HQ. Somehow, Epsilon always knows when we're about to strike. We minimize that happening by keeping it with just us. So eighty percent we succeed. And that's pretty good when it comes to odds." He dropped his hand. "Because Sundown is really a negative Nancy." Reno glanced over at Kenzie. "A total Debbie Downer."

"But almost always right, damn it." Kenzie's pushed him further from her. She wanted to be pissed at him, but Lust whined for Madness when they touched, making that impossible with that fuzzy fucking feeling. And Kenzie really wanted to be angry. But he might be right this time. She also wanted more than anything to make this world safer before the baby arrived. "Fine. I'm in."

28

"I changed my mind. We can't do this."

Tyrus took Jade for another ride on the bike to the same spot they had hatched the plan and surprised her with a moonlit picnic—complete with her favorite pizza, a food denied to her growing up. He topped it off with breadsticks and bottles of soda, then introduced Jade to his favorite red velvet cake as dessert.

The Keepers unanimously agreed. It would happen. Discussion included Bounce's anger and the likely fallout. Sundown gave high odds the Grid would demand punishment for not using the protocol and backup resources. They could only hope the fact they finally locked Epsilon away proved worthy enough for some leniency. For the son of Lucifer to stand trial in front of the High Council. Jade questioned why Lucifer would vote to convict. She had received a round of laughter. Apparently, the father hated the son and vice versa. Jade thought her family was festered with envy and resentment. No, the family tree of Lucifer was crumbled with rot at the core.

They would trick Epsilon with Envy as bait with Jade safely hidden away. And if things went as planned, they'd capture Epsilon.

It sounded like such a good idea yesterday. Tonight, the morning before they attempted it—not so much.

"Princess, don't worry. The others are just as hardcore about you being safe as I am. He's not going to get close to you." He had his arms wrapped around her. She sat between his legs to lean back against his chest. Envy purred in their heads. It would have been the perfect first date as he had called it, but the worry, try as she might, ruined it. The fear it would go very wrong ate away at the delight of having a boyfriend like Tyrus. Strong and handsome. The kindest and most patient boyfriend imaginable.

And tomorrow... the one with the greatest risk if they failed.

"It's not me I'm worried about. I told you that I'm scared for you. Tyrus, we're taking this risk because we want to be together. And yes, catching Epsilon will end or be the beginning of the end, but if something happens to you, none of it..." She wiped angry tears—she hated that once again, her body gave in to emotions she was determined to resist. Why did it have to be tears? Why couldn't it be anything but that—tears were weak. Lily told her it was not a sign of it. She and her sisters did it, too, but Jade hated it. "It's selfish for us to do this! We don't want the war to end because it needs to! We want it over so we can be together. In every way like a couple. That's fucking selfish." Her eyes widened the moment the f-bomb dropped. Even Tyrus appeared surprised it had fallen from her lips. "We need to stop this. We *have* to stop this, Tyrus."

Tyrus silenced her with a tender kiss. His fingers tenderly wiped away her tears. Jade learned that he was very good at kissing. They had done it several times now, and each time, it made her mind warm and fuzzy. It also chased away her fears and quelled suffocating anxiety. Envy had always been her friend and solace, but Tyrus was quickly becoming so much more—warmth, strength, and safety. He possessed the ability to make Jade laugh at the drop of a hat. And when he smiled? One of those rare, perfect easy ones that Jade felt were her and hers alone. They gave each other courage and understanding. And tomorrow, they may lose it all.

"You know I can't think when you do that." Jade tucked her head under his chin and wrapped their hands together. "Can't we send Epsilon word of a deal any other way? Tell him we're willing to do it that *doesn't* include you doing it? Right there where he can hurt you?" Her voice began to tremble, and she bit her bottom lip. "Or worse."

"Sweetheart, come on. We talked about this. There is no fucking way I'm letting him stop me from being with you. And generally, death—if you're not a Keeper—has a hell of a way of forcing a messy, damn breakup." He lowered down to be able to see her face. "It will. Not. Happen." There was a milder version of his open smile she loved. "I won't let it. Envy won't let it. And she'll be right there with me." The smile grew. "She likes me better than you do."

Envy laughed in Jade's head, but instead of amusing Jade, it angered her. She jumped to her feet and faced him. "This isn't funny. None of this is funny." She threw her arms out to the side. "Maybe it's because this is all new to me. This world. How things are done. But I'm *scared!*" She put a hand on her chest. "I am so scared that everyone is risking everything for me!"

"Because no one has?" Tyrus moved to stand in front of her and cupped her face in his hands. His thumb stroked along her jaw as he met her eyes. "That's over. The Grid risks everything for everyone. Every single day, Jade. It may be new to you, but it's the same ole, same ole for the rest of us." He dipped his head to place a gentle kiss on her lips. "We got this, Princess. Trust us. This is what we do. We're badasses."

While his words did nothing to lower Jade's anxiety, the attempt gave her strength enough to push it to a manageable level. "Oh, how could I have forgotten? Your father has said it a few times. Badasses," he said in unison with her, "with style."

"That's right. You are learning." He leaned back to smile at her fully. "Jade Shen, you're fucking smart."

Jade rolled her eyes and wrapped him in a hug. She laid her cheek on his chest and closed her eyes to tune in to the thud within.

"I've been told that before." She smiled softly. "I think you should confirm you mean it with another kiss."

Tyrus smiled when she lifted her head, and his mouth came down to hers. "See. I told you. So damn smart."

❧

"MASTER, there is someone at the gate."

Epsilon stood in front of the mirror. His fingers touched the jagged edges of scars on his face, his left eye opaque white and blind. His upper lip curled up on the same side in a grimaced smile. He looked as much of a monster on the outside as the inside. Envy made sure she poisoned the flesh during her attack. She used Jade's light to decompose the darkness of his, so he healed with a constant reminder. The dark power and the girl's bond… interesting. Ah, he would have enjoyed playing with them both. But the girl died, and Envy roamed the earth once more. Never mind that he was the cause of Jade's death.

"Why would I give a single damn for who is at our gate?" He shifted his gaze to meet his underling's gaze. One that lowered quickly. His name? Epsilon did not recall, nor did he care. They were all just tools for his use. Easily disposed of. The man shifted more to avoid the sight of Epsilon's deformed features. "Who is it?"

"The traitor. Tyrus."

❧

THEY USED a listing of every single facility Grid suspected Epsilon ran. All empty. Tyrus began to lose hope the bastard even remained in the city. He stood in front of the final one listed, and his hope renewed when one of the guards met Tyrus from behind the gate. One Tyrus knew Epsilon kept among the small number of a personal squad. Men and women he thought either too loyal or too chicken shit to betray him. If that man was here, that meant Epsilon hid in the old warehouse beyond.

The man left and came back with a smirk. Epsilon must be here. Tyrus shifted his focus from the asshole to the lit windows behind. Epsilon watched. Tyrus felt it. Like knowing that a spider hid in the corner of the bedroom. Sleep impossible as you waited for it to strike. He shifted and brought Jade's bracelet in front of him. It glowed bright green with Envy stirring inside. "Tell him I want back in. I'm sick and tired of the bullshit patrols. They put me guarding a bunch of brats at their new school. And the pay"—he snorted—"it's laughable. Tell him I offer this." He stepped to the side to give Epsilon a clear view and yelled. "Envy. They captured it when the girl died. I fucking stole it." He smiled and no longer spoke to the guard but his master. "For you."

The door opened, and a shaft of light hit the crumbling concrete parking lot in front of the place. Tyrus forced himself from shuddering in disgust at Epsilon's appearance when the bastard stood in front of him behind the gate. The night was dark, with the moon hidden behind a clouded sky. But the green glow from Envy shone on Epsilon's mangled face. It was horrifying. Jade and Envy told him they had fought to escape, but damn.

"Hello, Traitor. Like what you see?" Epsilon spoke to Tyrus, but his eyes were locked on Envy, swirling in the bracelet. "And hello, Envy. It is indeed a pleasure to have you visit."

Envy slapped the sides of her container, causing it to jerk in his grasp. Tyrus felt the power's glee to see the damage she and Jade accomplished.

"What do you want? Do you actually believe I would let you back into my ranks after what you did? And being that halfling mutt's son?" Epsilon laughed. It sounded slightly fucked up and garbled. There were more hideous scars on the man's throat, too.

"Intel. I've been with them for months. I know every move. Every access code. Everything you would need to take the do-gooders down." Tyrus stepped closer and smiled. He hoped Reno was right. Greed would not be able to pass up on such a goody bag of an offer. "I'll tell you everything. I'll give you Envy, and you give me a chance to prove that you can trust me." He came in as close as the chain link between them allowed. "You know I'm the only one you ever trusted fully, and there's a reason for that. We are not that different. Our fathers thought us garbage. Tossed us away. And the more I've gotten to know Marcus, the more I've learned how true all that is. Let me help you. Give me a chance."

Epsilon was silent, and it had Tyrus nervous. The man usually gloated or bluffed. Silence was neither.

"I want more."

Tyrus frowned at those three words. He opened his mouth to respond but stopped himself. What could Epsilon want beyond everything on the Grid? Why would he pass up on a raw, unfiltered dark power? Moments from their past played in his head, and he took a step back with shock. Of course, Epsilon wanted more. Or, in this case, what he had been denied. "Kenzie? You still want your favorite toy back?"

Epsilon smiled and shrugged. "A man wants what he wants. If you mean what you say, that you truly want back in my favor, I will take you, your information, the power you hold, and bring Kenzie to me. It's very simple." Epsilon brought a hand up. "And not up for negotiation. Those are my demands."

29

"What?" Reno stared so hard at Tyrus that he was surprised his eyes didn't shatter. "No. We can't do it. No." He shook his head and paced the back room of the noodle shop. "We're stopping this."

"Oh, I see. It's okay to put my ass on the line but not one of yours?" Tyrus stepped up to him, full of accusations in tone and expression.

Sundown must have agreed. A growl filled Reno's head. Adrenaline pumped through his system to prepare for a fight.

"Enough." Marcus stepped up to put his arm between them.

Reno narrowed his eyes, but he backed off—this time. But Marcus's kid was becoming a pain in the ass every day.

"It's quite clear this has gone sideways," Marcus stated. "And I agree, this cannot move forward."

Tyrus wised up a bit to move out of Reno's personal space. Good. Breaking the man's nose to bleed all over the floor would have made Ms. Woo hate Reno more.

Marcus rumbled a growl at both of them. "We attempted. We failed. And it cannot reach its conclusion as we wished."

Tyrus blew out his anger as he leaned against the wall, crossing his arms and ankles. "I tried. And he bought my whole bullshit reasoning of wanting to come back. I think he liked the thought of my going against you, Pops." He rubbed a hand over his face. "But it's not enough. He has yet to stop his crazed obsession with Kenzie. It makes zero fucking sense, but it is what it is. Greed had a bite of her. It's not willing to let her go."

Reno squeezed his eyes shut and brought his arms up to wrap around his head. It pounded with stress and exhaustion. That and coupled with the guilt of not telling Witch they decided to do it without asking Bounce. In fact, when she asked what Bounce said, he avoided giving her an answer but grabbed onto the out she offered him when she said that maybe it was for the best by not correcting her. The pressure to keep all of this under wraps from the Grid while praying one of the moles they never found wouldn't learn of it… It all crushed in on him. And maybe its failure had eased a small amount of the stress.

However, the desperation Reno felt to stop what careened toward their future only grew. Known or not. "Yeah. We can't give him Kenzie. We can't let that even come close to happening." It was the reason Kenzie was not invited to the meeting. "We can't ask that of her. I won't let it happen." His arms dropped with a heavy sigh. "We're done."

"I'll do it."

Reno heard the voice, and he glanced back over his shoulder in shock to find Kenzie stood in the doorway. He had been so off his game with the stress that he had not felt her arrive. He went fish faced as he sputtered in failure to respond.

Kenzie walked up to him and brought a finger up to park against his forehead. "Madness begged Lust to stop me from doing something but didn't say what. I knew you were all here. Lust can always lead me to you, Reno." She gave him a resigned smile. "And I overheard. This way, you don't have to ask me. Because I'm offering to do it."

"No, you can't." Reno shook his head. "I won't let you. You can't let him get you. You *cannot* give him that chance. Kenzie"—he brought a hand up to cup her cheek—"please. It's over. It's done."

She smiled. "But it's not. He's out there. And I'm about to have a baby with the woman I love. A woman he tried to kill. Just like he tried to kill Emma. And you, Marcus." She turned her head to regard every other person in the room. "Tyrus. Jade. He's hurt us all. He has tried to kill us and destroy us." She swallowed and brought her gaze back to Reno's. And god, did he hate to see such strong determination mixed with fear in those lavender eyes. "That has to end. It must end. Don't you understand, Reno? It has to. End." She moved away and addressed the others. "We vote, like every other time." She gave him a nod. "Team Keeper rules."

Reno swallowed. Not a single word could counter what she said —because he knew she was right. "I'll agree if everyone else does. But you know this is not what I want."

Kenzie smiled. "I know. But it's all we have."

JADE SAT in a booth with her legs drawn up and arms wrapped around them. When Tyrus had returned with Envy and informed the Keepers of Epsilon's demands, it made her both sad and happy. Even though the idea had been hers, something about it did not settle right when the group discussed it. It was stupid for her to think this would go their way. She may not have been with the Grid for long, but in that short time, she'd learned that Epsilon was close to impossible to outthink. They all thought Jade smart, but apparently, the devil's offspring ran circles around them all.

Jade listened to Reno and Kenzie go back and forth. Jade may not have Sundown to do the odds, but it didn't take that talent to know this would go bad. Very, very bad. Her new family was going to be ripped apart right down the middle. Both funny and heartbreaking for her to reflect how she used to pray that her parents would tell her grandmother to go to hell. How she wished her father would find the strength to walk away from the money, the power, and the esteem, family reputation, be damned.

When Kenzie said they had to vote, Jade was unsure how many times they called her name before she actually heard it and found them all staring at her. Blinking, she frowned. "Me? You want me to vote? I haven't even been part of the team for very long. Do I really have to vote?"

Tyrus moved over to squat in front of her. "Yes, Princess. You do. And right now, you're the swing one."

Jade jerked her eyes to the others and did the math. Marcus would have voted no—he hated putting his son at risk, to begin with. Tyrus would have voted yes. Anything to bring Epsilon down. Reno already said he wasn't going to vote, but she knew he was against it. And Kenzie, yes. She would sacrifice herself to end the war and keep her love and child safe. "Me? Tyrus, I can't. I..."

Child, be smart. Use those beautiful brains. Who is right? Who is wrong? Vote as your soul tells you to, Jade. I'll be there for you. And I am pretty sure all of them will be, too. It's okay, Jade.

Hadn't Jade been telling everyone she was no longer a kid? That she wasn't a child? Not anymore. She looked down and did as Envy suggested—used her brains. Jade realized Envy wasn't the only constant in her life. She had her intelligence and the ability to handle whatever test was given, not only passing it but exceeding expectations. Reno's eyes pleaded her to say no without saying a word. Kenzie's looked lost but resolved. And Tyrus? Of course, he held complete faith in her. She closed her eyes and slowly exhaled. Yes, she always exceeded expectations when it came to tests, and she would do that once again in this. "Yes. I vote yes."

30

"Why must you force me to ask this?"

Epsilon froze his movement. His hand paused in the air as the voice sounded behind him. "Father. Of course." Exhaling, he turned to face Lucifer. "Ask me what?"

Lucifer wore a perfectly tailored suit. He stepped over, grasped his chin and angled Epsilon's face to observe its damaged detail. "That is rather unfortunate. Gruesome and ugly. I could easily repair the damage, but as I told you last year, I am done cleaning up your messes. So it shall always remain." Lucifer's fingers dug into Epsilon's flesh. The area still ached from the damage. His father's cruelly applied pressure made it throb more in pain. "Why are you making deals for the Keeper of Lust? When you had a power *right there* for the taking? You are an idiot." He let Epsilon go and stepped back to straighten his jacket. Lucifer pulled out his pocket square to wipe the fingers that had touched him as if his own son's skin had stained his. "That is not news, is it, son?"

Son. Such a short, simple word. Three letters usually stated with the affection of a father or mother to their male child. But when his sire voiced it, those letters dripped with such venom that it hung in the air between them like the vilest curse word in any and every language.

Epsilon worked his jaw in his hand with a grimace. "I thought you stated you were no longer involved in my affairs, Father. Nice to see you, too. And I want her because... She. Is. Mine."

Lucifer laughed. "She was never yours. Everything belongs to me. Nothing is yours, and I am always highly entertained when you think *anything* is." He turned to Epsilon and met his eyes. "Do not do this. Let her and this plan go. You are well aware I have other measures soon to be in play. And you dabbling in your obsession to play with McKenzie Miller and her dark power is not worth detouring my plans. In fact"—he ran his fingers along Epsilon's lapel before bringing his hand up to fist his son's hair. Epsilon hissed when his head was jerked back painfully—"I want you to surrender to them. Give yourself up. Tell your men to do the same."

"What?" Epsilon snarled. "I would never do that. You can't ask me to!"

Lucifer's hold tightened. The roots of his hair protested with a sharp pain to let Epsilon know they were about to leave his scalp. "I can. And I did. And you will. You will offer yourself to the Grid. You will be locked away. And there you will go in front of the High Council and throw yourself to their mercy."

"No. I will not." He shoved his father away and felt the roots rip and give. A small price to pay if it meant he could sway his father. "Why would I do that? Why—" His words halted at Lucifer's smug smile. Realization numbed the pain his father caused. Even his scarred injuries ceased to ache from the volume of bewilderment.

"You want me there. On the inside. You want my men and me there." Epsilon widened his eyes, and his jaw dropped. "You're planning on destroying the High Council?" Shock caused his breath to hang in his chest. "By the Omega, it's fucking insane." Yet brilliant. Epsilon always wondered why his father played along with the treaty, the one between Heaven and Hell to fight the war that Lucifer not only blamed on Epsilon but also used his son to orchestrate. "And let me guess, you will be the remaining High Council member to live."

Lucifer nodded. "Yes. And I will call all the shots, which means I can choose to pardon anyone I wish. I can also place those loyal to me in the vacant seats on the council. And the realm of man?" He smiled and laughed—a sound more wicked than any sin when issued by the devil himself. "Omega himself won't be able to stop them from being under my control. He's an old, ancient god whose time has passed. Most of humanity no longer believes in him. Not anymore. But"—he angled his head and raised a brow as flames crackled in the irises of his eyes—"they'll have no choice but to believe in the devil."

Epsilon thought he knew how twisted Lucifer could be. Apparently not. "But my moles have said nothing of a plan at the Grid. I believe Tyrus is acting alone."

Lucifer let out an irritated sound. "Because it's the Keepers acting alone. And have no worry, the Grid will learn of the plan." He smiled as he put a condescending palm on Epsilon's scarred cheek. "There is only one mole. And that mole is me. Trust me, they will know. You just do as you are told."

"DANCER, WHERE ARE YOU?"

"In the kitchen, Snap."

Kenzie took a moment to soak in the sounds of home. Music playing, her heartbeat singing along—off-key. Lana danced ballet like an exotic nymph, but she sang like a drunken and deaf sailor. Kenzie moved down the hall and ran her fingertips across the ready bag for when Lana went into labor. She paused next to the pack-n-play given to them by Emma and Reno. The boxes of diapers sent by Marcus. And the stacks of clothes sent by all the members of the San Francisco Ballet company.

And she was taking a risk that may cause her to miss it all.

She turned to the kitchen to find Lana preparing food. Kenzie leaned against the doorway to watch. "I thought you were supposed to be resting. Not making dinner."

Lana giggled. "I don't think reheating day-old pizza is cooking. Nor is making garlic bread out of stale bread and the little bit of butter we have left. We really need to go grocery shopping before..." Lana's words halted. Her pretty face folded with worry, and she slid the pan of pizza to the stovetop. Kenzie sighed when she reached her. Lana brought her hands up to lower Kenzie's face so that their gazes met. "What happened? You look..." Her tongue came out to lick her bottom lip. Her frown deepened with worry. "You look like it's something bad. What happened?"

Kenzie brought her hand up and brushed the back of her knuckles along Lana's jaw. "We had a plan, and we thought it would work—Justus Keepers. We didn't even tell Bounce. We were *finally* going to get that fucker Epsilon where he belonged."

Lana's eyes widened, and her jaw dropped. "Oh, wow. Wait"—she cocked her head to the side—"you said you *had* a plan. Judging by how you look, it didn't work. Okay, but, Snap, why do you look like it's something else?"

Kenzie sighed. "Because there's a new plan, baby. And you're not going to like it."

31

"Can you guys hear me?" Jade sat in a van three blocks away from the facility Epsilon ordered Tyrus to deliver Kenzie and Envy to. They wore single-channel earpieces to keep lines of communication open. They needed to keep their stamps offline so the Grid couldn't detect their locations and activities. Team Keeper was on their own.

"I hear you, Princess. Relax. It shouldn't take long."

Reno cut his eyes over to Tyrus as the man answered. God, he hoped the guy was right. He rolled his head on his neck and shook his arms to loosen up. They were in a second van parked down the street. Kenzie sat on one of the benches. She had been silent since they left the noodle shop. "You sure about this? We can still call this off."

Kenzie lifted her chin. "No. We are here. Might as well get it done." She stood and adjusted her body-fitted Kevlar vest. It hid under an oddly light-hearted yellow shirt with a Care Bear on the front of it. She pulled her leather jacket over that and tugged her dark hair with its purple braids free of the collar. "Just remember, I have a baby on the way. And you think I get angry and stabby? You have no idea how violent a ballerina can get when you kill her baby mama."

Marcus checked Tyrus's gear. The big man was forced to stoop over under the van's ceiling. "Nor how angry I will be if my son is harmed or killed." He turned his head to regard Reno, eyes glowing amber to show Murder and he were in agreeance. "I will kill all involved. And that's from me, Marcus. Murder, of course, is always on board to slaughter."

Reno nodded in understanding. He closed his eyes, and his hand went to his stomach. He wanted to throw up. Go home, claim a sick day, and curl up with Witch in their room. Bring the kids in there, too, and they'd all camp out in the big bed and watch cartoons. But they couldn't do that. They were here, and this was about to happen.

"No one is dying. We're going to be fine. And this is going to work." He lifted his head, and his markings started to show. "There's a good place to fade in on the roof. Tyrus gets Epsilon to the gate. He will be so focused on Kenzie that he won't realize what's happening before it's too late. I swoop in and grab him. You guys isolate and eliminate his men." His wings unfurled from his back, and he rubbed his palms together to ease his nerves. "Let's get this done. Which means you, Tyrus, need to take Kenzie to him."

Reno stepped over to Kenzie. His vision went red as Sundown surfaced. They would work in tandem to up their odds of success. "Please don't make your baby mama hurt me for her Mommy poop getting hurt."

Kenzie rolled her eyes. "She told you? Great, just great." But the small smile given him was welcome, considering the circumstances —a boost Reno needed.

"For the kids. Let's end this war."

"OPEN THE GATES." Epsilon stood and checked his suit when he saw the traitor approaching the gate with McKenzie. Her steps were sluggish, and Tyrus shoved her to get her to walk. She stumbled along and did as she was told. Did he drug her? Jam her powers? It did not matter. She was here.

He exited the warehouse with four of his men following, each heavily armed and prepared. Epsilon reached the gate as it cranked open, and he smiled. "Tyrus. How delightful that you have recovered your loyalty to me. And here I thought it had vaporized with the onset of your hero complex."

Tyrus shoved Kenzie, and she went to her knees. "Whatever." He reached into his pocket and brought out the trinket with Envy trapped inside. Epsilon could see the power frantically beating within the device, trying to escape.

Tyrus held it out to Epsilon. "Now. I've brought you what you wanted. Can I come home?"

❧

"OKAY, let's go. The gates are closing." Reno threw open the van door, but a wash of bright light blinded both him and Marcus. Keepers' powers were useless in the light. Both of their powers shut down. Reno brought an arm up, and he pulled his gun free to fire. A familiar voice yelled for him not to do it. "Jess?"

Suddenly, his brother grabbed Reno and threw him against the van. "What the hell are you thinkin'? Making a deal like this? Are you more insane than the damn power you got inside of your fool head?"

Reno stared at Jess in confusion as the light went out. Standing on the other side of it was Jade. She stood next to Evan, who stood with a dozen attack-geared Recons. "Jade! You told them?" He snarled and took steps toward her, but Jess threw him back against the van.

"I thought…" But Jess cut off Jade's reply with a move to block her from Reno's view.

"No. We found her on the way in, which means Epsilon could

have." But Jade had a look of guilt, and Jess bullshitted to cover that she had been the one to bring him and the others there. Jess motioned to two Wires, and they led Jade back to an armored car. Jess stabbed a finger on Reno's chest. "Someone sent us the news and didn't sign their name for a thank-you card. And a damn good thing, too. Since you and I know you are terrible at decisions. And even worse with plannin' a single thing."

Jess stepped away but kept a hand braced on Reno's chest. He touched his stamp to command the others. "Move in. Get that asshole." His hand pulled away, but he pointed a finger in Reno's face. "You better be glad I talked Bounce into letting me run point on this. He wanted to turn your Keeper ass to dust. So do me a favor and help me go back to my retirement without wasting a few days mourning the loss of your handsome face. You stay out of it. We handle this. You've already done enough."

Beth stepped over wearing SFPD swat gear. "He gets the point, Cowboy. It's time to go." She met Reno's eyes with a look of understanding. Jess's... not so much. The two of them left him standing there. They merged with the others toward the warehouse. Marcus paused but then ran to join the battle. Most likely to make sure Tyrus didn't get caught in the middle.

Reno watched them go. He sagged back against the van and squeezed his eyes shut tight. Opening them, he looked up at the sky. "Sundown. Show me what could happen. What will happen."

Time seemed to slow down in the seconds it took for his dark half to do what he did best. Playing out all the ways this could go down. The right and the wrong. Both bad and good. Epsilon would stand trial. He'd be found guilty. He'd be locked away deep within the High Council's marble halls. Fed fine food and fancy wine. Scheming. Planning. Waiting. And Reno would always carry the fear... escaping.

And as his mind rejoined the flow of time in reality, he knew what he had to do.

32

Epsilon took Kenzie's arm and hauled her up. Her looseness reminded him of a rag doll. Good. Sedated was best until he secured her in the cell built for Jade. Tyrus still held out Envy. When Epsilon reached for the power, he caught movement coming up the winding drive of the building.

Grid. Dozens of them.

He flicked his eyes to Tyrus and smiled as he stepped closer. "Home. Such a figurative word. May Heaven or Hell be yours." He brought his head over to whisper in Tyrus's ear, "Once a traitor, always a traitor."

Shoving Kenzie behind him, he pulled out his pistol and shot Tyrus point-blank in the stomach. The ornament holding Envy hit the concrete, and the glass shattered. The dark power swarmed out to hover protectively over Tyrus, snapping at Epsilon. As Epsilon took Kenzie's arm and pulled her up, the rag-doll façade vanished. Rage-filled eyes met his, and she gave him a feral, deadly smile.

"You invited me, right?" His eyes shifted to a dagger that slid out of the sleeve of her jacket. Lust infused mist began to merge from her skin. "I'm more than ready to play this time, fucker."

They tricked him. His father had warned him this was the part where he dropped his gun and surrendered. But his father would be denied. Epsilon would pay for that betrayal—of that, he had no doubt.

Just like he had known that Kenzie would kill him, and even if she did not succeed, the hulking form of Marcus, running through the fighting force, would. Fuck his father's plans. He would not die for him or whatever schemes the devil had in mind.

Epsilon lifted his gun to aim it at Kenzie's head and walked backward. He knew there were only two ways to kill a Keeper. Bleed out or a well-aimed shot to the head. The latter would sever their brain stem. "I would hate to bring death to you, Kenzie. How would I have another chance for us to play in the future? But I will to save myself. I am Greed, after all. Do you not have a child to welcome into the world?" He smirked. "What would your dancer do without your help?"

She hesitated, which gave Epsilon the opportunity required to escape. He stepped behind the four guards who escorted him to the gate. He barked out an order to block Grid's entrance at all costs. As his forces rushed out to obey, he knew he sealed a death wish with his father. He'd had little intention of obeying, to begin with, but he had planned to enjoy Kenzie before Lucifer carried out the wish.

He entered the building as the battle waged in the parking lot beyond. His façade of calm control ruptured as he let out an angry roar. A table, cluttered with plans of the city, took the brunt of it as he kicked it. Greed roared in Epsilon's head at once, again not getting their denied toy. Epsilon, crazed with it, became aware a second too late to stop from being grabbed and thrown into the darkened warehouse beyond.

"How the *hell* did he get away?" Jess threw his helmet so hard it dented an ambulance being loaded with injured.

Kenzie paced at the entrance of the warehouse, a building being combed from wall to seedy wall to capture Epsilon. A whole cluster of his trained idiot mercs had been cornered. Another half a dozen lay dead on the grounds. Huge puddles of Eater goo were turning to slush, and yet… the son of a bitch had slipped away.

"Where's Reno?"

Jess glanced over at Kenzie as he braced his hands on his knees and looked up the sky. "Probably stomped off having a hissy fit because I told him to stay here." He straightened up and then twisted at the hips to look at the gathered Grid members doing cleanup and evac. "He's probably cryin' in his Kool-Aid somewhere." He scanned the faces of both Grid and San Francisco's finest to realize another face was missing. He grabbed a cop passing by. "Where's Detective Bailey? She in there?"

The man glanced at him before continuing on his way. "I didn't see her."

Fear spiked inside of Jess. He took off running, limping from his bad leg and a new bullet hole next to a fresh, shiny, bleeding stab wound neighboring that. Damn, this was the hardest retirement he had ever heard of. Maybe she worked in there doing documentation. Perhaps, she offered to be one of the cops to stay behind to catalog the dead and dying.

Or maybe…

"Nope. Not going to think that way. Ain't going to give it power." He reached the interior of the warehouse, and it was a mess. Thousands of shell casing littered the floor. Pools and splatters of blood. More than one blast mark from flash grenades and a few real ones. "Bailey. Has anyone seen Detective Bailey?" He did a quick cursory check of those he could see and saw not a sign of dark, short hair, hips he grabbed regularly, and the love of his life.

"She helped in a firefight. But that was during the fight. Haven't seen her since." A young officer pointed a pen down a long hall.

Giving the woman a nod of thanks, Jess held on to the hope she performed her job and nothing more. He refused to believe he'd find her body going cold. He blew out his panic as he passed other personnel traveling down the narrow corridor.

More than a dozen opened doors lined it from end to end, and he caught sight of corpses in the rooms. Some had rotted for a while. Others had just started to bloat. During the search, Jess heard they found documentation of Epsilon performing experiments. Disgusting. Sick ones. Sure, it was pretty much Epsilon's usual bad behavior. But it would never cease to hit Jess sideways at just how sick the man could be.

Jess asked for Beth a few more times. Finally, he was told she was in the last room on the right. He turned the crook of the hall, reached the open door, and froze.

Beth sat on the floor with her back to him. She softly whispered, her head down. Jess couldn't make out what she said.

"Beth?" She looked fine from where he stood. He entered the room and saw a produce box, a soft pink blanket draped over the side of it. Well, mostly pink, from what he could tell, beneath the dirt and stains.

When he reached Beth, he could see she held something in her arms. "Beth, darlin'?" He kept his voice calm and moved slowly so as not to make her skittish. He circled to sit on his haunches in front of her.

She held a baby.

A tiny, little bit of a child who sucked on his wife's knuckle. Beth's face was down, and her mouth moved as she spoke to the baby. A shock of red hair on the baby's head showed above the swaddle of Beth's jacket. Blue eyes blinked when the baby noticed him.

Something about seeing Beth sitting there as she held that baby had Jess going forward to his knees. He'd imagined this type of scene a million times. Dreamed about it even more. Of what it would be like to see his wife hold a baby... his baby.

And while this baby was most *definitely* not his, Jess also imagined this must be what it was like for any man to see his love and marriage come full circle. An absolutely gut-twisting fear, heavy with weighted anxiety, a heart about to burst with emotions.

Beth's pretty face was soft. Jess could tell her heart landed in the same place as his. For a baby, not even theirs.

"Beth," Jess whispered, afraid to break the spell. Reality would come crashing in. He'd find out he had taken a hit to the head. None of this had been real. He'd wake up in one of the ambulances or back at HQ medical. He'd have to resist telling Beth about this amazing, baffling dream. Jess had them often—dreams of holding their baby, showing his son or newest daughter how to ride a horse, being there for the first diaper and bottle. All the things he forced himself to miss with Sophia. This could not be real. It had to be another wishful dream. How could it be otherwise? A baby in this place full of death and destruction. A fresh life, surviving sick and perverted games.

"Cowboy." Beth's trembling voice brought Jess out of his disbelief.

He focused on her face, and reality reinstated itself. But it didn't change a damn thing. Beth's tears cascaded down her cheek. A streak of one made a path through a blood splatter on her cheek. "She was just in here. In a box. All alone and crying." She swallowed and began gently rocking the child. "She was crying. Screaming her lungs out all alone. I picked her up, and she stopped." Beth's hazel eyes darted up to Jess's and then back to the baby. "I put her down, and she started crying again. I think he just left her to die. I don't know."

Jess reached out to twist a small baby beaded bracelet on the infant's wrist. His thumb stroked over the letters engraved in each bead. "Mira," he whispered the name and brought his eyes up to Beth's. "Her name is Mira."

His hand moved to gently brush over that red hair, and those big blue eyes met his again. "Howdy, little nugget." When her fingers, all tiny five of them, wrapped around his one, his heart did another thing he had always imagined.

It fell completely. Totally, without a flip or flop, into the kind of fierce emotions of a man wanting to keep his wife and their baby safe.

And loved.

33

Jade had never seen a real gun battle, never witnessed bodies laid out. Groaning. Bleeding and dying. War was something that had never touched her life.

Until tonight.

She still felt the cold fear when the all-clear was announced. Medical was requested immediately to the warehouse grounds. The two Wires enlisted to keep her safe inside the armored car during the battle left it to stand outside. Jade used the opportunity to dash out of the passenger door. Frantic as she ran, she tried to reach Envy. "Please. Do you know where Tyrus is? Envy!"

The dark power shushed her. *Child, you don't want to see all this. It was a bloodbath. Do not come up the hill.*

There was zero comfort in Envy's words. Her motherly tone gave no solace. "I need to find him!" Jade screamed the words as she reached the broken gates. The sight in front of her halted her going forward. It was horrific. And somewhere, in all that horror, was the man she wanted to fall in love with.

If this war ever allowed them to.

As paramedics rushed by her, Jade didn't need to check for the Grid stamp, small and discreet, anywhere on them. Human heroes with mundane jobs, moonlighting while fighting the Grid's battles. Jade held zero doubt Bounce ran it as an efficient, secured Grid operation.

She followed the two men who carried a stretcher, hoping they led her to where the injured were taken, hoping that she would find Tyrus there rather than the opposite side of the lot where bodies were being placed and covered with a sheet.

"Tyrus!" She skirted past men and women in handcuffs—an obvious clue to which side they had fought on. She arrived at another row of wounded, and her hope was about to crumble until a hand grabbed her arm. She screamed in alarm only to be pulled against a chest.

A broad chest with solid, strong arms attached that wrapped around her, and warmth, greater than a human—Tyrus.

She fisted his shirt and broke out into sobs. The force of emotions shook both of them. Or perhaps an earthquake shook under their feet. The planet's moorings loosened by all the blood that soaked under its skin from the dead. "I thought…" She choked out, "I thought…"

"I know, Princess. I know." He tried to step back, but Jade wouldn't let him. She needed him close. There, with her. His hand combed over her hair as he brought his head down to press his lips over her ear. "I'm bleeding all over you."

Jade's head snapped up and let out a scream for help as he crumpled to the ground at her feet.

That had been two hours ago. Jade had ridden with Tyrus in the ambulance. She held one hand while Marcus held the other. When they arrived, Tyrus was triaged and rushed into surgery. It had taken an hour to dig out the bullet and repair the damage done in its path. Now, she and Marcus resumed their vigil next to Tyrus bed in HQ medical—she held one of his hands and Marcus the other. Just like in the ambulance.

Jade must have dozed off. When Marcus pressed his hand gently on her head, she sat up, startled.

"It's okay, Jade. You stay here with him. I am needed for debriefing. He will want one of us here." Marcus gave her a soft smile and nodded. "He would want you here. As do I." He then bent down and placed a kiss on her forehead. Jade felt tears at the tenderness of it. Her father had done that before bedtime when she was very young. Marcus did it now, and it offered her as much calming assurance as it had then. She missed it.

"Hey, Princess."

Jade turned her head to find Tyrus had awoken. His hazed gaze from the pain killers and hand squeezing around hers buoyed her strength, even with its weakness.

"Hi. You got shot." She moved to sit on the edge of the bed to press a palm against his forehead. "You scared me." She let out a tearful laugh. "Please, don't get yourself shot again."

Tyrus smiled. "Ah, Jade. I've been shot before. It's a thing." He smirked. "It will most likely happen again."

How he could be so flippant about it, Jade would never understand. But the fact that he could have her throwing herself down to hug him tight—until he grunted in pain. She still held him tight but was more careful about it. "Never let me go, Tyrus." She punched him in the shoulder, and he grunted again. "And at least *try* not to get shot."

"Too late, Princess," he stated with a grimace. "Guess they didn't tell you I got shot twice, huh?"

Jade looked down to where her fist hit to see a bandage. She squeaked and jerked to sit up. He dared to laugh at her unintentional disregard for his injuries. She could not help but smile through her tears. "Asshole."

Tyrus barked a laugh in surprise. "First, an f-bomb and now a-hole?" He shook his head in amusement. "Wow, my girl has spunk." He pulled her back down to cuddle. "Damn," he stated with a whistle of appreciation. "But I already knew you were. You should let it come out more often. I like it." He then kissed Jade to show her how much. And she liked that.

❧

"WE HAVE NINE INJURED. But no fatalities on Grid's side. We have a body count of eight on the other side, which we are working on identifying. But considering the real ones are most likely buried under layers of fake ones, it will take some time. We have contained seven of Epsilon's mercs in security. Medical was dispatched to care for their wounds under hot weapon orders." Evan glanced up at Bounce as he continued to read off the stats of the night. "They aren't talking per the usual behavior. But we shall see. We ended about a dozen Eaters by fighter counts but no way to know for sure."

"We have three still in surgery but not for serious injuries. The other six have either been sent home on medical leave or in our recovery." Emma paused, glanced around, and then back down to focus on her report as the head Healer. "The baby that Beth found among the deceased is fairly healthy. Only a few days old, but there were no pregnant women among the dead. So we aren't sure who her mother is." Emma scrolled through digital records on her table. "We did find a written document where, apparently, Epsilon hoped to bond Envy to the baby." Emma pressed her lips together. "His sickness never ceases to amaze me. And not in a good way."

Bounce stood in the comms room with the two of them. He knew why Emma's attention was torn. She was split between doing her duty and worrying about her husband, whose stamp was offline. And she kept touching her own on the back of her neck. He knew she hoped their fuse could be felt. His vitals, such as they were with being a Keeper, indicated he had not become less than his current state. Keepers were already dead. Bounce nor anyone knew where they went next. However, Reno remained on the realm of the living. He just did not want to be found.

Emma had told Bounce she knew of the Keeper's plans. She also said that Reno had promised to tell him about it, to seek Bounce's approval, or they wouldn't do it. Bounce had spent the last two hours on the phone with the deputy mayor of San Francisco. He assured his contacts within the city's government that the attack on the warehouse *had been* sanctioned by him—even though no prior authorization had been obtained from them to do so per official protocol. If he had to say "urgent action" one more fucking time to cover for this shit show, he would have a stroke.

Evan passed the tablet to Bounce when Emma suddenly broke away and rushed to the opposite side of the room. All turned to observe the commotion. She had run over to throw her arms around her husband.

"Take this." Bounce thrust the tablet back against Evan's chest. The man tried to stop him, but Bounce was laser-focused on the Keeper. Reno looked fine. He did have a cut and bruise on his cheek, and a possible black eye. Nothing compared to those of the Grid having surgery that very minute.

Bounce reached the couple and said Emma's name sternly. She turned, and her mouth opened to appeal. It would have been wasted breath, and he moved her carefully to the side. Bounce's fist came up, swung wide, and sent the Keeper careening into the wall with a punch. Gasps sounded, and yells of alarm could be heard. Emma grabbed Bounce's arm only to be pulled free by Jess, lifting her off her feet. She continued to scream in protest to stop. Good thing Jess had the foresight to keep her back. Bounce was not even close to being done.

Bounce bent over to haul Reno up. The ascent continued when he wrapped a hand around the Keeper's throat and lifted him off the floor. "You and your insane need to cause me and mine continued aggravation and danger has come to an end." If the man had been a rag doll, Reno's head would have wobbled off with the force Bounce shook him with.

"Why? Have I not given you everything you needed as a member of the Grid? I rewrote the rules for you! Accepted you and the others without a bat of an eye." Bounce let him go and didn't care if the man landed on his feet. "You are suspended for thirty days. Without pay. Without benefits. Without a goddamn thing."

Reno hit the floor upright and stood there without saying a word. It was good that he did because Bounce would have bashed his face against the wall. And the other wall. The floor. And possibly the ceiling.

"If I so much as *hear* your name in my presence during that time, I will suspend whoever dared to speak it." He stepped close to the Keeper, his lips curling off his fangs as he narrowed his eyes. "And he got away. *All* of this was for *nothing!*" Adding a hard shove, Bounce turned on his heel and left.

❧

"WHERE WERE YOU?"

Reno sat in medical, hands cupped over the back of his head and eyes downcast to focus on the floor in silence. He hadn't said a damn thing. Jess found his behavior real odd. After Jess pulled Emma back to give Bounce his pound of flesh, he figured Reno would fight back. Given some excuse or even tried to defend any of this.

But nope. Reno stayed silent from the time he arrived. Kept mum when Emma led her husband here to medical to check over his injures. Quiet to right now as they sat in the hall to wait on the others.

"I asked, where were you, Reno? Where did you go?" Jess moved to sit next to his brother and looked sideways at him. "You weren't hurt. You look like you went a couple of rounds. But you weren't in the fight with us." He angled his head to try to get a read off Reno's expression—if there had been one, which there wasn't. "Reno..." He put a hand on the man's shoulder. "Talk to me." Something felt off, way off. And the longer Reno remained silent, the surer of it Jess became.

"He got away. You know that, right? But no one died on our side.

And you know Bounce. Take the thirty days. Give him time, and he'll get over it, little brother." Jess thought about little Mira and smiled. "There was this baby. In the warehouse. You should have seen Beth with her. It was something..."

That elicited a subtle response from Reno. He turned his head to look at Jess. His mouth opened to say something finally.

"Guys! It's Lana!"

Both of them looked up to see Kenzie rush into the hall. She looked more frantic than she had been earlier facing down her biggest fear, Epsilon. She was turning left and right but going nowhere at the same time. It would have been hilarious, except she looked about as panicked as a person could look. "She's in labor! They're bringing her here! Oh, my god."

Jess was on his feet to rush over. "That's great!" Kenzie pitched forward, and Jess caught her before she face-planted the floor. "Are you going to faint? Baby Jesus in a tub of Jell-O. Head between your knees, badass." He laughed and looked behind him.

Reno was gone.

34

"Is it supposed to hurt this much?"

If Emma could count how many times couples asked that question during labor and delivery, she could give up her Grid paycheck. She gave Kenzie and Lana a smile and nodded to assure them both. "It does. And should." She placed her hand over the fetal monitor strapped to Lana's belly and checked her vital signs. "Everything is great. We're doing well."

Lana was fully dilated, and a contraction coursed its way. The former ballerina was doing surprisingly well after her water broke and six hours of labor. Dawn touched the sky above the facility. They would all be both exhausted but happy when the baby was born and could take some well-earned rest, especially considering the battle that had taken place last night. Not to mention the events Emma knew had transpired but didn't know the details of. But she forced herself to once again not worry about where Reno was or what he was doing. Her job had to take priority. A baby needed her. Delivering babies was Emma's favorite thing to do. She brushed Lana's hair away from her sweat-covered brow and smiled. "It's time, Lana. I'm going to need you to push, okay?"

Kenzie met Emma's eyes for a moment. The gaze held the same

as other partners. Helplessness. A paralyzing fear that something would go wrong. All well-founded emotions. After all, pregnant women and children were the highest priority targets for Epsilon. The three heavily armed men guarding medical were due to that man's evilness. Emma could not help but wonder if that measure would not be needed if Epsilon had been caught last night.

Dang it, Emma, she thought to herself. She needed to focus.

"Okay, let's bring a baby into the world."

❧

"SHE'S BEAUTIFUL." Emma quietly entered the medical suite, where Lana slept in the bed.

Kenzie slowly walked the room as she held her newborn daughter. Exams, footprints, blood work, and all the required procedures completed. So far, so good. A healthy and normal baby.

Kenzie looked up at Emma's whisper and smiled. "She is, isn't she? So fucking tiny. I keep thinking I'm going to break her." She brought the infant up to kiss her on the forehead. "I wish she would have told us she was a girl before this. I admit that I've got a long fucking list of boy names. Not girl ones."

"Stop cussing around our baby, Snap."

Both she and Kenzie looked back at Lana. Emma chuckled to find the woman still asleep.

"Damn, I mean dang. She's bitching, I mean, shit..." Kenzie gave up. "In her sleep at me." She chuckled, but the humor didn't last as her smile vanished. She looked over at Emma and sighed. "No word, huh?" She sucked on her fangs and hissed. "I'm going to kick his ass. He promised to be here. For me. And for this." She jerked her head up when she realized how that might have wounded Emma. "I mean, sorry."

Understanding, Emma smiled as she stood next to Kenzie. She reached out with one hand to touch the baby's soft cheek. The other splayed over her growing baby belly. Yeah, she and Kenzie were once at complete, angry odds with each other. Not only had the Keeper fed Reno when he was close to bleeding out, but Emma had a very difficult time understanding and forgiving the link via their powers. The draw of her husband to another woman—responsible for it or not—was a tough one to swallow and accept. "That's in the past. But I agree. He should have been here. He would have loved it. He should have been here for us both."

"You need to find him." Kenzie laid the baby in the bassinet by the bed. When Lana's hand reached for them both, she placed it on their daughter. Watching as Lana settled, Kenzie nodded her chin toward the door, and Emma followed her into the hall.

"You need to go find him—wherever he is. Something's wrong. Off." Kenzie leaned against the wall and kicked a combat boot up to rest on its toe as she crossed her arms. "It can't just be the fact that Bounce jumped his ass, Emma. That's happened a dozen times. Sometimes, all in one day." She frowned. "I'm worried. And not because of..." She rolled her eyes. "I'm worried because he's my friend. And something is just not sitting right with me. About him."

Emma chewed on her bottom lip as Kenzie spoke the very thoughts Emma attempted to keep at bay all night. Now that the delivery was complete and the baby safe, worry took over. She could no longer be distracted from it. She needed to deal with it. "I know. It's not just you. The fact he left when you said Lana was in labor, that's enough to worry that something is wrong. I'm told he wasn't in the battle, but he was beaten up. I skimmed the reports, and he was not seen in that warehouse. Nor after." She brought a finger up to vex its nail with her teeth. "I've had my stamp open all night. It's still open. Our fuse, too. There's no chatter of him being sighted or returning."

She looked over at Kenzie and found the woman's lavender eyes full of compassion and understanding. "I just want to know what happened between that battle breaking out and him showing up here." Emma brought her hand up to tug on her ponytail and tuck loose strands of hair behind her ear. "I don't even know where to look. Or if he even wants me to."

Kenzie pulled Emma into an uncharacteristic hug. If asked a year ago if she would have tolerated it, Emma would have said "heck no." But right now, it was perfectly timed and wanted.

"Think, Emma. No one knows him better than you. When he's lost, where would he go?" Kenzie pulled back and smiled at her. "That's where he is."

❧

RENO WOULD BE PISSED that Emma waved off her usual security to go home, but she'd deal with his anger later. Emma pulled up at the house and let out a weary exhale as she rested her forehead on the steering wheel. Her rounded belly with their twins barely fitting under it gave her a calm she desperately needed. Almost as much as she needed to find her husband.

Entering the dark house, she was relieved that Jade and Lily took the kids to their home to watch over that morning. She dropped her keys on the table by the door as she slid out of her jacket and shoes. "Reno?"

Emma moved quietly through the house. She should have been on alert—Epsilon had been tricked and cornered. Reno and their family were often the targets of his wrath. She glanced over to see the alarm system still engaged, her stamp acting as a token that allowed access. It confirmed no danger waited in the empty rooms.

She moved toward the master bedroom and saw the door cracked. She pushed it open fully with her foot. "Reno?" She turned on the bedside lamp and let out a relieved breath to see he sat in the corner. "Candyman…"

She walked over and went to her knees in front of him. He sat with his back against the wall, knees drawn up against his chest. His arms were wrapped tight around his legs with his head lowered between them.

Emma reached out to tenderly brush her fingers through his soft hair and whispered his name again. No response. When she said it a third time, he moved. Still curled up, he laid his head in her lap, his face pressing against her baby bump. She wanted to cry with how lost he seemed. "I'm here. I'm right here." She continued to comb her fingers in his hair while the other hand rubbed his back. "Their baby is fine. A beautiful baby girl. Healthy and as she should be." She kept her voice a soft, calm whisper, the type used to soothe a wounded animal to gain its trust. Afraid it would flee before it could be cared for. "We'll go see her later. For now, let's just be right here."

Reno's arms curled around her. Emma felt his skin warm and his heart start to beat. She felt each beat with her own. His body trembled as the tension began to leave it.

Emma was unsure how long they sat there, but the soft morning light began to creep across the floor through the windows overlooking the bay. Reno might have fallen asleep. He breathed slow and deep as if he had.

Emma wouldn't have moved if the house caught on fire. When he finally stirred, she watched him intently as he sat up in front of her. She reached out and palmed his cheek, brushing her thumb over a bruise on his cheek. His eyes swung to hers. They were focused and clear.

That worry of something being off had retreated a little, but it returned to gnaw under the edges of her exhaustion. "Where were you? Where did you go?" She searched his eyes. Usually, she could find love and safety in her husband's gaze. But this time, there lurked something else. Something Emma didn't recognize. "Reno. What did you do?"

He leaned forward and moved one hand to hers, where it splayed over the twins. He brought his forehead to rest against hers, met her eyes, and said softly, "What I had to do."

35

It had been three weeks since the failed Epsilon capture mess, and things at the Grid were falling back into its usual cadence. Bounce worked most days at HQ and spent nights at the club until dawn—then started the routine over again.

Epsilon had gone quiet. He had not been sighted since the battle.

His men were still contained in the security area at HQ. Some had begun to realize that they would stay there until Bounce saw fit to change that. Human ones had wives, children, and life beyond working for the wrong side. Each had a heartbreaking story of why they accepted the job and payment from Epsilon—but Bounce was not in a forgiving mood.

Yet.

Reno Sundown had one week of leave remaining and took Bounce's threat to heart. He had not seen the Keeper since that night. Marcus, once again, ran the Keepers and the squad that assisted that class of beings. Jade quickly developed into a useful resource with not only her intelligence but a willingness to be of value, so she and Envy trained to learn to fight. He had no worries about her proving herself. He still felt concerned about her relationship with Tyrus. They, in turn, assured him they understood the consequences. He could do nothing more in regard to that. Destiny would deal whatever it dealt—he could do nothing to prevent it.

He regarded the form his fingers tapped on, and he picked up his pen to sign it. Jess and Beth Bailey wanted permission to adopt the infant found in Epsilon's facility. That, along with the birth of Lana and Kenzie's daughter, had been the only bright spots as of late. He approved the adoption and shoved it, along with the pen, away from him.

Children were everywhere. And soon, two more would be added to that number when Emma gave birth.

Bounce had tried to ask her if Reno had any additional intel from the battle. She said no. Apparently, she just as baffled as he that her husband had nothing to say. Nor did Reno wish to discuss it. Odd. So fucking odd. Bounce stood, and his phone lit up with an encrypted message. Opening it, he found a snapped photo of a little boy with dark brown hair, olive skin, and eyes of blue. That could also be green. Or orange. Or even red—when angered.

Like his father.

Lacy did that sometimes. She would catch their son with a smile or a good shot of him playing with other children and send it to Bounce. No message. No salutations. Nothing. That had been at Bounce's request. It was his greatest desire to keep her safe and their child a secret. Aside from Evan, who covered for Bounce when he went to watch the goddess and Ryker from afar like a pitiful creeper, no one else knew.

It's where he should have been that very afternoon.

And he had missed going the week before that.

And the one before that... and on and on.

"Not fair." Bounce's frustration bubbled up, mixed with his loneliness, and spewed outward in action. He swept everything off his desk. The phone was sent flying and shattered on the wall. The desk was his next target. He gripped the side of it and flipped it airborne. An overburdened bulletin board took the next blow and clattered to the floor. Pushpins, papers, and other items scattered to join the mess. He raged and yelled until the club's office appeared as if a tornado had swirled within its walls. Club Bounce doors were locked during the day, opening late at night for those who sought pulsing music and other means of escape in their lives.

A life Bounce found less and less escape from himself.

Bounce let out a frustrated yell as he seethed. He rested his hands on his hips, blood dripping from his knuckles. He fixated his eyes on the ceiling above as his emotions drained to where they had to be kept. It was not often he lost his shit, and he could repair the damage done with a snap of his fingers. Restore everything in its place in a blink and manifest any items destroyed.

But not this time. Bounce needed to burn this frustration by performing something physical and busy. Other immortals used sex. But sex was something Bounce avoided.

Instead, he spent the next hour cleaning up the rubble and putting things back in their proper place. He'd need a new desk. There were plenty at HQ that he could have sent to the club. He scooped up his broken phone and passed his hand over the glass. It instantly returned to its undamaged state with the picture of Ryker, smiling, on the screen.

He stared at it until it welcomingly meshed into his gray matter. Then he hit delete, and it vanished from the phone. He never kept any of the photos. He couldn't risk being hacked—secured or not. He had lost Tanya and their baby. He would not lose Lacy and Ryker.

Picking up the two large black contractor bags of rubble, he walked through the dark club and out of the service entrance to the alley behind the large three-storied brick building. Opening the dumpster, he dropped them in and was about to go home to his apartment on the third story when he heard a whimper.

He crouched down and saw some sort of light-gray animal hiding under the dumpster. "What are you?" The animal cowered to move as far as it could when Bounce attempted to touch it. Bounce could see it shook in fear. Standing, he moved the dumpster, and the animal attempted to scurry away. When it did, Bounce was able to catch it by the scuff to hold at arm's length in front of him.

"You are a dog, which is good. I am not sure how I would have handled it if I picked up a city rat who likes to drink our stale beer and discarded trash pretzels." The dog was scruffy, some sort of poodle-terrier mix. And now that Bounce was able to see it in a better light, it was not gray but white under the grime and dirt. He pulled it closer to hold in one arm and saw a green leather collar on the dog's neck with a name tag.

"Murphy. What an odd name for a dog." He looked down at the dog and smiled at the fellow's big brown eyes and half-folded ears. And an adorably amusing big black bop worthy nose. "Are you lost, Murphy?"

The dog was wearing a shirt, and it was clear someone loved the animal a great deal. But now the dog could not find his home, or perhaps his home was no more. Murphy issued a quirky yip and licked Bounce's nose. Bounce laughed, and the weight of stress about all he had and could not have melted away.

"Well, consider yourself found." He scratched the dog's head and turned to reenter the club. "Do you enjoy video games? Should I lecture you not to chew on Rubik's Cubes or piss in my shoes?" The dog cocked his head. His ears even perked as if he understood human. Bounce smirked. "I am glad you aren't scared of me," he whispered. "Many are. But no need to be frightened of me, my furry new friend. You can stay. Because, here in our world, the good ones live forever." He opened the door of the club, and as it swung closed behind them, he said, "Welcome to the Grid."

"YOU'RE JADE, RIGHT?"

Jade sat in the cafeteria of Edge Academy. The very same school her grandmother had tried to buy admittance to, and the one where Envy had sought help. It was also where Jade met Tyrus. The doors had since opened, and Jade thought it the most amazing place she had ever been.

However, she did not attend as a student. She held a job as a teacher's assistant. The position allowed her to do her training—learning about Grid operations with the other students—while assisting Lily and the teachers. She snuck moments with Tyrus as he continued working security at the school. Jade was the happiest she had ever been. Even Envy had settled into their life now. The power was learning how to giggle. Yes, giggle.

Jade looked up at the young girl who appeared around ten years old and smiled. The girl had dark, curly hair and light brown eyes. Sun-kissed skin with freckles across her nose made it clear she spent time outside, unlike most kids her age. She even wore scuffed cowboy boots below a red polka dot sundress. "I am Jade Shen. And you are?"

The girl smiled, and without asking permission, she took a seat across from Jade. "I'm Sophia Bailey. And I heard about you! My candy daddy told me about you." The girl rested her chin on her upraised hands and wrinkled her nose. "You're the new Keeper. That's so cool. And you get to live with my Aunt Lily. That is also cool. She has the best books."

As Sophia babbled on, Jade became enchanted by the girl as she spoke in a rambling manner. Jade wondered if any breath held a chance to happen between one statement to the next. "Bailey. As in Jess Bailey?" Jade's jaw dropped. "You're the daughter of Jess and Reno. Your mother is Emma, correct?" Now that Jade knew, it was impossible not to see in Sophia's features those of Emma and Jess. She was pretty like Emma, but her nose came from her father, and she had his eyes. But the babbling way of speaking in rapid verbal fashion—definitely Reno.

"I am! I have one mommy. Two daddies. A brother. And going to have two more somethings." Sophia rolled her eyes. "We don't know what they are—boys or girls—just that there are two of them in Mommy's tummy. Like kittens." Sophia sat forward and clasped her hands together on the table between them. "So, what can you do?"

Jade raised a brow and gave the girl a puzzled look. "Do? As in my job here?"

Sophia giggled. "No. Powers. Keepers have the coolest powers. Marcus has puppies." She gave Jade a proud look. "He says I'm the only one allowed to pet them. Well, me and Eli. Brotherrsss. Gosh." But Jade could tell Sophia loved him and just kidded. "Kenzie has the prettiest purple flowers. And my daddy, he's the best Keeper. He was the very first one. He has Sundown. But I get to call him Sundy. Oh, and Madness. And wings! I love his wings." She looked up, deep in thought. "I wonder if I will get wings? Maybe when I become a grown-up, I'll get them. That would be so cool. I would fly around and go places..."

Jade let out a delighted laugh. The little girl had verbally wandered off as Reno often did. "Wings would be nice."

Sophia blinked and brought her focus back to Jade. "Oh, yes. Powers. What are yours?"

Jade laughed again, and Sophia met it with a wide smile. So precocious and fun. "Well, uh..." Jade looked around, unsure if she was allowed. She knew that they were all here from Grid families. Some were the offspring of supernatural parents, and many had inherited the same generational powers as them. But Jade had hidden Envy for so long that it felt strange to be so open now.

"I can do magic," Sophia said as she sat back and appeared very proud of herself. "I got that from my mommy." She held her hand out, and her lips moved in silence. The apple from Jade's tray floated up in the air and spun.

Jade's eyes widened, and she clapped. "That is amazing!"

Sophia stood to take a bow. And, apparently, forgot about the apple. It fell, hit Jade's plate with a very loud thump, and splashed in the gravy. "Oops. I forget the ending part sometimes." Both of them laughed.

Jade wanted to fit in with this new world. But the memories of being bullied and harmed for being different were still fresh in her mind. She looked up to see Tyrus.

He gave her that butterfly-inducing smile and mouthed, "You can do it, Princess," from across the room. Lily and Jess stood at the entrance, and they both gave her encouraging smiles.

She nodded and lifted her right hand, where a new bracelet for Envy circled her wrist. Bounce had created a second one after the first had broken. "Envy, would you like to say hello?"

Of course, child. I love children.

Green power mist swam out of bracelet and began to take form. A jade dragon appeared, then flew up and swept over the cafeteria. Every single child and adult watched it, enthralled as Envy twisted and turned. Envy came back to the table and settled on the end, curling up like a cat, complete with a tail sweeping the air like a happy cat.

All the kids ran over to "Ooh" and "Ahh" over the show and introduce themselves to Jade and Envy.

Sophia Bailey elbowed her way through them all and grabbed Jade's hand. The little girl proclaimed in a very possessive way, "Get back. She's my best friend. Gosh."

AND… BEFORE THE END

Reno avoided taking the trip on the sightseeing boat from the shore across the bay to Alcatraz Island for more than a week. Between getting Eli and Sophia started at the Academy and getting the nursery ready for the twins, he kept busy during his suspension from work. But, to be perfectly honest, the real reason he delayed was he just didn't want to do it. He stood on the bow, his head back and eyes closed as the mist from the bay touched his chilled skin. He held a bag as he disembarked with the tourists. A guide began speaking into a bullhorn for the tour to begin.

Reno didn't need the tour. And if asked for a ticket, he would be found not having one. He let the group wander their way down the cracked cement as he stepped behind the building. He swung a rusted cover off a new high-tech keypad and entered the code to unlock a deceptively rusty new iron door, created to blend into the age and architect of the old building. He glanced around to make sure he could enter unseen and closed the door behind him.

He faded to the lowest level and appeared in the long hallway deep under the old jail. One light after the other came on as he walked. He purposely left them turned off since his last visit. He swung the bag and started to whistle as he journeyed to the last cell.

It was unoccupied three weeks ago.

That wasn't the case now.

Keying in another code, a partition in the thick ballistic glass door opened. He tossed in the bag and leaned against the glass as he shut the opening. "Food. Water. You're welcome."

Reno didn't even flinch when the prisoner threw himself against the door.

Epsilon looked much different now. His designer suit was grimy. The jacket of it was bunched up after being used as a pillow on the bare cot. The once white dress shirt was spotted with both blue and black blood. A white beard had begun to grow, but its progression was uneven due to the grotesque scarring on the man's face. The bruises they both wore when they fought in the warehouse were faded. A fight Reno won—obviously.

When Epsilon grabbed the bag and scurried away, Reno smiled. Epsilon's condition made all three of him happy. He watched the man rip into the food and down a bottle of water so fast it dribbled on the floor. He felt smugly satisfied at the thought of Epsilon sitting in the dark. In the cold. No sound. Nothing.

For weeks.

"What is your plan, freak?" Epsilon snarled around bites of his sandwich as he crouched in the corner. His eyes bore into Reno with such hatred, but that was okay. Reno was pretty sure Epsilon found the same in his.

"Oh, freak? Do you think that word bothers me? Nope. Nothing you say impacts at all. It's just mouth vomit. Yada. Yada. Yada." Reno lowered himself to his haunches and cocked his head to the side. "Oh, I have plans for you. The first was making sure you suffered. Making sure you didn't get put in a fancy holding cell at the High Council and fed grapes and treated like a celebrity. I accomplished that." Reno slowly smiled and showed his fangs within its curving spread. "No one knows you're here. In fact, no one even knows this place exists. It's just you, me, Sundown, and Madness."

Epsilon lunged toward the door, and Reno stood. The glass was the only thing between them. Reno could smell the stench of the bastard through the small holes they spoke through.

Epsilon sneered. It made his face contort into a strange smile. "You are nothing. You have no spine. You have no balls. You have no courage. You think you scare me? No. Leave me to rot. I'm immortal. I'm going nowhere. Feed me no food. Let me starve, yet I will not die. But one day, I will escape. You know that, right, freak?" He slammed his palm against the glass. "And I will get your wife. Your children. And my toy. And I'll make you watch while I rape them. Slaughter them in front of you. I will make you pay for this."

Reno's smile remained. In the past, Epsilon's threats would have got under his skin. Sent him into a frantic panic as he waited for when they'd be carried out. But that was before he gained the position to make them.

And carry them out.

"Really? You see, I kind of thought you'd say that." Reno brought his palm up, and black wisps formed a ball of Madness to float above his hand. "I'm not a freak. I am not nothing. I am something who captured you. I'm the Keeper of Madness, the good side to Sundown's bad. I'm a father. I'm a husband. And I'm a friend. And you aren't going anywhere. We both know that."

Epsilon's eyes slid to regard Madness. "You can't do a thing with your power here. It's jammed. I already tried, and Greed can do nothing." He laughed. "You don't even know your own design! Stop boring me with your useless tactics."

Reno returned with a laugh of his own. "Oh, I do. It's why I had it engineered to allow mine. But only mine."

Epsilon paled and backed up. "Wait. Let's discuss this." He chanced a step back to the glass in desperation. "We could become partners. You're right. I am impressed by all that you have done. You outsmarted and defeated me. Imagine if we joined forces? Turned our combined abilities and desires on him? Take his throne." His voice took on the edge of pleading yet still attempted to sound important. Superior. It all rang as bullshit to Reno, but Epsilon continued in the effort.

"I want nothing of the world of mankind. It is yours. I just want Hell, a realm that should have been mine, not yours. You don't want it. Give it to me. Together we can control them both. The war will end." Epsilon took another step back as Reno keyed the code to open the panel. "I promise. You have my vow that your children, your wife..." He took another step back. "I'll leave Kenzie and the rest alone. Think about it!"

Reno paused and met Epsilon's eyes. "I have. I have thought about it all for so long. And each time you hurt someone I loved, one of my friends, I thought about it some more. And this is what I have decided to do." The panel opened, and Reno put his hand inside to release Madness. Epsilon stumbled away, but the wall behind him did not allow him to get far. "First, Madness is going to have some fun. He's going to burrow inside of you. Burn through every pore of your body until he crawls under your skin and claws into your brain. He will destroy and feed on Greed and hollow you out. Until you are nothing more than an empty man."

Epsilon desperately sought to find an escape, some crack not found before, but Reno knew there were none.

"And then, when he's fed and bloated with your power, it's going to be Sundown's turn. He's going to feed his way on your pain by beating, ripping, and torturing you. Making you scream and beg. Bleed and cry. He's very good at that." Reno gave him a deadly smile, baring his fangs. "And you will feel it all. Without any help of your power to take it away."

Epsilon glared at him. "You are insane. This isn't you. You are the happy, fun one!" The man spat the words out with a yell. "You are not smart enough to end me! Your plan will fail because *you are a failure!"*

Reno clicked his tongue, and Madness began to expand inside the cell. He brought his hand up to wag a finger right before he closed the panel with a slam. "Tsk-tsk. Now see, you make the same mistake as everyone else. You underestimate me. Write me off as not smart. Or unable to have the upper hand. I know everyone believes that. And it's to my advantage." He rested his shoulder on the glass and crossed his arms on his chest. "But you interrupted me, gosh. I wasn't finished telling my plan."

He turned his head and met Epsilon's eyes. The smile vanished, and he spoke with a growl through his fangs. "When Sundown is done, when you are left as a beaten, sack of wasted flesh, I'm going to have my time. I am going to make sure you feel every bit of fear you ever made my Witch feel. Be scared of the bad things like my kids have. Over. And over again. And then, we might start all over again." He pushed away from the wall and lifted his chin. "And if you beg to die and think it might happen, it won't." Reno turned on his heel to go and left Madness there to start the fun. "I know how to bring people back from the dead. It's not that hard. So you won't be dying."

"You think you know everything, freak! I bet you don't." Epsilon tried one last tactic as Reno reached the end of the hall, the lights going off as he walked.

Reno frowned and looked back over his shoulder toward the cell. Epsilon was pressed against the glass, the view already almost obscured as Madness spread out to feed.

Epsilon smiled. "He's your father. Lucifer. You are his son. Not mine," Epsilon spoke with a snarl. "You are my brother. And he's lied to you. Because he knows it."

Reno faced forward and swallowed. He tried to reason the purpose of Epsilon's reveal. Could it be true? Could it be? There was something about the way Epsilon said it. The way Lucifer had been in Heaven all those years ago when he helped Reno become a Keeper.

He knew it had been no desperate tactic.

You may not want to know this, but that has a one hundred percent of being fucking true.

It wasn't a lie. Epsilon spoke the truth.

It changed everything—except what was about to happen to the man. Reno straightened up, shook it off, and keyed in the code to open the door.

It closed behind Reno. But not before Epsilon's laughter at telling the secret abruptly cut off—because it's impossible to laugh when screaming is all you can do.

SNEAK PEEK: CHAOS

AN EXCITING SNEAK PEEK OF BOOK SIX OF THE SHADOW-KEEPERS SERIES

CHAOS: A PRELUDE

THE SHADOW-KEEPERS SERIES: BOOK SIX

"Vadim, I don't think this is a good idea." Valya must have told her brother that a dozen times as they made the way through San Francisco. They now stood in front of a grand mansion in one of the most beautiful neighborhoods she had ever seen. It was not an issue of not trusting her brother's ability to scope out a target for burglary. No, they had been doing petty crimes since they were kids. Her brother had as much talent in their side work as he did their primary. Only recently had they evolved into more illegal activities.

"Do you really want to go to bed hungry?" He had coaxed her to do all their crimes with a promise of onion rings smothered in nacho cheese. She and Vadim were crouched behind a row of topiary hedges. She could tell at one time they had been in the form of animals. But they and the rest of the landscape were overgrown and neglected. "We'll never be able to leave the circus if we don't get some money."

Valya knew her twin brother was right. They were identical in every way except for their genders. Black hair, thick hair from their mother. Bright light gray eyes from their father. Tall and athletic lean after being raised to carry on their family tradition of performing acrobat. They were born into the Circus of Night, a flea-bitten, low-cost circus of various talented performers. Deformed individuals worked the freak show carnival row of it. Their parents, Vadim and Valyria Petrov, had come to America as Russian refugees with no money. And no immigration status. The circus had been willing to harbor them if they worked within the performers" ranks. Their parents were talented acrobats in their home country. Even a part of the Russian Olympic team as teens. They fit easily into the talent pool. At one time, the circus was well maintained, famous, and glamourous, but, over time and with the invention of the internet, social media, and cynic disbelief in all things fantastical, it fell on hard times.

Their parents died from a fire when she and Vadim were only ten years old. That was when they learned the true hold the aging owner and his son had on the family. Their parents had been nothing more than indentured servants. And their children were added to the ownership at birth. Their parents feared deportation; therefore, they had never attempted to get their U.S. citizenship. It was a death sentence to leave as they had. The owner used to reveal them to the authorities as a leash to control them.

The twins were born in the United States—it was simple for them to gain the status of citizens. But it cost money, and Vadim refused to become homeless and broke. Valya wasn't sure if that would be any worse than their lives were now. The owners deducted the pitiful pay the performers received for food, lodging, and "other benefits." At times, if she and her brother missed a performance like she did when she sprained her ankle dismounting the high wire, they owed the circus. The elder owner even deducted from their parent's pay when their mother was unable to perform the last months of her pregnancy. A debt that had gone unpaid even with Vadim Senior working double jobs as performer and laborer.

The twin's housing consisted of a tent, their bathrooms, the porta-potties. They cleaned up in the same water tank the skinny and abused animals drank from. Their kitchen was the mess tent with the others. The meals were often scant and disgusting, but it was better than being homeless, Vadim had stated. Barely, but still. It was something.

The agreement the owners made with them to leave the service with the circus was a joke. Threats of calling the law for stealing and reporting them. Neither twin was sure his threats could be carried out. But they did not want to take the chance. The man demanded an absurd amount of money, one they had no chance of funding, hence the turn to crimes to hoard the cash within the carefully cut pockets in the folds of their sleeping bags.

"Look, I've been coming here every night the past week after performances. The old lady is alone. I never see her leave and no hired staff that I've seen. She paces in front of the windows, talking to herself. She's nuts. I bet she won't even notice a few things are missing." Vadim pointed to the expanse of windows in front of the home. "There she is. See? Walking and talking to herself." He brought his focus back to Valya. "And do I need to remind you that we're leaving San Francisco after the final performance tomorrow night?"

The circus always packed up and left in the middle of the night. Valya wasn't exactly sure why, but it was an easy guess—the owners most likely never paid the ground fees or contracted food carts. They left each city in the dark of night, slinking off to the next quietly, gone before the debts came due to the vendors the following day.

Her brother was right. If they were going to do this, it had to be tonight. "Okay. But remember, we don't hurt the woman." She didn't need to tell her brother that, but she always did. They had both vowed to the other they would never harm anyone in their crimes. So far, they hadn't put themselves in the situation to break the vow.

Handspringing over the hedges, they moved silently to the back door. Valya kept watch as Vadim began to pick the lock, only to find it unlocked. Exchanging glances, they both stepped inside the dim interior. It showed more neglected on the inside than it did on the outside. Trash cluttered the home, unwashed dishes in the sink with shards of busted china on the floor. They crept through the room, careful not to crunch the pieces with their shoes.

Crouching by the kitchen door, they could see the woman pacing. Her hair wild and her pajamas grimy from poor hygiene. Vadim must be right. The woman had lost her mind.

The woman talked to herself—some language Valya didn't recognize, but the woman was clearly of Asian descent, so maybe Chinese or Japanese? It didn't matter. They would do this and go quickly. Vadim nodded and waited as the woman turned her back to them in her pacing. They ran to the stairs and climbed them fast to the top floor.

Valya paused at one bedroom, obviously a teenager's room, but the walls were scrawled with Asian letters. The bed was ripped in two and destroyed. The mirror over the dresser was shattered, streaked with dried blood. God, she hoped whatever kid inhabited that room was long gone and safe. Maybe that's what sent the old woman into insanity.

"Valya. Come on."

Glancing down the hall to where Vadim stood in a second doorway, she nodded and joined him. Stepping into the large master bedroom, she found the mirrors shattered in there and the master bedroom, as well.

Vadim tossed the dresser drawers, and she moved over to a large jewelry armoire in the corner. When she opened the door, she found a mess of bundled chains. She stepped back to see most of the items tossed to the floor. A piece of jade caught her eye, and she bent over to pull it free of the mess. It looked like a dragon pendant, and it hung from a silver chain. Shoving it in her pocket, she squatted down to dig through the mess.

"Shh, she's coming."

At Vadim's warning, they both ducked on the opposite side of the bed as the old woman walked into the room. She tore at her hair and continued to talk to herself as before. She seemed tormented. Valya felt sorry for her.

They tracked the woman as she approached the two French doors that led to a balcony beyond. Vadim stood and took Valya's hand, and they moved downstairs to search for valuables there.

The moment they stood, Vadim jerked Valya back down. She went to question why when something else moved into the room. Something... not a person. Not a pet. But... something.

It looked like a cloud of fog, but fog wasn't green. It didn't make a hissing sound. It almost sounded like whispered words. Vadim appeared just as shocked and confused as she was.

The green fog moved across the room to circle the woman. The hissing became louder. The woman, in turn, spoke to it, her words broken with sobs. She then started ranting, batting her hands at the fog as if it were solid, trying to choke it, fingers clawing at it.

"We should help her," Valya whispered and went to stand again. And once again, Vadim jerked her down. She turned her head to glare at him. He was not this heartless, but he stared past her at the door.

Swiveling her head, she covered her mouth as a second fog entered the room. This one consisted of dozens of hues mixed together. It made Valya think of an oil slick on water. It should have been cheerful like a rainbow—instead, it was more horrifying than the green one.

The green fog reacted with a louder, sharper hiss, coiling, and faced the approaching second being. The rainbow mist let out a loud growl. The green snapped and then disappeared in a rush over the balcony rail. The multi-colored one followed.

Valya let out the breath she held and met her brother's confused look with one of her own. "We need to go," he said. This time, he pulled her up with him.

"No. We can at least bring her back into the house." Valya released his hand to approach the balcony.

He grabbed her wrist. "Didn't you see those things? Those were real or we both wouldn't have seen them! Whatever is in this place is evil. You had to feel that too!"

Valya swung her eyes back to the woman. "But they left. We need to help her."

Vadim let out the word "fuck" through his teeth but gave her a nod.

Valya touched his cheek in gratitude as she carefully navigated the destroyed room. She was close. Only a few yards away when the woman became more frantic and agitated. Did she realize they were there? No. She looked out into the city.

And then she climbed up on the rail.

Both Valya and Vadim ran to stop her.

It was too late as the woman let out a sigh. It almost sounded relieved before she let herself fall.

Running to the rail, they both looked down to see the woman lying akimbo on the curved driveway. Her limbs and body in an unnatural angle when it hit, the blood pooling under her body—the fall had killed her.

Valya covered her mouth, a sob breaking through. Vadim stepped back. "Valya..."

She pivoted toward him to leave. That's when she saw what he had seen.

The rainbow mist hovered in the air outside the balcony. And Valya could have sworn it stared at them.

And, oh God, was it smiling?

Horror replaced the shock of the woman's death. She and Vadim ran out of the room and down the stairs. Neither of them bothered with being stealthy in exiting the mansion—nor did they slow down once they had.

But Valya felt a strange cold breath on the back of her neck.

She dared a look back.

No one was there.

THE GRID GLOSSARY

THERE ARE MANY TYPES OF BEINGS ON THE GRID. HERE ARE JUST A FEW:

Breakers: Supernatural heroes with a dark past. When they are bought from Hell by Bounce for the price of a coin, they become part of The Grid to help fight the darkness and destroy the demons from Hell which are called Eaters. If they do their job well when the war ends, or when they find love, they get a second chance of life if found worthy, as well as a chance to join the Source and be eternal upon death.

RELAYS: HUMAN AND OTHER COUNTERPARTS OF THE GRID. THERE ARE SEVERAL KINDS JUST AS WITH ANY ARMY.

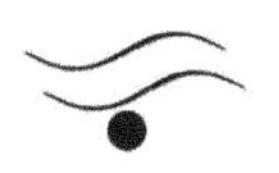

Tech Relays: The computer and technical side of The Grid. They Monitor and maintain the vast Grid located in Fort Pearce under the Golden Gate Bridge. Techs have limited fighting skills but incredible analytical abilities.

Recon Relays: The human counterparts who are trained to have both fighting and tactical skills as well as trained as snipers. They work with the Wires, which are the top of the Breaker food chain in reinforcing the laws and balance from inside The Grid. They are the ones who hunt down those wishing to destroy or harm The Grid on the inside..

Healer Relays: Humans and deities who serve to heal those on The Grid. Gifted with the talent of touch-electrotherapy, they are able to tap into their own spark to heal another. Tap too much? Their spark goes dark and they die.

Bridge Relays: The designers of The Grid. The engineers who not only worked closely with Tesla in its design but are constantly designing new technology to ensure it stays ahead of the war to assist those on The Grid.

Municipal (Muni) Relays: These are humans who work for the various branches of government and agencies in the city. They are aware of The Grid and use their positions to keep it hidden. Examples: Deputy Mayor, Police Officers and Firemen.

SHADOW-KEEPERS: KNOWN AS KEEPERS, THEY ARE THE TOP OF THE FOOD CHAIN ON THE GRID.

These beings are animated by the dark-power that must exist to keep the balance of dark and light. The Keepers walk the shadow in-between by feeding their powers yet keeping them controlled so the darkness never grows too strong.

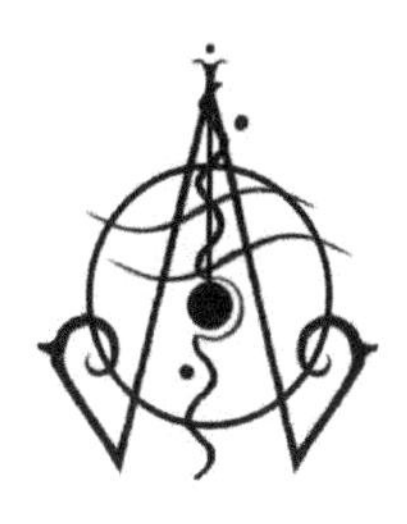

Reno Sundown

Keeper of Madness and former Breaker on the Grid.

———

McKenzie Miller

Keeper of Lust. Former human and now part of the Grid.

———

Marcus DeMonte

Keeper of Murder. Former Elite Assassin for Lucifer.

Jade Shen

Keeper of Envy. Youngest and only Keeper to not lose her life to become one.

A NOTE FROM JAS T. WARD

"I am the product of several realities making the whole: a troubled childhood, domestic violence survivor, homeless person, single mother and a suicide survivor. But in every single one of those realities, one thing remained true—my imagination. "Reading and writing were always my escape. It helped me deal with the harshness of my existence at the time and made me grateful for the escapism books gave me. Now, as a writer, I seek to give that gift back to someone who may need the same haven that saved my soul and my creativity as I once had." —Jas T. Ward

WORKS BY JAS T. WARD

Shorts & Poetry

Bits and Pieces: Tales and Sonnets

Contemporary Romance

Love's Bitter Harvest

A Little Pill Called Love

The Shadow-Keepers Series

CANDYMAN: Before the Madness

MADNESS

BOUNCE

LUST

COWBOY

MURDER

ENVY

www.AuthorJasTWard.com

ABOUT THE AUTHOR

Born and raised in Texas and spending time living in Kentucky, Ms. Ward spends her days and nights writing as therapy to handle the past. She is the proud parent of three very independent grown children and grandmother to three delightful grandchildren.

She has furbabies that sit and ponder why their human is talking to herself late into the night as she writes out colorful and diverse if not twisted characters and tales.

Ms. Ward is also the founder and CEO of Ink-N-Flow Management Group, helping others in the publishing and talent industries.

You can find more information here:
www.InkNFlowManagementGroup.com

She can be reached via social media at:
Facebook: facebook.com/AuthorJasTWard
Website: www.AuthorJasTWard.com

Lightning Source UK Ltd.
Milton Keynes UK
UKHW040959250420
362198UK00001B/185

9 781648 713828